Greetings from the FLIPSIDE

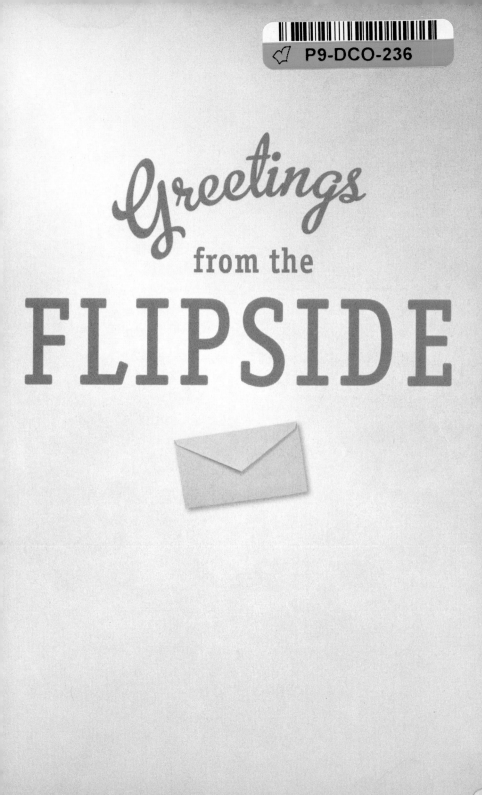

Greetings from the FLIPSIDE

RENE GUTTERIDGE
CHERYL McKAY

B&H PUBLISHING GROUP
Nashville, Tennessee

Printed in the United States of America

978-1-4336-7689-5

Published by B&H Publishing Group
Nashville, Tennessee

Dewey Decimal Classification: F
Subject Heading: LOVE STORIES \ GREETING CARDS—FICTION

1 2 3 4 5 6 7 • 17 16 15 14 13

Acknowledgments

Rene Gutteridge

The first time I read one of Cheryl McKay's screenplays, I knew I had to hunt this woman down. I finally found her and gushed like a rabid fan. Thankfully I didn't scare her away, but I really wanted her to know what a phenomenal screenwriter she was. I never guessed that over the course of several more years, we would end up working together as a comedy writing duo, turning her fabulous scripts into novels.

Collaborations, especially between two writers, can often be tricky, but our working relationship has flowed seamlessly, and I couldn't be more grateful for it. What started as a writing partnership has transformed into a deep friendship that I count on every day. So, special thanks to Cheryl, who, in writing and in life, continues to show deep wisdom, unending love, and triumphant hope.

I'm also thankful for the support the B&H team gave us during this project. Julie Gwinn and Karen Ball, thanks for making the journey safe and encouraging and thanks for all your notes and insights into the manuscript.

As always, I'm grateful for my agent, Janet Kobobel Grant, whose faith in me often exceeds the faith I have in myself. And to my family, who blesses me with love when I doubt myself and acceptance no matter what. Sean, John, and Cate, I love you!

Last but not least, thank you to Jesus, who uses every story and every character to better my life story and increase my own character. And, thanks to what he did on the cross, I can be eternally grateful for all of it.

Visit Rene at www.renegutteridge.com, and on Twitter and Facebook.

Cheryl McKay

When I originally wrote this story, I was single and frustrated in the wait to find love. I took out my frustrations through writing Hope's story as she tried to focus on her career instead of love. Romans 8:28 has always been one of my favorite Bible verses. What spoke to me most while penning Hope's journey was how important it is to find the good in the painful things that happen to us.

I'm very grateful to everyone who had a part in bringing this story to life. To Rene Gutteridge, for always being so brilliant at taking my scripts and turning them into novels. I love the way you expand the inner life of the characters.

I would like to offer a special thanks to Art Within, who helped me develop the story while writing the screenplay: Bryan Coley, Terri Measel Adams, Jeanna Bagley, Sean Gaffney, Brent Sweitzer, Kathleen Snow (my prayer warrior), and my fellow fellows in the writing program: Liz Beachy Hansen, Miguel Almendarez, Jim Krueger, and Jared Romero. You all encouraged me develop the most unique set of characters I've ever put together on the same page. From our lively table read of the script, I'd like to thank Kelly Delany, who was the first actress to read Hope's character out loud and show me how funny she could be, and Belle Adams, for bringing Mikaela to life. I must also thank Susan Rohrer, Brian Belknap, and Nathan Scoggins, for all the supportive calls and writing life advice.

Thanks to Janet Kobobel Grant, for her unending support of Rene and me doing these script-to-book novelizations and for believing in us as a romantic-comedy duo. And to the B&H Publishing team, for all of their help and support during this project, and especially Julie Gwinn, Karen Ball, Jennifer Lyell, and Kim Stanford.

Lastly, I must thank my wonderful family, my parents, Tom and Denise, for their constant cheerleading, my sister, Heather, and to my husband, Chris, for his unending love and support of me—and for showing up at the altar. (That's a little Hope Landon humor.) And to God, without whom I wouldn't be able to do what I do.

Please visit Cheryl McKay online at: www.purplepenworks.com or www.finallyone.com

1

Suck it in. Come on, suck it in.”

“My stomach is on the other side of my spine,” Hope wheezed, barely enough air in her lungs to finish the sentence. Becca tugged and jiggled the zipper while trying to maintain a smile for the crowd of elderly residents who’d gathered around for the fitting. Normally Hope would be leading them into the bingo hall, but today was different. Special. There was a certain excitement on all the faces of those who’d managed to stay conscious. “Are you sure you gave them the right measurements?” Hope whispered to Becca.

“Are you sure you haven’t been eating cheese? Or Popsicles? Both?”

Then, with one final tug, the zipper slid up the teeth and the dress closed. Hope let out the breath she was holding, her stomach pooching a little. She prayed she wouldn't blow the seams out.

She turned and smiled for her seamstresses, every one of which was in a wheelchair or held steady by a walker.

"Oh, honey!" Mrs. Teasley gasped. "It looks beautiful. You're stunning!"

Miss Gertie, who had worked as a seamstress her whole life, wheeled closer. "Did you notice the hem, Hope? It's done the old-fashioned way. These days, nobody takes time on the hem, rushing through it as if it doesn't matter. It is the most important part!"

"Miss Gertie, it's perfect." Hope whirled around, glancing in the mirror they'd brought out for her. She'd been hesitant when the nursing-home gang offered to make her dress. But she was barely making over minimum wage here, and her mother certainly didn't have any money to help. It had been a gamble, and for once, she won.

Mr. Collins's hearing aid went off, sounding like a dying fire alarm. "Mr. Collins!" Hope tapped on her ear to let him know. She twirled again, her fingers sweeping over the hand-stitched pearls and the lace on the sleeves.

"Sam will love me no matter what I look like," she said to Becca. "But I look awfully good, don't I?"

Becca clapped. Miss Gertie wheeled even closer to Hope. "I'm so glad this is your last day."

Hope laughed. "I know you mean that in the nicest way."

"You're too good for this place. You've got to go out in this world, make a name for yourself!"

That was the plan, to flee Poughkeepsie and move to New York City with Sam right after the wedding. She'd dreamed of it her whole life, and it was almost here. She glanced at Miss Gertie and Mrs. Teasley, both of whom had their hands clasped together, pure delight shining in their eyes.

Hope leaned in for hugs. "I'm going to miss you both."

Miss Gertie sat up a little straighter in her chair. "Listen, we need to talk."

"About what?"

"I know this may come as a startle, but when you get married, you're going to have duties."

It was something about the way she said *duties* under her breath that made Hope realize Miss Gertie wasn't talking about vacuuming. "We don't really need . . . we don't have to talk . . ."

"Doesn't take long, dearie." Mrs. Teasley patted her hand. "Just endure it."

"I bet she'll be pregnant by Christmas!" Miss Gertie said to the room full of hearing aids. At the word *pregnant* seven of the ten ladies woke to attention. Ms. Cane was looking at her own belly.

A hot flush crept up Hope's neck. "Miss Gertie, really, it's okay—"

Suddenly Mr. Snow shuffled in, moving faster than anyone on a walker should. His bright white hair was blown back and he leaned way forward on his walker, making him look like he was fighting a stiff north wind. Hope knew he was looking for her but probably wasn't recognizing her in the long, white dress.

"Mr. Snow, over here!"

"Ah! There you are. Didn't see you." He shuffled her way, smiling, his always-clean dentures sparkling under the fluorescent lights. He let go of his walker, which normally didn't turn out well for him, and grabbed her hand as he wobbled. "I'm going to miss you, Hopeful."

"I'm going to miss you too, Snowball."

He reached into the small bag that hung off the side of his walker and pulled out a card. "I couldn't let you leave without giving you a card to rewrite."

Hope read it aloud. "'There are five stages of grief.'" Hope looked at Mr. Snow. "I'm sorry. Who died?"

"My cousin, Burt. He was one hundred and three years old and wanted to die two decades ago."

"Ah." Hope opened the card. "'Let the Lord help you with each stage, one step at a time.'"

Mr. Snow took out a pen from his bag and handed it to her. Hope thought for a moment, then scratched out the fancy italics, wrote beside them, then handed the card back to Mr. Snow. He slid his reading glasses on. "'There are five stages of grief.'" His shaky hand opened the card. "'You've been in denial for a while. Can I help you move on to anger?'"

The room was suddenly quiet. Hope fidgeted . . . too snarky? Too insensitive?

Then Mr. Snow threw his head back and laughed. Everyone else joined in and soon the room was filled with chuckles. Mr. Snow slapped her on the back. "Good one."

Becca looked at her. "We're going to have to go soon."

Hope nodded. She knew it was time to say her good-byes. One by one, she bent down to hug each person, careful to avoid any mishaps with the dress. Some of them hugged back. Some of them didn't. But they all knew she loved them.

She made her way to Miss Gertie and knelt by her wheelchair. "Will you make sure my grandmother's fresh flower arrives every day?"

"Only if, when you find that job making your own greeting cards, you send me a new card every day. They sure do make me giggle."

"I promise."

Becca tapped her watch. "We've got about forty more things to do today."

"Just a few more minutes." Hope hiked her dress up to her shins, headed down Wing Two. She smiled and nodded at all the familiar faces: Mr. Speigel, a once-successful CEO for a large bank, who hadn't had a single visitor in the last four years; Aunt Jackie, as she liked to be called, who suffered a stroke in September and lost the ability to move any muscles in her face—but there was life in those green eyes of hers; Old Benny, once a major-league baseball player, now with amputations at both knees because of diabetes. He lost his sight and his mind back in '08.

The door to Hope's grandmother's room was open, like always. Two towels were tossed on the floor. Hope dutifully stooped to pick them up and throw them in the hamper. Her grandmother sat by the window, staring out at nothing more than an empty lot washed in hazy sunlight, twirling a Columbine flower in her hand.

Hope scooped up tissues, flattened the silky bedspread, fluffed the pillows, wiped clean the sink, and replaced the tissue box. Five cards lined the same table that held the tissues. Ten more sat across Grandmother's nightstand, and another ten on the cabinet. There were weeks when Hope wrote a card a day and brought them to her grandmother's room. Sometimes they didn't move, other times her grandmother would give them away or, when she was more lucid, mail them. Mostly they just sat with all the others, simply signed *Hope*. A glance at one of the wittier lines she wrote caused her to laugh, and her grandmother looked her way.

"Thank you, young lady." Her grandmother's smile, though feeble, was gentle and genuine. She didn't seem to take notice of the long, white dress Hope wore.

Hope stooped by her wheelchair. "Grandma, it's me."

"Okay."

"I wanted you to see me in my dress. It's finally happening. This weekend."

"Okay."

"I wish you could be there, but I know you'll be there in your heart."

"Okay."

"Did I tell you that Sam is writing me a song? I probably did. He's been writing it for a long time. I thought he was going to have it ready at Christmas, but he said he needed a little more time. He hasn't said it, but I'm pretty sure he's going to debut it at the wedding. I heard he's been inquiring about getting a grand piano into the church." The thought made her smile. She'd been dying to hear the song, imagining it over and over in her head. "So, Grandma, Sam and I are moving to New York City. That's right. I'm finally getting out of Poughkeepsie, just like you always wanted." Hope paused, searching the elderly woman's eyes. She laughed at the memory of her grandmother, before she lost her mind, trying to talk her into some boy from Hope's school days. "I have a feeling about him," she would say.

But Grandma also always wanted bigger and better for Hope, and everyone knew bigger and better was not to be found in Poughkeepsie. The name itself implied its own identity crisis. Few knew how to even pronounce the name and those in the know disagreed as to whether it was *puh* or *poo* or *poe*. The *kips-see* was generally acknowledged by all as the proper way to end the word, but then there was the question as to whether Poughkeepsie was upstate or downstate. Also in question was the matter of the town and the city. For no reason anyone could identify, Poughkeepsie was split into the *Town* of Poughkeepsie and the *City* of Poughkeepsie. The town boasted enormous houses and even larger taxes. The city had low taxes and lower housing.

To grow up in the Spackenkill District was to go to its privileged high school, where lockers didn't even need locks. Hope did not live near nor even infrequently visit that district, but overall Poughkeepsie was a decent place to grow up, with a glorious view of the Hudson at dusk. The smog did wonders for the color spectrum. It was home to Vassar College and the Culinary Institute of America and city-dwellers were flocking to Poughkeepsie, pushing the population over thirty-five thousand.

She looked out the window her grandmother stared out of every day. It was a colorless view of warehouses and smokestacks. Her grandmother was born and raised here and as far as Hope was concerned, she was Poughkeepsie's shining star. But eleven major-league baseball players also hailed from Poughkeepsie, as did professional poker player Hevad Khan and the inventor of Scrabble, Alfred Mosher Butts, who sold his invention to entrepreneur James Brunot. Brunot renamed it *Scrabble*, from the Dutch word *scrabben*, meaning "to grope frantically, to scrape or scratch."

It was that word, *scrabble*, that defined what Hope always felt about this city and her place in it. The word pointed her toward the escape chute, so to speak. She always felt, someday, she would make a disorderly haste straight out of this town, clambering and scraping and climbing her way to freedom.

Ironically, or perhaps not, the word was also used to mean the act or instance of scribbling or doodling and that . . . *that* . . . was her ticket out of Poughkeepsie. Simple doodling would set her free.

That, and Sam.

She turned to her grandmother, stroked her knobby shoulder with the back of her hand. "I won't be able to see you every day."

"Okay."

"But the ladies will make sure you always have a new flower. And Mom will of course come by to see you." Tears stung Hope's eyes as she looked into her grandmother's bright blue gaze, twinkling with a life Grandma no longer remembered. Hope knew—her grandmother loved this dress. Would love the wedding day if she could go, and would love Sam if she could ever know him.

A soft knock came at the door. "Hope, we have to get to the church," Becca said.

Hope squeezed the hand that didn't have the flower. "I will send you a card as soon as I get to New York City, okay?" She stood and kissed her on the cheek, which smelled like baby lotion. "I love you," Hope whispered into her ear.

"Okay."

JAKE TRIED NOT to seem too obvious as he watched Mrs. Dungard's expression. He lifted the bouquet from below the counter, handing it over like it was a newborn baby. But it was the expressions that always made his day. Mrs. Dungard's whole face opened in delight, her eyes shining with pure joy as she grappled for words.

"Oh, Jake! You've outdone yourself this time!" Her fingers delicately stroked the petals of the Egyptian lotus, which he'd encircled with some baby's breath.

"It's called the Sacred Lily of the Nile," Jake said. "They were grown along the Nile thousands of years ago and the Egyptians ate their roots, which were edible."

"The color is astounding. And I love how it's all wrapped in lilies! Susan will love these! Did I tell you it's her birthday?"

"You did." Jake smiled. "And I also remembered, from last year, that hot pink is her favorite color."

Mrs. Dungard's eyes shone with tears. She patted Jake on the hand. "You don't know how much this means to me."

He did know. He always knew that a simple bouquet of flowers could reset a fractured relationship, bring hope to something hopeless, say a thousand things without whispering a word.

"How is Susan doing?"

"She's holding her own. But the chemo is taking its toll."

Jake went around the counter to the small rack of handmade cards he kept in the shop, usually only ten or fifteen at a time. He pulled the one showcasing summer, a field of yellow flowers in the distance that perfectly matched the setting sun. He'd written the poem inside himself.

"Take this and give it to her too."

"Thank you, Jake. Your cards are so beautiful." She cradled the bouquet. "Thank you so much for this too. It's just breathtaking."

"You're welcome."

Mrs. Dungard left and Jake closed the shop for the evening. He liked this time of day, when the sun was settling to bed and the shop was quiet.

He closed the register and found Mindy, his assistant, in the back.

"Hey Mindy, you can go on home."

"But we've still got a lot to do for the wedding this weekend," she said as she measured some ribbon.

"I'll finish it up."

"You're sure?"

"Definitely. Go home and see that baby girl of yours." He grinned extra wide to let her know it was okay. Mindy tended to feel guilty about doing things for herself.

She grabbed her bag. "I'm nervous about this one. The mother is kind of . . . strange, I guess you could say. She's the same lady that has us send that Columbine flower to the nursing home every day, right?"

It was true. She wanted it every day. And when their driver was sick, he took the flower himself.

"Yes."

"She was having a hard time articulating what her daughter wanted, or I was having a hard time understanding. Either way . . . I'm nervous."

"No worries. I already have an idea what to do."

Relief flooded Mindy's features. "You rock, Jake. Seriously. You never fail. Why was I worried?"

"See you tomorrow."

Alone in the back room he sat on his favorite old stool, the one his father had carved for him when he was ten years old, and began his final sketch of the bouquet. She wasn't frilly. Or girly. But she was feminine and pretty. Tough but vulnerable. At least, that's how he remembered her.

A lot of his youthful memories had faded, but he would never in his life forget the day he gave Hope Landon a card in the first grade. It was Mrs. Mosley's class.

It had taken every nerve he had to do it. The night before, with a flashlight under his covers, he wrote the card, practicing good penmanship and making sure he spelled the important words correctly. The next day in class he'd managed to add some crayon to it, for a final touch. Then he stuffed it down his pants to hide it from Mrs. Mosley—in hindsight, possibly a mistake.

Then it was time. Art class. They were painting spring cards. He was watching her from across the room as she fervently worked, as if the whole world depended on the card she was creating. Her passion—and her dimples—fascinated him.

He finished his spring card in five minutes, which he intended for his mother, and started painting the easel itself. If caught, no recess for him.

Admittedly, he was just delaying because he was nervous. This was the first girl that hadn't grossed him out.

He was a scrawny thing with big magnifier glasses and wispy hair that even back then seemed too old for him. High-priced hair gel couldn't hide the fact that even at seven his hair was receding like the tide on the shoreline.

He watched her and then, she stopped painting. Her hand rested on her knee, the paintbrush poking out between two fingers. She slumped a little, observing whatever it was she was painting. In one spectacular moment, he'd found a burst of confidence. He stood and walked to her with a strut he'd only seen on TV, his shoulders back, his chin tipped upward enough to make him at least an inch taller, he estimated.

Then came the sudden realization, only four feet away from her, that he'd forgotten to take the card out of his pants. He had to think fast. And he did. Halfway through his stride, he turned, pulled it out, kept walking.

Very smooth.

But with each step closer, his confidence faded. By the time he got to her, he was shaking. But she didn't notice. She didn't even look at him. He cleared his throat. Nothing.

There he stood. It was a very Charlie Brown moment.

So he dropped the card in her lap and ran off.

To his surprise, forty minutes later during free time in their class, she stood by his desk.

"I appreciate the thought," she said, towering over him. "But this is cliché." He didn't know what that word meant. She slapped the card down on his desk and opened it up. "See here? *Do you like me? Yes, no, maybe so.* The rhyming is good, but I think you can do better. Something funny, like 'Do you like me? I also come in chocolate and strawberry.' Girls like boys who are funny. Also, you're not telling me how you *feel* about me." She grabbed his pencil and pointed to the front of the card.

"And stick figures? At least give them expression. Personality. Enthusiasm. It's got to catch my eye."

And that was the end of it. She walked off and never checked a box.

But she never stopped being his Lucy, either. By the time they got to their senior year of high school, he was pretty sure she didn't even recognize him anymore.

And now, he was arranging flowers for her wedding. Bittersweet, to say the least. She probably didn't even know it was him. Her mother was the one who came in and made all the arrangements.

No matter. His life was not one he wanted to share anymore. But he was going to give her the most beautiful bouquet he'd ever designed. She deserved that. His whole young life, she stood out as the girl who deserved better than what she had.

His pencil flowed over the paper. Two hours later, he was still working.

THE DAY RETREATED and night settled over the old, wooden frame house she'd lived in her whole life. It was drafty, creaky, sometimes moody in a way. A lingering smell of cooked cabbage that to this day could not be explained. A tar-black woodstove in the kitchen held its own against some of the more modern appliances. A beautiful, hand-carved mantel stretched the length of the living room, with bookshelves on either side.

The house had character, but if it were human, Hope would be taking care of it at the nursing home.

Hope was in her room, doodling out some fun wedding cards she'd been imagining when her mother's thin voice rattled the even thinner wooden door of her bedroom. "I'm home!"

"Okay! Just a sec." Hope sat at the small white desk she'd had since elementary school, her knees bumping into all parts of it if she didn't try to stretch her legs out. Sticking out between each finger of her left hand were five colored pencils, her signature colors: red, black, blue, white, and flesh tone. Colors she'd be known for if she ever made it big, which she had every intention of doing.

The plain white, heavy card stock sat centered on her desk, and she sketched the long and lean bride, one sassy hip poked out and a delicate hand set atop it. Hope pressed the pencil to the paper, drawing a grin that said, *I've got something to say, but I'm holding it in out of politeness.*

"Hope?"

She set down her pencils, cracked her knuckles, and decided she would have to work on the groom later. It was time to talk wedding details with her mom, but she wasn't sure she was up for it. The pre-exhaustion that usually set in before she had to try to have a normal conversation with her mom was wilting her resolve by the second. With a long sigh, she put the Scrabble box that sat on her bed back on her desk, covering the card. She didn't like anyone seeing them before they were done. And the Scrabble game was a constant reminder of her task at hand.

At the door of her room, she closed her eyes, then forced herself to turn the knob and walk out into the hallway. Her sneakers dragged against the carpet but she kept her focus on the end result . . . the wedding and the race out of Poughkeepsie. She had a dream to fulfill. Five hundred cards, all carefully packed away in the garage, needed her to be strong. They had a dream too . . . to make someone, somewhere, laugh.

Hope found her mother at the kitchen table, still surrounded by mustard yellow chairs that came in and out of style all in the same year: 1975. Her mother was dumping a sack of fake flowers and mismatched ribbon out onto the table. Hope sat down with the kind of caution that is normally reserved for people in dangerous occupations like alligator wrestling or rattlesnake wrangling or customer service.

"Look what I bought! It was all on sale. Clearanced at 90 percent off! I figured we could use it somehow. We must have some decor at your wedding."

At the word *decor*, Hope's attention drifted to the rust-colored walls of the kitchen. It was still unclear in what year the color had been popular. In the living room, the paisley print couch sat atop a green shag carpet. On the end tables were two lamps she swore came straight from the set of *The Brady Bunch*.

Her mom hadn't updated anything since 1979, including herself. Everything about her—from her frizzy, unkempt hair to her polyester floral skirt—seemed a bit faded, like an old photo. Hope watched as her mom continued to rummage through her craft store goodies. As she often did, she imagined they were having a normal conversation, a conversation any mother and daughter might have before a wedding. She'd done this since she was little, sit close to her mother and pretend they were conversing about school or boys or an upcoming dance. That made her feel better. That . . .

And Popsicles.

"When I make the pigs in a blanket, do you want Swiss or provolone? I'm thinking cheddar."

"Cheddar is fine." It was the pigs in a blanket that worried her. She'd agreed to let her mother cater only because there were no other options. They couldn't afford to have it professionally done, and their circle of friends was only about an inch across, thanks to her mother's unusual outlook on life.

On the brighter side, her mother had agreed they could pay a florist to do her bouquet and a few other arrangements. She was looking forward to seeing what he was planning. Rumor was that he always sketched out his bouquets before designing them, to get the client approval. It made her feel like she was from Spackenkill.

"So provolone?" her mother asked.

With her mother catering, she feared her wedding might look more like a backyard barbecue, complete with American flags and sparklers if she happened to find them in a discount bin somewhere.

Her mother chattered on about the pigs in a blanket, and Hope grabbed one of the ribbons, running it through her fingers. So much rode on her mother and Hope knew all too well that things dependent upon her mom were in a world of trouble. Hope bit her lip, desperately wanting to ask the same question she'd asked for four weeks now. But why would she assume the answer would be different this time?

Except Hope always seemed to live up to her name.

"Mom, did the travel documents come yet?" She held her breath.

Her mother blinked, as if trying to remember what a travel document was.

"For whatever this surprise honeymoon is that you've been talking about." Well, Mom mentioned it only once, but that was enough to get Hope's hope up.

"Documents! Yes!" Her mother jumped from the chair and hurried to the kitchen. "Came today!" She returned, clutching an envelope close to her heart, gazing at Hope with her head tilted to the side. She said nothing, just stared at Hope like she was a famous monument.

A tinge of excitement rose up in Hope and she couldn't help it: a grin hit her face like it was catapulted there. "So . . . are we going somewhere tropical?"

Her mother smiled and handed her the envelope.

Hope ripped it open, snatching up the folded contents. Tickets! Actual airline tickets! She turned them over to try to find the destination. A thrill rushed through her as she read the destination.

Then read it again.

Hope slowly lowered the tickets, placing them on the table.

Idaho.

The state.

The place nobody would go to for an exotic honeymoon. Her grin was still slapped onto her expression, but it began to quiver. She was about to burst into tears, but she had to hold it in. Crying extracted the strangest of all her mother's behaviors.

"It's a bed and breakfast!" her mother stated, her enthusiastic expression equivalent to Oprah's when she gives away new cars. "That B and B harvests *their own potatoes*!"

"We're spending our honeymoon in potato country."

"I know how much you love your mashed potatoes."

"Is this refundable?"

"Nope! Paid in full, my dear!" She smiled, missing the grave disappointment sinking into Hope's expression. Her mother started messing with the ribbon again.

What was there to say? She couldn't be ungrateful. She was certain her mother saved for months for this. A sharp pain cramped her stomach. Her mother reached across the table, patted her hand, grinned widely enough for the two of them.

"By the way, if your daddy shows up at the wedding, how about we both take an arm?"

No. Not now. Not talk about Daddy. "Sure, Mom."

Then the dim mood of the room was undone by what could only be described as the spontaneous prayer version of Tourette's syndrome. "Lord! Please hear this our prayer!" Her mother shouted, like there was some racket she needed to be heard over.

She waved one hand in the air. "Bring Hope's daddy back in time for her vows!"

Her mother's eyes were squeezed shut so Hope rose, went to the freezer, and grabbed a blue Popsicle. She'd gone through ten or twelve Popsicles a day when her dad left. Now she only needed them every once in a while . . . like now. They had a calming effect, maybe because they temporarily froze her brain.

"Bring her daddy home, dear Lord!"

Hope returned to the table, sat down, sucked on her Popsicle.

"And please, please, please Lord, convince Hope and Sam they don't need to move away."

Hope's heart sank. Her mother was having a hard time with it, and it kind of broke her heart. But she needed to leave. She had to.

"It's going to be okay, Mom," Hope said, patting her on the hand. "I'm tired. I'm going to bed. Good-night. I love you."

In her bedroom, against her will, she picked up the picture of her dad, the one where he grinned like he could see their whole future together and it was magnificent. It was winter and they were bundled tightly together. His mustache was thick enough that it seemed it could keep them both warm. She always wondered what he'd look like now, whether he'd still sport that mustache or not.

"I'm not going to get any silly ideas about you coming to the wedding," she said to the photograph. "There's a new man in my life now. He is my family. He is the one that will be there tomorrow. Not you." She tossed the frame aside and grabbed her cell phone, speed-dialing the man who would take her away from this place, forever.

His voice mail picked up. "Hey, it's Sam. I'm probably off playing some outrageously sick gig right now. But if you're important, maybe I'll ring you." A guitar vamp roared through the phone, followed by a delicate beep.

"Hey, it's me. I love you and can't wait to walk down the aisle. I can't wait to hear the song you're writing for me. I can't wait"—she glanced at the picture of her dad on the bedspread, still grinning—"to not live in Poughkeepsie anymore . . ." She was talking as if the voice mail might converse back. "You know what, I'm just rambling now. I've got lots to do, so I'll catch ya on the flipside."

Outside her room, her mother sang some gospel music or something. Hope hopped off her bed and went to her closet, where her beautiful white gown hung, wrapped in plastic, off the back of the door.

She was actually getting married. Crazy was about to be a distant memory and normal was where she planned to relocate.

2

In solid sheets of white, rain gushed over the 1972 Oldsmobile that Hope drove along at fifteen miles an hour because, starting in 1994, her mother refused to drive in anything but pure sunshine. Wouldn't even drive on a cloudy day.

And as luck would have it, on their way to the church, the windshield wipers stopped working. Her mother now hung out the window and loudly declared the wipers to be HEALED!

"Oh God!" she wailed, soaked to the bone on her right side, "Come! Heal these wipers."

When the wind shifted, rain splattered against Hope's cheek. Good thing she never had any grand ambitions about her wedding day. She hadn't pictured frills and carriages and perfect weather. Of course, she hadn't pictured her mother hanging out the car window praying over the windshield wipers either, but things could always be worse.

"Mother!" Hope yelled over the rain.

But her mom couldn't hear her. She still hung out the window, trying to fix the wiper blades, half her body teetering out of the car and one arm wrapped around the car frame. She wouldn't drive on a cloudy day but had no problem with this.

"Lord! Hear our prayer!"

Hope glanced down at the speedometer. She was now going thirteen miles an hour.

Her mother started manually moving the wipers back and forth across the windshield. Hope slumped in her seat. At this point, frills and carriages and an ounce of sunshine wouldn't kill her.

God, please . . .

Suddenly, the wipers squeaked to life again. Her mom emerged from the rain. "There! Sometimes when the wipers of life get stuck, you gotta arm wrestle them to life."

Hope smiled, trying her best to enjoy each moment of this day. This would turn out to be one of those memories you laughed about. Later.

The downpour started up again. "So today's the big day!" her mom shouted over the racket of the rain and the squeak of the wipers. "You finally get to hear the song Sam's been working on for you!"

This brought a genuine smile to her face. "I know!"

"That boy has some God-given talent! I see him in a church one day," she declared, lifting her hand toward the windshield like it was a portal into heaven. "Yes, yes, yes I do. Leading a choir of hundreds."

Over his dead body. But Hope kept her mouth shut. Sam had wanted to wed at Pairaview Hall, where Black Sabbath once played. She'd told him that wasn't going to fly.

Hope wasn't a big church attender, but a church seemed like the proper place to wed . . . a good way to start off the whole deal. There would be lots of things coming against a marriage. God shouldn't be one of them.

Finally they arrived at the Poughkeepsie Community Church, quaint but colorless on this dreary day. The wedding dress was double-wrapped and her mother insisted on carrying it in. Hope resisted twice. Her mom insisted three times.

As she watched her mom maneuver the dress up the steps of the church, Hope was certain something catastrophic was going to happen on its way through the front doors.

Potato-farm catastrophic.

Hope held her breath and wondered how she was going to break the news to Sam that they were going to Idaho. It was supposed to be a big surprise. Well, it was surprising all right.

Okay, so . . . their first big disappointment to tackle. Fine. They could do it. Besides, Sam was a pretty laid-back guy. He could find the fun in anything, which was what first attracted Hope to him. He'd probably suggest they go cow-tipping or something.

Hope pulled her mom's industrial-sized raincoat over her head and raced toward the church. Inside, she found her mom in the room where Hope was to get ready. It smelled musty and the carpet was dense, dark, and old. The rain thumped loudly against the wooden roof and poured down onto the concrete sidewalk just outside the window.

Her mother joined her at the window. "This is going to be the perfect day, my dear. Just perfect. Who cares about the gloom outside? It's going to be warm and sunshiny inside, just like you!" She gave Hope a tight, sideways squeeze. Sometimes her mom's misplaced enthusiasm came in handy.

Her mom disappeared into a side room to change and Hope stood and watched the rain. She wondered how her mom could see her as warm and sunshiny. She wasn't that person. Witty, yes. Sarcastic, nearly always. She just didn't smile that much. But her mom, well, she saw reality a little differently.

"Hope Landon, you should be smiling. It's your wedding day!" Becca breezed in, carrying her sapphire-blue matron of honor dress, made especially for her pregnant body. She hung it on the door and frowned. "Why aren't you dressed? And what's going on with your hair?"

"Just waiting for you." Hope moved away from the window, smiling for Becca's sake. Hope plopped down in a chair and pointed to her hair.

"No kidding," Becca said. "Looks like you drove here with the top down!" She fluffed Hope's hair with her fingers. "But no worries. I can fix it. I brought all my magic." She grabbed a large bag off the floor.

"This is my wedding day." The breath in her lungs felt inadequate. "It seems surreal."

"You're going to look stunning. The hair's definitely going up."

And for the next thirty minutes, Becca sprayed and combed until her hair looked sassy and elegant and part of this decade. She then went to work on Hope's makeup.

"Take a look," Becca said, handing her a mirror.

Hope gasped. "I *do* look good!"

"Dress time!" Becca sang. She helped Hope into it, tugging on the zipper as Hope sucked in. Her mother flitted back into the room, twirling in her new outfit: cream and almost no polyester except her floral vest, which was trimmed with burgundy piping. Hope thought she looked pretty, with her hair pinned back by jeweled-toned clippies. Her lipstick was vibrant—enough to come with a radiation warning—but even that looked right on her today.

"Gorgeous, Mom."

"Me? Look at you! Good heavens, Lord Almighty! You are a drop of sunshine in a bucket of chemical cleaner, my dear. You're like the smell-good in the Pine-Sol."

Hope leaned toward the window. "There are actual cars out there! People are coming! I thought nobody would show up."

"Are you kidding?" Becca said. "Now suck in, or they're going to see more than they bargained for."

Hope obeyed. "I'm sorry, I ate a Popsicle last night."

"Hope Landon, I thought we agreed to no sugar for the last three days?"

"Oh God!" her mother shouted. "Please cause that zipper to—"

"Got it!" The zipper slipped up her back and the dress closed. Hope turned, gazing at herself in the long mirror.

"Are my hips wide?"

"Shush," Becca said. "This is your wedding day. Nothing is going to ruin it for you."

Her mom walked over, observing her daughter with complete delight. "Oh, I nearly forgot!" She handed Hope a small envelope. "The best man gave this to me to give to you."

"Lyle." Hope smiled. Sam's ever-faithful band mate. It was probably the marriage certificate they applied for.

She turned and gazed at herself in the mirror again. She'd never felt prettier in her life. Her mother walked up behind her, placed her hands on Hope's shoulders, just like in the commercials that all the normal families can relate to.

"Oh, Hope . . ."

Hope felt her eyes swell with tears.

"You are gorgeous," her mom continued. "Just like a perfect turkey, right out of the oven!"

Becca glanced at her and gave her a playful shrug. Becca knew her mom. There was never a need to explain away the odd remarks. She tapped her watch. "It's almost time, friend."

Her breath caught in her throat and she nodded. She opened the envelope in her hand to make sure it was the wedding license. It wasn't.

Instead, she pulled out a handwritten note.

"What is it?" Becca asked.

"It's a note from Sam," Hope gushed. "Sam wasn't happy about the tradition of not seeing the bride before the wedding. So I guess this letter is his way of peeking."

Becca patted her heart. "That is so cute."

Hope unfolded the note and began to read.

> *Dear Lan,*
>
> *Last night I made one final attempt to write your song. Nothing came, nothing flowed. Which can only mean one thing. We're not supposed to be together. I'm sorry. Good-bye.*
>
> *Sam*

The letter slipped from her hand, gliding against the invisible air, floating like it was angelic, until it landed and lay perfectly still.

All of Hope's senses roared to life. The air conditioner blew cold against her skin. The sunlight broke through the clouds and sent blinding light into the room. The faint murmur of the crowd that had gathered outside sounded like a thousand haunting voices. The room grew small. The musty smell overwhelmed her.

She looked up. Becca stared at her, unblinking, not moving a muscle. Then she started toward her, her expression intensifying with each step.

"What's the matter?" Becca grabbed her arm like Hope might tip over if she wasn't held steady.

A clap of thunder shook the church and the wink of sunlight now disappeared under the sudden downpour.

"It's okay, dear!" her mother shouted from across the room. "The show must go on! A little thunder never killed anybody. Now lightning, well, that's a different story . . ."

Hope snapped her attention to Becca and lowered her voice to a whisper. "Can you distract her?"

Becca searched her eyes, then looked at the note on the ground between them. "Okay."

Becca moved toward Hope's mom, taking her by the arm and guiding her to the window where they struck up some conversation about rain. Her mother's hands shot in the air and she was no doubt praying for the rain to stop.

Too late.

Lightning had already struck. And scorched her soul.

Hope grabbed her bag, which sat by the door, and slipped out. To her right, the hallway led to the sanctuary, where she heard people's conversations. Did they already know?

To her left was a side door.

Hope hiked up her dress, instinctively perhaps, to keep it from dragging on the wet ground. Thunder grumbled above.

She darted into the heavy downpour. It had nothing on the sobs that escaped from her, loud and heartbreaking, but nevertheless swallowed up by the sound of the rain. She ran across the sidewalk, stupidly trying to save her dress. She was soaked to the bone within seconds.

She hated herself for crying, even though she knew if ever there was a proper time to cry, this was it. But she didn't want to let *another* man abandoning her cause her this much pain. She swore she would always guard her heart.

She screamed into the noise and racket of the storm, but she couldn't even hear herself. The dress made it hard to run, but she kept running, dragging the dress on one side, her overnight bag hanging off the opposite arm. She got to the Oldsmobile and dropped her bag onto the ground, causing a small splash against her ankles. She plunged her hand into the side pocket and withdrew the keys.

But her hands were shaking and she couldn't get the key into the hole. She sobbed louder and louder, cursing and scratching the car as the key slid back and forth everywhere except into the hole.

"Get in that hole!" Her hands shook more and the rain got louder.

She stood there for a moment, her dress growing heavier as it took on more water. She was going to have to get a grip. If she didn't hurry, people were going to start trying to find her.

She took three deep breaths, during which she noticed a white delivery van parked by the church, the writing across its side partially blocked by an SUV. So it only read HEAVE.

Normally that would be delicious and ironic and funny and land somehow in a card, but on this day it was only a dreadful cue. Right there on the pavement, she heaved.

She stood up and felt a little better. She tried the key again, begging herself to hold it steady.

"Got it!" But the words had barely left her mouth when a sharp pain splintered through her skull. She fell against the window of the car, her cheek smashing against the glass. Her body slowly slid down the side, her face knocking against the door handle as she slumped to the ground. She tried to reach for the side mirror, but she had no control of her body.

She spilled onto the wet blacktop, face down.

Something heavier than rain trickled down her forehead, around her cheek, and over her lips. She turned over, tried to open her eyes, but everything was a blur. A shadowy figure stood over her, a young girl, maybe a teenager. She wore a purple winter jacket.

Then, without her permission, her eyes closed.

3

En route to the wedding, Jake decided to get over the irony of it all. Besides, he had better things to do with his time than revisit old losses and regrets. But he did regret quite a bit that he never tried again with Hope Landon, that he didn't get over his fear of rejection and just tell her how he felt.

There he was again, with the regret. He'd just about talked himself out of letting it go, too. His only hope, he supposed, was to finish up this delivery and get it over with. Maybe then, with the flowers delivered, he could move on.

He'd already brought most of them in, wrapped in sheets of plastic to protect them from the rain. The only thing left was the bouquet. It was his tradition to always hand-deliver the bouquet straight to the bride, with a card attached for well wishes and a personal good wish from him as well.

But in this case, he was having second thoughts. Then again, maybe seeing her in her dress, ready to walk down the aisle, would give him closure. He was sure not to make a good impression either way, because he was already soaking wet from this horrible storm. What a day to get married. He had no doubt Hope had some witty and snappy remark about it, probably already written out in a card—if she still wrote cards.

He stood at the front doors of the church and decided to hand-deliver the bouquet. It was the least he could do, to wish her well and hope for her happiness. He was about to dart back to his van, which was parked at the side door, when he noticed something in the back end of the parking lot. At first he thought it was a white trash bag. But the more he peered through the rain, the more he realized it wasn't a trash bag fluttering against the wind.

It was a wedding dress. And the woman wearing it wasn't moving.

Ducking into the rain, he began to run toward her, noticing a car speeding away from the church.

He hurried toward her. He could see she was missing a shoe. Her toenails were painted bright pink. The only thing moving was her wedding dress.

"Hope?" he yelled through the rain. He rushed to her side and knelt, trying to take in everything. Blood trickled across the side of her face and dripped into a small puddle beneath her. Her eyes were closed and she wasn't responding to him.

"Hope? Hope, can you hear me?"

He could barely hear himself with the rain and the noise of the storm. Lightning cracked in a wicked flash overhead, followed by a thundering clap. He leaned over her, made sure she was breathing. He tried to wipe the blood with the sleeve of his coat, but it was gushing, running off her head like water off a gutter. "Help! Somebody *help*!"

But there wasn't a soul around.

His cell phone was in his truck. With no time to waste, he went to retrieve it. By the time he returned, Hope's mother, CiCi, was running out of the church, her eyes frantic. A small group of people huddled around Hope's seemingly lifeless body.

"Hope! Hope!" her mother screamed.

Others from the wedding attended to her, and Jake stepped back, calling 911. He gave the address and all the pertinent information.

What in the world had happened to this beautiful bride-to-be, struck down in a parking lot on her wedding day?

He wanted to dive into the crowd and grab Hope's hand, plead with her to hang on. But she was swallowed up by everyone else.

So he prayed, his heart as heavy as his rain-soaked body.

GREETINGS FROM MY LIFE

I can sum myself and my life up like this . . . I have trouble stepping onto escalators. It's all about the timing, you see, and I am either too early and stumble or too late and then my legs awkwardly stretch away from one another and people instinctively reach out to help me.

To be exact, right now the escalator analogy doesn't really apply because I'm more in a state of free fall from the second story of a mall.

Perhaps that's too bloody of an example. People don't normally live when they fall off something that high. I'm definitely alive.

Let me go back to the escalator. Maybe it's like I'm wearing flip-flops and get my toe stuck. Well, shoot. I'm not stuck. I'm actually in just the opposite state.

Okay, I've got it. It's like I stepped onto the escalator, fully expecting it to continue as it does every second of every day for everybody else. But when it comes to me, it jolts to a stop, throwing me forward as I tumble all the way down the thing and land at the bottom, somehow managing to live through it but wishing I hadn't.

Yes, that's it. That's exactly what I'm trying to convey.

To catch you up, I got dumped at the altar. Not at the actual altar. It was before I got to the altar but after I got myself into my dress. It came by way of a handwritten note from Sam, my fiancé, right before I was to walk out of the dressing room and into the sanctuary.

I guess nobody knows exactly how they'll react in a situation like that. I can tell you that I surprised myself by grabbing my bag and bolting for the side door. There was a terrible storm that day and it had been pouring rain since morning. I was in my dress, trying to raise it up so it wouldn't get wet as I splashed through the puddles. I remember my hands were so shaky I couldn't even get the key into the car. I just wanted to leave. Flee. Bolt.

After that, things get a little fuzzy. To tell you the truth, I think I went into shock. Sam was not only the love of my life, but my ticket out of Poughkeepsie.

I cannot tell you why, but now I am at a diner, missing one shoe. Hobbling in with my bag, my hair falling out of its chignon, my dress muddy and sopping, I stand at the Coca-Cola door and look over the decor. It is fifties-nostalgic with an old soda fountain and black-red-and-white-checkered counter tops. Pictures of classic cars line the walls. A sign above the register says *Odyssey's*. It is charming enough that I take another step inside, hardly noticing that I'm leaving a puddle every few feet. A girl in a purple jacket brushes by me, knocking my shoulder, not even apologizing.

Nearby is a booth of locals enjoying their lunches. A waitress stands over them, a rag flopped over her hand, the other hand planted into her hip, chatting it up. All at once, they look over at me. Look me up and down. I try to smile. Maybe I grimaced.

Whatever the case, the waitress who is smacking radioactive-colored gum stops chewing and walks to me like I'm in desperate need of assistance.

"You lost, Sugar?"

"No. I, um . . . I'm just on my way to the . . ." I glance outside through the large window to see that my car is no longer there. I swear I just parked it, but there is nothing but empty space. "I just need . . ."

"Oh, sweet baby." The waitress takes her rag and reaches for my forehead, swiping her rag across. When she's done, we both look at the rag. It's covered in bright red blood.

I'm bleeding?

"That's going to need stitches," she says, eyeing it. "We'll need to take care of that right now."

I step backward. The woman looks like she might just pull out a needle and thread right this moment.

"No, um. No. I'm fine. Thank you."

She steps toward me and the next thing I know I'm in her warm embrace. Then another. And another. All the locals are surrounding me with one big bear hug. I kind of need it so I just stand there and let them hug me, as awkward as it is.

Soon enough I'm standing with only the waitress again.

"Where you headed, darling?"

"Can someone take me to the airport?"

"I'm not sure, you, um . . ."

"My mom, she already paid for this stupid honeymoo—vacation to Idaho." I look at her. There is a soft, rhythmic dripping onto the laminate floor beneath me, like my bladder is leaking one drop at a time. "I need to get away."

Then I jolt awake even though I did not think I was asleep. I am on an airplane. I can feel the plane touching down. "Welcome to Idaho, folks!" says the flight attendant.

I sit up straight, blinking away the fog, and peek over the heads of the rest of the passengers.

The flight attendant, holding the P.A. mic, has a plastic smile—and a head that is shaped like a potato.

Literally.

I slide back down in my seat. *What* have I gotten myself into? And why does my head hurt? At least I don't seem to be bleeding anymore.

Three days later I begin to understand there might be hope that I'm going to make it through this mess.

I am sitting on the veranda, overstuffed from my breakfast of hash browns, sweet potato fries, and cheddar mashed potatoes. Carol, the nice lady that runs the place, said I'd be in a coma for a while, and she wasn't kidding. With this much carb consumption, who wouldn't be? I like the outside because inside there are a lot of animal heads nailed to the walls. Deer. Moose. Lots and lots of antlers and beady eyes. Wasn't doing much for my creativity.

Outside, it's actually quite beautiful and the weather is gorgeous. A light breeze lifts the edge of my drawing pad every so often. The lodge sits atop a mountain and overlooks the breathtaking Kootenai Valley. Next to my pad are my five colored pencils, newly sharpened. So far I've sketched out twenty-seven cards on this trip. But it is the twenty-eighth that manages to catch my attention.

In a stroke of genius that began with the caption *Boy Meets Girl, Boy Loses Girl,* I realize I have discovered an untapped market for greeting cards.

I kind of bolt backward in my chair, standing, staring at it, gesturing at it like it might give me a response. I know I have a winner. Carol comes out to the veranda, asking if I'd like sweet potato flavored tea.

"I've just struck gold, Carol," I say, gesturing in wild strokes toward my pad of paper. "Right now! Right here!"

Carol smiles vacantly. "Wonderful, sweetheart. Did you say yes to the tea?"

"I'll pass." I put my hands on my hips and grin widely enough to think there might be some Cheshire in my ancestry. "Now I just have to help you find your way," I say to the little card.

I stare at it with reverence and deep emotion. This is my ticket out. Right here in front of me. Tears drip into my hash browns.

First, I must return to Poughkeepsie and finish some business.

4

Nothing else in the world made Jake more uncomfortable than hospitals. The smells, everything from the cafeteria food to the floor cleaner, nauseated him. And he didn't think of himself as a germaphobe, but in a hospital, sometimes it felt like things were crawling off the walls and right onto him. Every place there was a foam disinfectant dispenser, Jake used it.

But this particular visit was growing increasingly uncomfortable for other reasons that had nothing to do with the hospital. First, he was ushered to the hospital with Hope's family and closest friend. He was definitely the odd man out. He hadn't explained he knew her from school. He hadn't explained anything. Her friend, Becca, had insisted he come, and then stay, calling him a hero for finding Hope. On and on.

Jake didn't do anything extraordinary. He was just in the right place at the right time. Unfortunately for Hope, it seemed she'd been in the wrong place at the wrong time.

As they stood in the hallway now, just outside Hope's room in the ICU, Becca explained everything in a very hushed tone, patting her pregnant belly to underline certain important facts.

Hope was dumped at the altar.

She had plans to leave Poughkeepsie.

She never saw this coming.

None of them did.

But even weirder than Becca's trust in him, was Hope's mother. Jake had met her a couple of times, when she came in to order the flowers. She never seemed particularly odd, though Mindy had mentioned she was a bit . . . off. Perhaps she was outdated but that was all he noticed. Now, though, she was wailing. And not in a crying or grieving sense, although she was obviously sad. But it was more in uncontrollable bursts of . . . prayer? He wasn't even sure. But he heard God mentioned a few times. Jesus twice. She wasn't swearing. Just . . . praying.

Becca was able to handle her, but Jake was afraid to say or do anything. Mostly he just wanted to sink into the wall and keep an eye on Hope.

She'd been unconscious since he'd found her. They'd taken her immediately to get a CT scan. Now the doctor and two nurses were in the room examining her. Jake watched CiCi while listening to Becca talk about how sad she was for Hope.

Jake understood that sadness. If he'd only been there a few minutes earlier, maybe he could've stopped the attack.

Just outside the ICU, through the small windows in the automatic doors, two cops waited to see if she would wake up. They wanted to try to get a description of whoever did this to her. Jake had already told them everything he knew, which was nothing.

"JESUS!" CiCi belted. Jake jumped toward Becca.

Becca patted his shoulder. "You'll get used to it."

He doubted that.

The sliding glass door that led to her room opened and the doctor emerged, his expression not betraying a hint of what he was about to say. He held a chart in his hand, scribbled something down, and handed it off to the nurse before approaching CiCi.

"Doctor, please tell me she is going to be all right. Please. She's my only child!" CiCi clung to the doctor's arm. He didn't look like he was used to being touched. Becca gathered her into her arms.

"The wound is deep. She's definitely going to need stitches and we're going to need to take care of that immediately," the doctor said. "The CT scan shows swelling on the brain. She is in a coma."

"What?" CiCi looked like she was about to collapse. "A *coma*?"

"There is no way of telling how long she'll be in the coma." The doctor shifted his weight from one leg to another and then took a step back. "Or *if* she will come out of it."

CiCi began to cry. She turned and clung to both Jake and Becca, taking an arm from each of them. Her fingers dug into the flesh of his bicep.

The doctor's attention focused on Jake, since CiCi had turned away from him. "Traumatic brain injuries are tricky, and they don't follow a pattern or formula. We'll keep an eye on her vitals." His expression dropping into solemn stillness. "And hope for the best."

He left and they all turned toward Hope's room, staring at her. She looked like she was asleep. She had no ventilator in. A few IVs dangled from her arm. Otherwise, she looked like she was napping on a rainy day. Jake wondered if he should stay or go, but CiCi turned right to him, her eyes locked into him like a deadbolt. "Are you coming?" She nodded toward the room.

"I, um, wasn't sure if I should stay or—"

"Honey, we need all the prayers we can get in there." She reached for his hand, which he'd stuffed in his pocket. "We're goin' in like a college marching band and we're going to blow our faith horns like it's bedlam!" She stepped toward him. "You do pray, don't you?"

"Sure. Of course." Not really. His prayer life wasn't all it used to be. Luckily, it didn't sound like he was going to be the one leading the pack of three. He glanced at Becca who seemed all at once sad and startled.

CiCi turned and actually marched right in. All she was missing was a baton. She pumped her hand into the air.

"I'm just warning you," Becca said out of the side of her mouth, "that it could get interesting. Don't get me wrong. That woman loves Hope with all her heart. But she's got her own way of doing things, and—"

Becca's words were cut short by a loud wailing that sounded like a shofar he'd once heard in church.

"Enough said," Becca said with a tense smile. "Let's go."

Jake took a moment to catch his breath before stepping into the room, but was then nearly knocked to the ground by a nurse going in at the same time. She elbowed her way into the room, gasping and looking around.

"It's okay," Jake said. "Everything's okay. It's just her mother. She's very . . . upset."

"Lord! Heal her! Heal her, Lord Almighty! Bring her back, Lord! Bring her back!"

The nurse froze, listening for a moment. Then she nodded and turned toward Jake. "Gotcha," she said with a warm smile.

When Jake saw her face, she was way older than he expected, with sagging skin and wiry gray hair that looked as if it hadn't been tamed a day in its life, though it seemed she probably gave it a good try every morning. She wore no makeup except a thin line of red lipstick that was barely inside its border. She touched his arm, a kind touch, like a grandmother about to dispense advice you might carry with you for the rest of your life. "Just remember, there is evidence that coma patients can hear what's going on around them."

"Bring her back," CiCi wailed, "from the clutches of death!"

The nurse gave him a knowing look and then left.

Jake needed to stay. He wasn't sure what he was supposed to do, but maybe it was to insert a little bit of reality into the situation.

The reality was—and he knew this firsthand—God was sometimes in the habit of not answering prayers.

GREETINGS FROM MY LIFE

I stand at the curb of my house, fishing for cash to pay the cab driver whose cab made an inexplicable beeping noise the entire trip. Despite that annoyance, I'd handed him one of the cards I'd made while in Idaho, and to my everlasting delight, he is laughing. And not just a chuckle. I'm talking a full-fledged belly laugh. He's actually leaning over, slapping his knee.

I start to hand him the cash, but he waves me on, pointing to the card, indicating that's all the payment he needs. I grin. Yeah, I feel like it's worth a good $3.95, but a whole fare's worth from the airport?

I shrug. Well, so be it.

The cab pulls away and I stand there in my yard, my duffel bag around my shoulder and a ten-pound sack of Idaho potatoes by my side.

The high I just got off the greeting card pat-on-the-back drains right out of me. In its place comes sadness. I really, really, really thought I was off to New York City. I really, really, *really* thought I'd found a man who wouldn't leave.

Now I'm back in Poughkeepsie, and I'm back at this little old house, that leans a little to the left and whose shutters are nailed in such a way that they appear to be a good half foot off from one another. The electric garage door hasn't worked since 1992. The grass is full of weeds and the mailbox is about to fall off the siding by the front door.

I long to see my mom. I guess everyone needs their mothers when they're in a crisis, and I'm no different, even if my mom is. I guess I've learned to live with her quirks. I don't cringe anymore, because no good comes from it. There was a point, around the age of sixteen, that I thought a person could actually drop dead from cringing too often.

I am kind of looking forward to a big hug from her, and Lord knows I could use a prayer or two, which I'm certain she'll offer up straight out of the gate.

The front door is unlocked, and I walk on in. The smell hits me first. Nothing's changed. The house is dark. Mom only turns on one light at a time, depending on which room she's in. She likes the drapes pulled too, yet somehow, from somewhere, light always seems to seep in.

I pass the dining table and do a double take. Cards. Lots of them. At least fifty. They make cards saying "I'm sorry your daughter got dumped at the altar"? Wow. That doesn't seem like a lucrative market.

Or maybe they're for me. But still . . . ? I make a note to read them later. I wonder out loud about taking my new card ideas to whoever might be selling "dumped at the altar" cards. Then I notice a box. And another box. And a third, set against the far wall. All labeled "Hope's Stuff." I'm about to go examine this when I hear movement down the hall.

My mother emerges through the darkness. I can tell it's her because her hair is backlit by the nightlight I insisted she install in the hallway. She flips on the living room lights.

And screams.

And not one of my mom's normal screams either. That wouldn't even make me blink. But this is like a blood-curdling scream, and for a moment I think we're about to both be murdered by someone I can't see. She is actually turning pale. I wait for the arms to shoot in the air and her to shout something about the devil, but nothing. She just keeps screaming.

So, instinctively, I scream too. We're both screaming. She seems to know why. I don't have a clue. We sound like squealing tires. Then she stops, so I do as well.

"What are you screaming about?" I am breathing so hard my bangs lift and fall from my forehead every second or so.

My mother rushes over to me, grabs my head, shakes it like she's listening for change in a piggy bank. "You! You, you, you, you!"

"Me, me. Me what?"

"You're here."

"I live here." I eye the boxes in the corner. "But you've got to give me credit. I did a heck of a job trying to move out. Almost got there, too." I smile, hoping to break the awkwardness, though the awkwardness doesn't seem to be coming from the fact that I got dumped at the altar.

"But you're dead. Dead people don't live."

"Funny. Yes, it felt like death. Heartbreak often does."

"But I had your funeral."

This is the moment when I realize that she may not be speaking metaphorically. Especially when she falls straight back and faints.

"Oh, wow . . ." I hurry to the kitchen and get a washcloth and then drag her to the couch and heave her up onto it. I drape the washcloth across her forehead and watch her breathe. "Come on, wake up. *Wake up*. I'm not dead." I prod her a little.

And that's when I see a super skinny dude walking toward me, rolling an IV stand alongside himself, looking like a cautionary tale for some sort of vice that will eventually kill you.

I might not be dead. But maybe I'm going crazy.

The dude is so skinny his britches are hanging halfway down his backside, but not in a fashion-senseless sort of way. He's got a belt and everything but they're just too big for his small, skeletal frame.

The IV stand rattles loudly as he slips toward us. He weighs so little I can't even hear his footsteps.

"Oh, man . . . she okay?"

"Who are you?" I stand up straight, bow my chest, but truthfully, I could totally kill this guy with my left pinky. If I blew hard, he'd fall down.

"I'm renting a room." He pitches a (by all standards, rather fat) thumb over his shoulder, toward the hallway. "The old lady's daughter just died."

I swing my arm wide toward my mom, who is peacefully sleeping away. "She is not old. Yes, she is current-decade challenged, but she's not old."

"She's like a Ford Pinto in a dress. Who are you?"

"I'm the Pinto's daughter." I sit on the edge of the couch next to Mom. Nobody calls my mom a Pinto. I stroke her hand. She is *so* Pinto-ish though. But in a good way. You know when you drive down the street and see a Pinto carrying large pieces of plywood in the back and you realize your coupe could never do that? That's my mom.

He huffs. "Well, welcome back from the grave. Does this mean I have to give up your twin bed? I already paid the rent for this month."

Mom's eyes fly open. She taps my face lightly on the cheek. "You are here! Is it you?" Her taps suddenly turn into repetitive slapping.

Skinny just stands there and watches like he is still waiting for an answer about his rent.

I feel like crying. "What is going on?"

Skinny gestures toward a stack of newspapers on the coffee table. "It is all over the news."

"What is?"

Skinny picks up a paper and reads. "Witnesses say the car plunged into the Hudson River. While authorities haven't been able to find the body, the driver is presumed dead." He looks at me. "They should've said 'allegedly presumed dead.'" He turns the newspaper around. It's front page. There are pictures! There's one of me, my face as big as a playing card. "Gettin' dead got you famous, girl."

I grab the newspaper and read the caption: *"Hope Landon of Poughkeepsie, Daughter of CiCi Landon, 31, Never Married."*

My eyes quickly scan the article, which is two columns in length. Is that what happened to my car? Someone stole it? Admittedly, everything was fuzzy up to the potato farm.

I read quickly, eyeing all the quotes:

"I'm not surprised she did it. She had a panic attack at my cake shop."

They're quoting someone I don't even know! My eyes dart from sentence to sentence.

"Today, on her wedding day, she was left at the altar by musician Sam Vanderbilt. Our department is handling this as a suicide," said the Poughkeepsie Police Department's captain, Jerry Wilburn.

I turn to mom. "Tell me this is a joke! A nightmare! That I'm going to wake up!"

"Look," Skinny says, "do you think I like this IV stuck in my arm? Dripping incessantly? Do you hear that drip? Over and over. Drip. Drip. Drip. We all got our things, lady."

"Do you mind?" I say to him. "You can go now."

He turns and heads to my room, grumbling all the way about rent and Pintos.

Mom tries to sit up. "You should have been there for your funeral. We had azaleas, lilies, and a whole tree built out of greeting cards. Just for you."

"Mom, how could you think I killed myself?"

"Well, what do you expect me to think when you drive my car off a bridge?"

"I didn't."

"Did you swim out the window? Sometimes it gets stuck."

"I didn't crash the car. It was stolen . . ." I remember now, the girl in the purple jacket, racing by me . . . did *she* drive the car off the bridge?

Mom slaps my arm so hard it feels like a needle prick. "I'm your mother. You let me think you were dead. Where've you been?"

I slump and sigh all at once. "Idaho."

"Why didn't you call me?"

"Clearly you don't have the humiliation gene, Mom. I didn't call anyone."

"I shouldn't have applied for your death certificate, huh?"

"I'm gone one month. One. And you rent out my room, have my funeral, *and* apply for my death certificate?"

"Upon grief I became extremely productive."

"Mom." I gaze at the boxes lining the walls. "Dad's been gone for two decades and you still keep a closet of his stuff."

Suddenly mom grabs my hands, forcing them together. I don't have to ask. I know what is coming next. "Good Lord, you said I could have the desires of my heart . . . be still, oh my heart, it worked on Hope. Now, how 'bout bringing me her daddy? And a new hubby for Hope to share those gifts with?"

My head snaps up. "What gifts?"

Mom leaps off the couch and opens the coat closet. Gifts are shoved in there so tightly it looks like a wall of wrapping paper.

"Mom! Why didn't you send the gifts home with the guests?"

She shrugs mildly. "Souvenirs? Speaking of . . . look what I kept!" She holds up the bride and groom that were supposed to be on top of the cake.

I put my head in my hands. This is too much for me to take. I'm overwhelmed with the idea that I was dead and everybody thought I was dead. Not just dead. Suicide dead. That's a step below just plain old death.

Mom is beside me now, with her lanky arm wrapped around my shoulder. "There's always a bright side, my dear. Always a bright side. The best part about Sam leaving you is that I get to keep you here with me."

My heart sinks so low I think it hits my bladder.

"I bet," she says with an excitable ring to her voice, "you can get your old job back!"

The doors *swoosh* open at the nursing home. I didn't notice the smell much when I worked here, but now it's making me nauseated. I hold my breath as I hurry to Mrs. Barrow's office, which is down the hall from the cafeteria. I have to gasp for air about the time I pass the cafeteria, and I'm overwhelmed by a whole new set of smells—egg substitute mixed with the burnt smell of a coffee urn sizzling on a hot burner somewhere unnoticed.

I hurry as fast as I can and round the corner, bursting into Mrs. Barrow's office the way nobody who is thought to be dead should ever burst into a former boss's office. Luckily, I called earlier to let her know I was alive and wanted to see her.

Still, her mouth has dropped and her eyes are wide as full moons. I guess it's kind of hitting me at this moment how dead people really thought I was. As I cautiously sit in the chair in front of her desk, she rises with the same slowness. Now she's towering over me, not saying a word, just searching me up and down like I might vanish before her eyes.

"Hope . . ." It's all she says.

I sit up straight and pretend this isn't at all awkward. I put on my best "I'm-here-for-an-interview" smile so we can get on with business. I think about cracking some sort of "back from the dead" joke but Mrs. Barrow doesn't seem like she'd be able to take it at the moment.

As slowly as she rose, she sits back down, both hands flat on her desk as if she might bolt at any second. Why isn't my "all-is-normal" smile working?

"So," I say, "as I said on the phone, I was hoping we could talk about me getting my job back."

Mrs. Barrow relaxes a bit, tugging at a blouse that is gaping in all the wrong places. She's got my folder out on the desk, looking it over for who knows what. I wonder if it has "dead" stamped across it anywhere.

"Hope . . ." She shakes her head ever so slightly. It's not so much a shake as a wobble, like her head isn't sitting quite right on her neck and it's causing an imbalance. "You quit . . ." She presses her lips together like she might break into a low hum of some sort. "You told us you were moving . . . and then you died. You quit and died. You see my predicament?"

I nod, but Mrs. Barrow doesn't seem to see mine. I've been dumped at the altar and declared dead by suicide. As predicaments go, I feel mine trumps hers. But you can't say that at a job re-interview.

"Mrs. Barrow, I've worked here seven years. My grandmother is here." I clasp my hands together, hoping to either appear angelic or desperate.

She drums her fingers against the folder, pinky to thumb, over and over. "Well, you have been a model employee. The way you keep up with the laundry . . ."

"I fervently oppose laundry pileups."

"And the bed pans . . ."

"Nobody is more enthusiastic about bed pans than I am."

Finally she sighs and closes my folder. My eye twitches a little as I watch her do it. The book has been closed on me once. It's like she's putting the lid on my coffin.

"I can check with H.R. about letting your replacement go." Mrs. Barrow smiles. She's got the kind of smile that makes everything else on her face temporarily obsolete. Those big teeth gleam and twinkle. Her lips are spread wide and tight. And even as I return the smile, a sudden wave of doubt slips over me like a silky nightgown. I don't think the smile makes it all the way to my lips. I only know this because Mrs. Barrow is now looking at me with the kind of expression that denotes alarm.

"You know what?"

She obviously doesn't. Her eyebrows are raised halfway up her forehead like she can't possibly anticipate what's going to happen next.

"Maybe I . . ." My heart is beating silly in my sternum. My palms are moist and spongy, like a higher-end cake mix. The air conditioning blows uncomfortably at my ankles. "Maybe I don't want to be known as the Best Bed Panner for the rest of my life."

"But you are. You really are. I should've gotten you a plaque."

"Thank you, but I'm realizing even as I sit here—"

Mrs. Barrow is starting to look desperate. "No, really. I can check for you. Who else will rewrite the ladies' greeting cards for them? Who else will make them smile?"

I stand suddenly. Now I tower over her. "I'm an artist. A writer!" It's all way too dramatic for a twelve-by-twelve office in a nursing home, but I'm having a moment. I'm having one of those life-changing revelations that you hope happens on top of a mountain or near a monument. She has a small plastic flag on her desk, held up by Snoopy while he stands on his doghouse. So I look at that. "This, here, it's not what I planned to do."

Mrs. Barrow's expression morphs back into that same expression she wore when I bolted into her office just a few minutes before. I stretch a charming smile across my face. "Why let a little thing like my pulse get between you and the new girl?"

I kneel by my grandmother's wheelchair and hold her hand.

". . . and obviously I realize it's very confusing, me having left, then died, then come back, and now I'm leaving again. People in their right minds are having trouble tracking with this. But the point is that I think I've found my way. For the first time in my life, Grandma, I think I've found my way."

"Okay."

"Yes. Yes! Okay indeed." I place the Columbine on her lap. "So, good-bye, Grandma."

"Okay."

I leave her room, trek down the same hallway I've trekked a hundred thousand times, and round the corner into the common room. Usually at this time, the residents are entranced by their soap opera, but there is an odd sight. They're all reading newspapers. Some of them can't even see.

I spot Gertie by her shoes, Reebok's under swollen ankles. "Gertie?"

She lowers her newspaper and smiles at me. The other residents lower theirs too. Everyone is staring at me.

"Oh honey!"

I embrace her. "Hi, Gertie."

"I was so glad to have read in the paper that you're not dead."

"No, I'm not de— . . . hold on. Paper? What do you mean, in the paper?"

Gertie hands me the newspaper, folded crisply and neatly the way I remember my dad reading it. I turn it over to see what she, and apparently everyone, is so enamored with.

There are the obituaries. And where normally there would be a large ad for funeral services or legal services or carpet cleaning, there I am, four inches tall, with a headline over my forehead: *"Alive and Available!"*

I gasp for the obvious reason—my mother has taken out an ad for me on the obituary page, where, of course, every hot-blooded male goes on the hunt for potential mates. But beyond that madness, she has managed to choose the quirkiest picture ever taken of me, one of those pictures where you're managing to have a bad hair day and a momentary lapse in judgment on clothing choice and facial expression. It's a complete train wreck. For no reason that is discernible, my arm is raised, and a shadow is cast right into my pit, looking like I've decided to go all Euro on my hygiene options.

I gasp again. One more and I'll be officially hyperventilating.

"It's official. I'm going to kill her." I glance at all the residents. They look as if no one really knows who *her* is. "My mother," I say flatly. "For putting this in the paper."

"Oh . . ." they all say in unison, nodding.

"Now, now," Gertie says. "Your momma means well."

"This is a nightmare . . ."

"You know what? After you get rid of them bad boys, that's when the good one sneaks right on up."

"The only people looking at obits for dates are gold diggers, Gertie."

"One day, mark my words, you'll be so thankful you're in all this pain. When the right boy answers this ad."

Maybe it's just me, but have you ever had a moment where you're so mad that you're engulfed by it? Like all facets of your mind are in gear, working out the angst, solving the problem of how to change your current circumstance? Some call it "seeing red," but I just call it blind-by-rage.

That's why I didn't see the van as I pulled into the driveway of my home. At that moment, I was rehearsing the speech I was going to slay my mother with.

It wasn't until I heard "Hope!" that I realized anyone was even there.

I look up to find a reporter stalking across the lawn of my home, a microphone extended out in front of her, a cameraman trailing behind, and a long cord snaking behind him. My eyes dart to the van. It's a news crew. The woman is wearing fuchsia head to toe—the kind that really only works if you're trying to overexaggerate your presence. Her hair is tied into the kind of bun that makes her look like she's in the middle of getting a face-lift.

"Ms. Landon," she says as she sidles up to me.

I slowly close the car door because the car is *dinging* a reminder I've left the keys in the ignition.

"How does it feel to be alive?"

"Great. Thank you for asking." I flash a smile because all the awkward photos of me are streaming through my mind and I'm hoping, if I'm lucky, this one gorgeous grin will make up for all the ones that have let me and every other single woman down.

I try to step to the side. She steps in front of me. I try the other side. She's right there, her heel planted so firmly that I think it might have actually sunk into the concrete of the driveway. All the while, she's smiling at me and angling herself to still look good on camera.

"We want to do a news series on you. You give hope to our audience."

I just stand there blinking. Me? Giving hope? What is she talking about? Hasn't she seen all that has happened? I can't give hope. I'm the polar opposite of hope. I'm Oedipus. I haven't killed my father and accidentally married my mother, but you've seen my life. You have to agree that all-in-all this is more Greek tragedy than inspiration. My mother alone is cause enough for despair.

The reporter is still going. Her eyes are all "aura and light," as if somehow her dream is coming true right before our eyes. "To come back from being left at the altar, back from a suicide attempt! Now you're ready to risk, to find love again."

"I'm . . . no, I'm not. I'm still coming to grips with the fact that I was dead. I am still feeling quite dead, to tell you the truth. Not totally dead. Just alive enough to wish I might've really been dead. It's complicated."

"Let us follow your story with our cameras until you find true love! You'd be inspiring many women out there who feel hopeless."

I'm slumping just like an eighth grade girl who is all at once dealing with acne and social dilemmas. Doesn't she see me for what I am? I'm no hero. I'm certainly no reality star. I'm trying to keep my mother from taking more ads out in the obituaries, for my death and for my life. This is not the picture of stardom or hope. This is the picture of complete dysfunction on nearly every level imaginable.

I look at the reporter. She is still smiling as if I'm missing the most exciting opportunity of my life. "What's your name?"

"Danielle Warren."

"Danielle, let me give you some advice. I'm assuming by the way you're looking at me that I'm offering you some hope in life, that you're single and you're looking for that one story that makes you believe true love can happen."

Danielle glances back at her cameraman, then back at me. She slowly nods. "I got dumped too."

Oh goody. We're all in the same club and they need a pack leader.

"So you can understand where I'm coming from when I say that this is not really my dream—to be dumped, presumed dead, only to rise again and find out that my life is way worse than I thought. You see what I'm saying? This is not the kind of story that Meg Ryan and Tom Hanks star in."

Danielle lowers the microphone, nods her head slowly.

I'm about to thank her for her time, hug her because, after all, she was dumped too, and bid her farewell when all of the sudden I hear a noise that causes me to freeze—it's the kind of noise you can't at first identify. But it becomes louder and the only thing that's moving in my entire body is a sudden flush of adrenaline, the kind that makes it possible to lift a car to save a life if need be.

What is that noise?

It almost sounds like a herd of elephants. Or geese. It's the weirdest sound. I look quickly at Danielle. She doesn't look alarmed. She looks . . . guilty.

I turn around, just in time to see it—the source of the noise: a dozen men are piling out of the news van, each and every one of them sweaty like they'd been stuffed inside a duffel bag for a while. They're gathering on the front lawn of my home, adjusting their shirts, feathering their hair, checking their armpits.

Now, I am just like any other American woman. I see a hot guy and even if I truly believe he's toxic and would eventually be the death of me, I strike a pose. I smile, maybe run my fingers through my hair. It's just instinct. Primitive, really, if you don't include the hair spray and the lip gloss.

So you'll understand what I mean when I say I don't strike a pose. I don't smile. At all. I'm just staring, that kind of awkward stare that you never want to be caught giving.

I count them one by one. Eleven. How did they all fit into that news truck?

I scan the crowd as they smile and wave. Four look like they should be at ComicCon. Three just got off the farm, literally. Two are wearing reds that don't match. And the other two don't look right. That's all I can say.

Danielle puts the microphone back in my face, her eyes wide with anticipation. "Every one of these men called today to answer your ad!" She makes a sweeping gesture, as if I'm royalty, these are all princes and I get to choose with which one I will live in eternal bliss.

A croaking noise comes up my throat. It shocks me because I can't remember another time I've actually croaked, besides when I supposedly died. And I'm no psychologist, but if I'm sticking with the fairy-tale analogy, I'm pretty sure somewhere in this scene there are toads. And I'm no amphibian, so . . .

The croaking sound erupts again from my throat. Danielle's face grows concerned. The cameraman tilts his head away from the viewfinder, takes a step back, as if preparing for me to yack. At this point, I can make no promises.

Now you're probably thinking that I'm going to say something clever. Or give the ComicCon guys a shot, because you and I both know that Nerd is super-hot right now. But I can't tell you the difference between Star Wars and Star Trek. That kind of ignorance can get you murdered at ComicCon.

It takes me a whole second to decide, but I realize I need to beat the next croak, because all I can see are five-second sound bites of me on the news, four seconds of which are me croaking like a frog.

So I bolt. Straight for the front door. I actually jump over the iron railing around the porch. I don't remember even opening the door. I am just suddenly inside, my back against the door, my pulse a thick, ticking thud against my neck.

"Mommy?"

It took me eighteen days to decide, but I did it. I stare at the duffel bag and rolling suitcase that are open on the couch. Both look like wide, gaping mouths that are ready to devour the hope and the future that God says I have. That's stenciled on my wall. Some of the letters have worn off through the years so now it reads: *I now the p ans I have for yo , pla s for a hope and a futu .*

I don't know what my *futu* holds, to tell you the truth, but anything has to be better than this. I realize that people have different thresholds for their low point. Anyone who has ever dealt with an alcoholic knows that just because you think they've hit bottom doesn't mean they have. But generally speaking, I'm pretty sure being dumped at the altar and then falsely declared dead by suicide is a low enough point to consider a new life plan.

My friend, Becca, disagrees. She's standing next to me, looking into the same gaping suitcase holes that I am, but with a completely different perspective. Her hands are on her hips, which is the first indication she believes she's right. The second is that her belly is swollen with new life growing inside, which changes the chemistry in women's brains to believe they have insight into all life, in any form, in any predicament, regardless of their own life experience. It doesn't say that in *What to Expect When You're Expecting*, but I'm certain a lot of men can confirm my suspicions.

"You're sure you're not just running away?"

I've assured her for seven days, ever since I told her my plan to go to New York City. But that hasn't taken. So I try a different approach. "I live in a small town that most of the country can't pronounce. Humiliation rests behind every corner. Why would I need to run away?"

She starts to answer but I interrupt her. "Example, and I'm just pulling this out of the pile of four dozen examples. But I was at the grocery store a few days ago. I have about six items in my basket. I get to the cash register to pay and the cashier says to me, 'It's paid for.' I ask her what she means. Apparently the lady in front of me handed the cashier a hundred dollars, asked her to pay for my groceries, and then wanted to give me the change."

Becca can't even sell it as it comes out of her mouth. "It was a nice gesture."

"It's pity, Becca. I don't want to be pitied. I don't want any of this. I want out." I gesture toward the small round table I'd eaten most of the meals at in my life. On top of it I've constructed a house of cards. A house of all the cards that have been sent since my death and all the new ones sent since my resurrection. There are of course no cards made for people rising from the dead, so people are sending awkward ones, like the one today meant for someone getting a promotion. *Congratulations! We know this is well deserved!* "Look at this house I built."

"Nice." She doesn't smile.

"That's what I've been doing for the past two weeks. Building a three-foot house of cards out of cards."

"I should get you a Popsicle. That's what you need. Just one of those blue Popsicles that makes you feel so good."

"You think a blue Popsicle is going to solve my problem?"

Becca sighed. "It's just that my grandmother said something to me once. She said if you are not happy, geography isn't going to change a thing."

"That of course insinuates that I am the problem. Save that psychobabble advice for the ladies at the nursing home—you know, the ones who have no control over their geography. They can't even choose whether they want to go to bingo or not. They just get wheeled in there, like it or not. I have the freedom to go and do and you're saying I shouldn't?"

Becca softens a little. Her hands leave her hips. Even that big, sassy ball sticking out of her tummy appears to deflate a bit. "It's just . . . by yourself? New York City by yourself?" She chews a nail that hasn't grown past the nail bed. "We're just small-town girls, Hope. I mean, what do we know of the big city? When you were going with Sam, that was different. He was with you. He'd lived there once. But how are you going to survive in a city like that? By yourself?"

"First, you've hit your quota for saying 'by yourself' to me. No more. Obviously, yes, I'm by myself. That was evident the day my wedding fell apart. So there's no reason to reiterate it. Second, why should I stop chasing my dream because Sam isn't coming with me?" I pull one of the cards off the house of cards. I flip it over and point to the New York City address and the "Heaven Sent" logo on the back.

Becca arches a brow. "You've already been to heaven. And back. And I'm not entirely sure about this, but if I'm guessing, heaven isn't in New York City."

"Becca, my entire life I've been too afraid to leave Poughkeepsie. To chase my dream of making cards professionally. These"—I point to the one in my hand—"well, yeah, they're kind of sappy. But they got published. And they're very popular. We received dozens of them when I came back from the dead. And I look at these, Becca, and I know . . . I can do better than this. I'm good at greeting cards." I say this with a grand gesture.

I bump the table. The entire house of cards falls down—revealing my mother, who was apparently standing there listening the whole time.

It's such a shocking exposure she actually covers her privates even though she's fully dressed. But indeed, she has been exposed.

"You can't leave! Your life is here!"

"Mother, what life?" I take a breath, realizing I'm going to have to defend this decision once again. That's why I need to get out of here, so I don't have to explain anything to anybody anymore. "Taken inventory lately? I even lost custody of my twin bed."

"I'm working on getting that back." Now my mom has her hands on her hips. "No one's going to publish your cards."

"Now that's just mean."

She nods heartily in agreement, her eyes watering. "I know it was. I'm just desperate."

I look down at the card in my hand. It's so sappy, like it came straight out of a tree. Sticky with the residue of a useless kind of hope, the kind one sits around and waits for instead of going out and getting. All these words, they're meaningless. Prayers that sound good on a page, rhyme well, tickle the ear, but have no use otherwise. Well, I refuse to write sap. Refuse it.

"Dad always loved my cards." Sure, they were all the ones I created when I was kid, but even then I had a certain edge, a certain way with words. I didn't care about butterflies and rainbows, I can tell you that. I once wrote an entire poem to give to the old lady that sacked our groceries, wishing her a windfall of money so she could sit and her ankles wouldn't swell. Just sayin', that's how I saw the world. It's how I *still* see the world. But now, I have an even newer perspective—one that most women don't have, but should.

I cover my face with my hand as my mom's hands shoot into the air. I always know it's coming yet each time it always feels misplaced—which obviously it is, but there's a pattern you'd think I would've settled into by now.

"Lord! Tell her if she stays she'll find love here!"

To my surprise, my hands shoot toward the ceiling. Becca stumbles backward. Even my mom looks caught off-guard. Her mouth is open, mid-prayer, but nothing is coming out.

I look up at the ceiling. Notice some cobwebs and a moldy patch from where the roof leaked in '88. I don't see the Almighty, but that doesn't stop me from shouting at him: "Tell *her* that love and all the pain that comes with it—I don't need it! None of it!"

My mom catches her second wind. Now she's back in gear. "You know love, Lord! It sneaks up on ya! Tell her it's sneaky!"

"Tell her that it's *my* time! It's my chance to be heard! Which has never been a part of my—"

"But you gotta be in that right place to be snuck up on, Lord! Like Poughkeepsie!"

I drop my hands. Becca gives me a wistful, sympathetic look. "Mom, I believe you just proved my point. I'm trying to state that I'm never heard and then you interrupt—"

"I hear the Empire State Building is a perfect place to find love." It's Becca this time who keeps my declaration from fully escaping, but at least she's now seen my perspective.

I turn to my mom. I take her hands. Tears, fat and bulbous, are welled in her eyes. I know this is so hard for her to understand. All she's ever known is me, Poughkeepsie, and our little way of life. "Mom, this is my chance to say something. To give something to people in pain. To help them laugh at pain."

She is so lost. "Oh, honey. Pain's not funny."

I realize it right then. No matter what, she will never understand I have a gift. She will never see what it does to my soul to see someone laugh at something I wrote. It's my balm, but it's not hers.

"Maybe it's not," I say to her as gently as I can. "But can you support me? Just this one time?"

My mom slides her hands to either side of my face, right at the cheeks. I don't know if she's going to slap me, squeeze me, or pop me. "At least I can take comfort."

I try to smile, but her hands are in the way.

"When this fails, you'll be back. I'll save the couch bed for you!"

5

It was the strangest feeling, to not be connected to someone for years and then to suddenly feel an inexplicable—even relentless at times—tug toward them. Yet Jake was, for all intents and purposes, just on the sidelines. An onlooker. At the right place at the right time . . . or seconds late, as he felt. So many regrets had been running through his mind over the past week. If he'd not stopped to get a drink on the way to the wedding, he might've been able to intervene, to save Hope from this terrible mess.

He felt helpless, too, unsure if he should visit her at the hospital. He'd gone a couple of times but always felt out of place, even when he was the only one in the room. Yet it seemed she didn't have a steady stream of people coming and going. It was mostly her mom and her friend, Becca. They couldn't be there all the time, so maybe he should be.

Then he would talk himself out of it again. This was how every day at the shop began and how every day ended.

"You should go see her."

Jake whipped around, holding cut stems in his hand that he intended to toss in the trash fifteen minutes ago. Once again, he'd gotten lost in his thoughts.

Mindy stood there, her head tilted to the side, a compassionate smile on her lips.

"I'm sorry, what?"

"Hope. You should go see Hope."

Jake blinked. How could she have read his mind like that?

Mindy grinned, stepped forward, patted his shoulder. "Jake, I've worked for you for several years now. I've always known you to stay on task and get things done." She glanced toward the front counter of the shop, where ticket orders were piling up.

Jake looked at his feet. "Mindy, I'm sorry. I know I've been distracted."

"Don't apologize. That's not what I'm saying. What I'm saying is that when we're consumed with something, we ought to figure out why. You witnessed something horrible to someone you once knew. The fact that you can't get her off your mind says something."

What did it say? He had no idea.

"It says that you need to go see her."

Jake walked to the counter, sifted through some of the tickets. "I've been to see her, Mindy. Twice since the day of the accident. I mean, I'm not family. I'm not even a friend. What am I supposed to do there? She's in a coma, so what's the point?"

"The point is, you can't stop thinking about her."

Jake held up the tickets in his hand. "I think we better get to these pronto."

She took the tickets from him. "I can handle these myself. Go to the hospital."

"No. Too much to do. I can't leave you here by yourself."

"I've got the sisters." She touched his arm. "Jake, you've been very good to me. The best employer I've ever had. You've always watched out for me and my family. It's the least I can do. There's a young woman in a coma after the worst day of her life. She needs somebody there."

Even as Jake shook his head in protest, he knew that's where he wanted to be. His mind was there already, every part of the day. His body should follow. Jake hugged Mindy.

"I'll come in tonight, help finish up these orders. Just leave them by the cash register before you lock up."

"Go."

The hospital was only fifteen minutes away, but it took him an hour to get there because he kept circling the building, then would head home, then turn around and come back. What was his hesitation? But then again, what was his obsession?

Finally, he made it inside the hospital elevators. When they swished open, he just stood there.

A little old lady, her purse clasped against her chest, stared at him. "Are you going to get off?"

He stepped off, but didn't move. The elevator missed pinching his backside by mere inches. He didn't bring flowers this time. He carried nothing except hesitation as he turned right and walked the shiny, white linoleum toward her room. Everything was so stark, so sickeningly clean and bright. The lights hurt his eyes. The sounds buzzed his ears. His head throbbed with uncertainty.

He paused right before her doorway. He could still leave now. He could just turn and go home and let fate carry Hope to wherever she was supposed to go. But for whatever reason, he didn't. Instead, he stepped into her room.

Her friend, Becca, was at her bedside. Sobbing. Jake immediately regretted his decision to come. He'd broken into a private moment. He took two steps backward, trying to quietly and gracefully exit.

But Becca suddenly looked up. Then she gasped. Jake gasped too, but he tried to suppress it, which caused his lips to press together like a waffle iron and his cheeks to inflate like balloons.

Becca wiped the streaming tears. "I thought I was alone."

Jake took a deep breath as Becca stood with effort, her belly round and protruding. "I'm so sorry," Jake said softly. "I didn't mean to interrupt."

"It's Jake, right?"

He nodded. They'd stood together the day of the accident, almost two weeks ago, but he'd barely seen her since.

"The flower guy?"

"Yes. I'll just come back another time—"

"No, please. Come in." She beckoned him with her hands. "I have needed to leave for twenty minutes but I hate leaving her alone."

"Where is her mom?"

"I'm not sure. She is here some, but she spends a lot of time down at the chapel and I don't know where else."

Jake felt the tension between his shoulder blades release a little. "She does seem to like to pray."

Becca raised a playful eyebrow. "You have no idea."

Jake stepped a little closer to the bed, for the first time looking at Hope. She lay still, her arms crossed over her belly, a little thinner now. They'd taken the bandage off her head wound and there was just a Band-Aid over it now. Dark purple seeped around its edges, and he wondered if she still had stitches in.

"How is she doing?"

Becca shrugged, casting a desperate look toward the bed. She pulled the blanket a little higher. "The doctors can't really tell us anything. They said it's a traumatic brain injury. They have no idea when she'll wake up. Or if." She grabbed her sweater off the back of the chair and stepped next to Jake. "It's so nice of you to come to check on her."

"I just feel so . . . bad, about everything."

"She definitely doesn't deserve this. She's such a great person. Talented, too."

"Did they ever catch the person who did this?"

Becca shook her head. She squeezed his arm. "Thank you for coming. I know she's not alone now."

Becca left and Jake just stood there for a long time, observing her and feeling guilty about it. She was truly as beautiful as the day he saw her all the way back in elementary school. He could still spot some of those features even now as she'd grown into a woman. Yet in this bed, she looked as fragile as a child. She probably hated the idea that people were just standing around staring at her.

"Hi, Hope. It's Jake. You won't remember me, but we . . ." He sighed. What a stupid thing to say.

"We what?"

Jake's head jerked up. Hope's mother stood in the doorway.

He jumped out of his seat while trying to keep a casual look on his face. By the way her mother eyed him, he could only assume his expression was betraying him in every way imaginable.

"I'm sorry. I was just leaving."

"Wait." Her hands were crossed at her chest. She was fully blocking the doorway. "Wait just a minute."

A sickness roiled through his stomach, the kind you get from a roller coaster or having your zipper down in public.

"You . . . I know you . . ."

"Um, well, yes. I'm Jake, from the other day. I found Hope—"

"No. I knew you before that."

"Yes. You ordered the flowers for the wedding from me. I was delivering them . . ."

"No. Before that." Her mother's eyes narrowed.

"We deliver the Columbine flower to your—"

"Before that."

Jake cleared his throat. "Hope and I went to the same school."

"That's it!" Her expression now beamed delight. "That's how you know my baby girl?"

"Well, I mean, no . . . we . . . you know, we didn't run in the same circles. I hardly remembered her, you know . . . just kind of the name . . . I put it together days later . . ." He was never good at lying.

CiCi, as she'd introduced herself the first day, walked into the room and looked at her daughter.

"I'll leave you two—"

"Oh no you will not. The doctor says we need to keep her stimulated." She eyed him. "You look like the kind of guy that can do that sort of thing."

"Oh . . . uh . . ."

"Talk to her. Carry on an interesting, one-sided conversation?"

"I sometimes have trouble even when it's two-sided."

"Oh, come now. Surely you can think of something interesting to say. Talk about your childhood memories, the school, the teachers, that sort of thing."

"But, I'm not really—"

"The doctors say she can hear what we're saying, so you must, must talk to her. You could be her only hope."

Jake's gaze cut to the bed. He sure hoped not.

And then CiCi raised her voice at the point that most people would lower theirs. "You must understand what dire straits this poor girl is in. She's been dumped . . . DUMPED . . . at the altar. Generally, people don't recover from that. But it must be said, one doesn't get dumped at the altar because the relationship is going well. And relationships generally don't go well when one or more of the parties lives in a dream world."

"You mean . . . the coma?"

"Before the coma. She believed she could make a living writing greeting cards." CiCi shook her head, made circular motions around her ear.

Jake couldn't help it, it just rolled off his tongue. "Believes."

"What?"

"Believes. Not believed. She's still with us."

Then her voice grew even louder. She was practically shouting. Or wailing. "My poor baby girl! Her life fell apart the day her daddy left and it's just getting worse and worse!"

Before she could shoot her hands in the air for another prayer, Jake gently put a finger to his own lips though he really wanted to put a hand over her mouth.

She stopped, looking curiously at him.

"If what they say is true"—he spoke in such a quiet whisper she had to lean in to hear—"and she can hear what we say, perhaps a better use of our time is to speak to her in a way that will encourage her to wake up."

CiCi looked as if she was trying to understand, but blinked as if she didn't. "I know the Lord hears my cries." And up her hands went.

But Jake whispered, "The sign down the hallway says he hears them more clearly in the chapel."

Her hands dropped. "What sign?"

"Down the hall, by the door, near the place that has the thing."

"What, wait . . . where?" CiCi's eyes widened. "If that's true . . ."

"Oh, it is."

She glanced at Hope. "You'll stay with her then?"

"Sure." The room was now very quiet, but the alternative, to have CiCi shouting her daughter's dysfunction all over the hospital corridor, didn't seem to be a good option either.

"Thank you, you dear one! Thank you!" She drew him in for a hug, but she was so wispy it felt like hugging a cheese cloth. Then she was gone.

He stood and watched Hope for a long time, wondering if she might, on a whim, just open her eyes. When she didn't, his gaze followed the crowd of cards and flowers, pushed into all the shelves and spaces in the room. He walked to where most of the cards were, gazing at their covers . . . a lot of mountains, waterfalls, bridges, clouds, rainbows, sunsets, grassy fields, barns . . . the most serene pictures that were ever caught on film.

"Excuse me, sir . . . ?"

He looked to the doorway, where a candy striper—in actual red and white stripes—stood holding a stack of cards. "These came for her."

"Oh . . ." Jake looked around. There wasn't really a place to put them. "Here. I guess I can take them."

"Thanks." The young girl couldn't have been more than sixteen. She glanced sideways, with a measure of guilt on her expression. "She looks so peaceful."

Jake nodded and thanked her again.

"Well," he said, sitting in the chair, counting the stack of cards. "It looks like ten more have arrived today for you."

He fingered the sharp corners of the envelopes. He should say something. Something real. Something profound. Something encouraging. But he was no different than that small boy who couldn't manage to speak when the girl rewrote his card. His tongue was tied even as his feelings were unraveling.

She was beautiful, even sleeping. Her hands held delicate and long fingers. He wanted to take them into his. He wanted to tell her that it was going to be all right, that she didn't deserve what happened to her—any part of it.

But instead, nothing came, and he chided himself for being unable to speak even the smallest amount of encouragement. Instead, he looked at the stack of cards on his lap and then tore open the first envelope. It was a pretty photograph of a gray sky with a vague hint of a rainbow. He opened it, a little sheepishly because he was reading someone else's mail, but it wasn't like she could read it. From a family called the Thompsons: "May

God bless you in the midst of your turmoil." He glanced at her. Well, this was turmoil all right. He supposed a blessing would be for her to wake up, but he guessed they didn't make "wake-up-from-your-coma" cards.

He filtered through the cards, a lot of handwritten notes like "hope you get better!" and "get well soon!" inscribed after some Bible Scripture or a simple poem about all the good that suffering can do when placed in God's hands. A lot of pictures of doves.

He opened the last one. It came in a slightly smaller envelope. When he pulled it out, he immediately recognized it. It came from his shop. It was a card he'd designed himself. He remembered taking the picture . . . it was of a creek at dusk. The water glowed a beautiful amber and reflected the fall leaves that shaded it. Small logs drifted in its water. A vine grew up one tree. A tiny butterfly floated just above a rock. He didn't have to open it. He knew what it said inside:

> *"The silence inside a perfect day*
> *Will help you find your way"*

He sat back and stared at it, then her. It was going to take more than a pretty picture to get her out of this mess. But whatever it took, he'd try to make every day he could, while she was in this awful mess, as perfect as it could be.

And maybe he could do a little better than just silence.

GREETINGS FROM MY LIFE

The train slows, then stops. I cannot believe it, but I am about to step right into Grand Central Station. It makes me smile because my friend Becca's mother used to almost use it as a cuss word when we were kids.

"What is this? Grand Central Station?!"

But here I am, at my destination. The dream is alive. I quickly tuck my drawing pad and pencils into my bag and wait for the door to open.

As it does, I'm hit with a strange odor, then a foggy, muggy kind of air, thick like syrup and odorous too. The light isn't quite right, either. I was thinking everything would be awash in sort of an amber light . . . more natural light, maybe. I'm not sure. But either way, it is time for me to step off. And step off I will!

When people fall, they don't really make a *splat* sound, you know? I mean, why do we even say that? It's more a *thud*. And a grunt. And then I hear my pencils rolling from my bag, one by one. I can't see anything but shoes as people walk around me like I'm some kind of mud puddle.

It was the strangest feeling that caused the fall, a sharp, shooting pain through my foot. I don't know why nobody is helping me up. I manage my way to my knees. My heel throbs but it's the least of my concerns. I locate my bag. It's three feet away. I reach for it but can't quite get to it. One foot after another, each adorned with some pretty impressive footwear, stomps on it.

Like a slug, I crawl toward it, panting against the suffocating humidity that apparently hovers two feet off the ground. I reach my bag. Scramble for my pencils. Dodge spiky heel after spiky heel.

It feels like hours, but finally I manage to get to my feet after the train traffic has cleared and get my luggage. I blow air into my bangs. I'm sweaty. Shaken. But. I. Am. Here.

As I walk out of the terminal, I make myself smile. What did I think? NYC was going to be a cakewalk? It's tough here and I have to get my game on. I hold my head high and my bag close and I march on.

Until I have to stop and look at a map.

Thanks to craigslist, I have a good idea of where I want to live. At least judging by price and location. Thanks to Google Maps, I also have a good idea of where I don't want to live. I'm three blocks away from gang territory, but supposedly it's a safe neighborhood in Westside Manhattan.

Except . . . the apartment doesn't look so . . . Manhattan-ish. At least how I envisioned it. But again, I have to keep an open mind. I once read about a couple who lived in a 400-square-foot apartment in Manhattan. It's my new way of life.

I walk up the steps, dragging my luggage. I knock gently on the door. The door cracks open and an old man peers at me with one eye. I can see he has a gray beard and a mole on his nose, but that's about it.

"Who are you?" he grumbles.

I beam with friendliness. "I'm here to inquire about the apartment you have for—"

"No cats!"

"Excuse me?"

"No cats!"

Just at that moment, I feel something brush my leg. It's soft and furry. I glance down and there is a calico cat circling me like we're well-acquainted. I shake it off. "It's not my—" And as if it multiplies right in front of my face, another cat appears. Except this one is a tabby. ". . . cat. Cats."

I'm not a fan of cats. Don't judge me. I know it's uncool to be prejudiced, but the irony of it is that I always feel like cats are judging me. They seem like they can see right into my soul, but maybe it's me. Or maybe it's their green eyes. I don't know. It's just weird how they're circling me like sharks.

The old man is still looking at me. "No cats!"

And then I try some New-York-City humor. I watched some YouTube videos to help me prepare. It's not an easy sense of humor to grasp, mind you, especially if you're not from the city. But I feel pretty confident I can get this guy to crack a smile.

"These aren't cats. They're dinner." I say this all straight-faced and calm like I really mean it.

The door slams.

I don't fare well at the next place either. She's a brick, this one–about 4'11, solid as a concrete birdbath.

"I'm here to inquire about the apartment for rent."

Meow.

Not the lady, the cats. They're seriously circling me like ground vultures.

"They're not mine," I say, a scowl cast toward them while I simultaneously cast a pleasant, I'm-dependable-and-catless grin at her.

Her frown is severe.

"I'd be a great tenant. I'm not married. Not engaged. No boyfriend and no plans for one. I'm here in New York City, following my dream of becoming—"

"No single people!"

I'm about to explain that (1) I haven't given the ring back yet so technically I'm still engaged. And (2) Statistics show that single people are better tenants. I don't have data to back that up, but I'm assuming that's true. Either way, I think I've just been discriminated against.

I wander the streets, pulling my cardigan, looking for an address that doesn't seem to exist. Sweat has soaked my bangs. And now I have a third cat following me. This one is black with small patches of white around the ears and nose. Perhaps adorable on any other day but this. Now it looks less feline and more leech.

I glance across the street and see a man trying to put a "for rent" sign up in the window. I hurry across, dragging my luggage and my cats, causing a taxi to lay on its horn. The man doesn't notice me at first. He's still working on getting that sign up in the window.

But he looks like the nicest man. I know, naive to go by looks. But he's wearing a cardigan. The kind with the wooden buttons. Again, no stats to prove it, but I'm pretty sure serial killers don't wear cardigans. Secondly, he's older. His back is hunched slightly. He's got a newspaper tucked under his armpit. He's got small tufts of hair growing out of each ear, but he's remarkably well groomed otherwise. He turns, notices me and smiles the kind of smile only dentures can pull off.

"Sir!" I don't mean to shout, I'm just excited and he's old. He turns down his hearing aid. "Sorry. I'm looking for an apartment."

He notices the cats. Who wouldn't? They're like a carousel around my feet.

"These are not my cats."

"They look awfully fond of you."

"New perfume. I think it's a little too catnip-ish." I can't think of another explanation.

"You seem nice enough. And I hate showing the place. You wouldn't believe all the crazies that show up when you have an apartment for rent." He pats my shoulder with a thick, swollen hand. "Your credit checks, it's yours."

"Thank you!"

"Come on inside."

I start to follow him, but suddenly my foot doesn't move. I glance down and the cats are still there, but none of them are holding my foot down. I try again, but it's stuck. With a lot of effort I pull one more time and then hear the strangest sound . . . like something coming unglued from something else.

I realize I've stepped in a glob of sap.

I quickly slip off my shoe and follow him in, but not without noticing that there is not a tree in sight.

Inside he is already seated at an old computer tucked in the corner. I hand him my driver's license and a sheet of paper with all the information he'll need to look up my credit.

Outside the cats are meowing their protest.

"Take a look around, see what you think."

With measured delight, I peek here and there. One bedroom. A tiny kitchen. A decent sized living room, at least large enough for a couch and a chair. The bathroom is swallowed up by a claw tub. The sink is crammed in so tightly it seems like an afterthought. But it's charming, nevertheless. Once I start bringing in some real money, I can think about getting something a little nicer. For now, this will do.

The man is now at the small kitchen table, barely big enough for three. Reading glasses are perched on his nose and several papers are spread out in front of him.

I sit down. "Well, the place is just lovely." It's not lovely, it's just what it is, but you shouldn't insult your landlord. Even I know that.

He peers at me over his glasses and then says, "You're dead, woman." I'm about to bolt for the door, realizing how stupid I am for assuming serial killers are opposed to cardigans, when he adds, "This report here says you're deceased."

My head drops to the table with a thud. "And yet," I mumble, "I'm not even feeling woozy." It is no use explaining my predicament, that I'm dead/alive by way of my crazy mother.

He grabs my shoulder, shoos me out with his big, fat hands. "I'm sure this is a shock," he says flatly. "If you need to sit down, there's the curb."

"Come on. Do I look dead to you?"

"That's the problem with this country!"

"Zombies?" I can tell this is going south all the way, so I figure I might as well be witty.

"You're dead to me, identity thief!" The door slams in my face.

I shout back through the door. "You think if I'd steal an identity, I'd choose *this one*?" As if he's looking through the peephole, I make wild gestures at myself, trying to paint a picture of my mother, my fiancé, my wedding day and other continued nightmares of my life. To the passersby, I probably look like I'm seizing out. The technical term is *conniption fit.*

At my feet are four cats. The color of the new one doesn't matter. At this point, it's just a mismatched quilt of fur.

It takes me an hour to scrape all the sap off my shoe. I'm seriously regretting my perfume choice, but if I can just get in a building somewhere for the night, I'm hoping these cats will lose interest.

While I'm rolling the small stick up and down the sole of my shoe, I notice a sign for the YMCA. It's only a block away, and already I can hear the sounds of the kids outside playing. I'm exhausted. This was not how I pictured my first day going, but I realize that I've got to stay focused on the goal. So for now, I need a place to stay until I can figure out how to rise from the dead, government style.

I walk the block or so, dragging way more than physical luggage, if you know what I mean. The kind I'm dragging doesn't have wheels and a pop-up handle. It's heavy too. Real heavy.

I stand outside the YMCA for a long time, trying to decide if I have the stomach for it. Say what you will about my mom, her house was always tidy and my sheets were always clean.

But again, it's my dream. I'm here. I've made it to New York City. So I should do what it takes. I can't help but wonder how different this would be if Sam were with me. He'd know what to do. He'd find us a place to live.

After several inquiries about whether there is a bed available, I am introduced to Morris. How to explain him. No neck to speak of. Lips the shade of a ripe plum. They're fat, too, the kind that women pay thousands for, but that look awkward with no neck. His eyes are small. I notice for a man of around forty or so, there are no laugh lines. That's worrisome. His shirt is buttoned up wrong and one pant leg hangs higher than the other. He gestures for me to follow him, keys dangling from his hand, and for no reason that I can identify, he squeaks with each step.

He talks over his shoulder as I trail. "Each week, you pay in advance and leave a credit card on file for IVs, antibiotics, and bed pans."

I laugh. Well, at least he has a sense of humor. But by the way his eyes cut toward me, I realize he isn't joking. Or he's a master of the deadpan delivery. I swallow and continue to follow.

We arrive at a door in the very tight hallway. The room says *11* above it. As he unlocks it, I notice an old woman, probably in her seventies, hunched over a mop, cleaning the floors at the end of the hall. She has a janitor uniform on.

"Welcome to paradise, Ms. Landon." Morris flips on the switch. We both stand there gazing into the closet. *Closet* is not the right word. It's slightly smaller. More like a very roomy file drawer. It's the smallest livable space I have ever seen. A hot plate in the other. A desk so small I think it's been sawed in half, sits with a chair pushed against it. And there, on the wall right in front of me, is a Murphy bed. I've always had a fear of Murphy beds. Doesn't everyone?

"Showers are down the hall." He squeaks away as I have flashbacks of junior high gym class.

It is late afternoon, but I'm only going by my watch. The room has a small window covered by small gray shades. The sun seeps through the sides. I decide I should unpack. Set on top of my now wrinkled clothes is the plastic bride and groom from my cake. *Mom*. I toss it in the wastebasket, which is also very small, like it belongs to an elf. I guess people in these circumstances have very little to throw away.

I have left my room door open. The air seems to circulate better out in the hall and I'm also starting to get claustrophobic. No one passes by for a long time, and then I hear footsteps. I look toward the doorway just in time to see her. She is a young girl, dressed in a plain T-shirt and baggy shorts. Her hair falls across her shoulders but is tangled. She glances in at me and I glance at her. Our eyes lock. She seems to see right through to my soul. I blink and she is gone.

A couple of hours later, I stand at the doorway of the showers. There are four, all with off-white shower curtains. The tile is stained in nearly every part of its grout. I thankfully brought flip-flops. A roach skitters across the floor. I am completely racked by fear but I'm also equally as terrified by my own body stench. So I take a step forward.

One shower is taken. I can see the feet under the curtain and they look a little cavewoman-ish. But there is singing. It kind of sets me at ease. It's an old hymn I remember singing in church but never knew the words to.

I manage my way through the shower. You've never seen an armpit scrubbed so fast. I'm back in my bedroom, hair wet and combed back from my face, sitting with the door closed on my very lumpy Murphy bed. It squeaks with every move I make. And it has to be said, there is a balancing act to these beds. One false move and you're a goner.

The next day, I oversleep. It is eleven a.m. and I haven't eaten in over twenty-four hours. I order Chinese takeout, eat in my room and try to figure out the subway map. There are a lot of dots and lines and color-coding that is supposed to make sense. An hour goes by and I finally manage to find the subway route I think I should take to get to the address that is on the back of the Heaven Sent card, when I realize I am within walking distance.

A knock at my door causes me to jump out of my skin, and that is just enough to throw the whole thing off-balance. Before I know it, the old Murphy bed is calling it quits on me, closing up fast. I'm trying to save my map and my Chinese food when I should've tried to save myself.

The next thing I know, I'm inside the wall.

So.

One is forced to examine one's life when trapped in the wall by a Murphy bed. Strangely, it's the perfect analogy for how I felt in Poughkeepsie—backed against a dark wall with nowhere to go.

Now, you're probably wondering at this point why I'm not screaming my freaking head off. Well, I was. But then someone came to rescue me. The same person who knocked on my door.

She hasn't gotten to the rescue part yet. She's currently in my room eating my food. I only know this because I can hear her slurping the lo mein noodles.

"So," she says, "what's your name?"

"Kid . . ." I am assuming it's the young girl who passed me earlier. I don't really know, but her voice sounds kid-ish. "Would you get me out of here?"

"Of course I'll rescue you. Just as soon as you answer my nine questions."

"Can it be three?"

"No."

"Kid. Please."

"Do you have a boyfriend?"

"It's getting kind of stuffy in here." I couldn't be sure, but I was guessing I was going to have major sheet marks on my cheek by the time I got out.

"Are you married?"

"Claustrophobic."

"Does that feel anything like being in love? Oh, wow. I thought the lo mein was good, but the orange chicken is amazing."

"Let! Me! *Out*!"

I didn't even hear her unlatch it. Suddenly I am falling and now I lay facedown on my mattress. I glance up. Yep. It's the same girl I saw before.

"Thank you." I take in one breath of air after another.

She holds a piece of chicken on the tip of her fork. "Here. You should try this."

I gather my maps and my pencils off the floor and everything else that was on the bed. "I gotta go see about a dream."

I grab my purse, my sketchpad, the Heaven Sent card, stuffing everything loosely in my bag, but the girl doesn't budge.

"It's good to have a dream. I'll hang here. Hold down our fort, sit here pondering my dreamy non-boyfriend." She plops down on the Murphy bed, but I open the door and wave her on out.

"Fine." She sighs, the first indication she's really a kid. Her face turns pouty. "I didn't catch your name."

"I didn't throw it." She walks out. "See you later, Room Eleven." And she swings out the door.

Within the hour, I am sandwiched between two people who did not scrub their armpits like I did. I decide to take the subway to get used to it. I should have walked. But finally I have arrived at my stop. I emerge from the underground into the light, squinting and trying to get my bearings.

It takes me a second to find North, but when I do, I'm only about three blocks away to the East. An easy walk without the baggage. I find myself walking more briskly than normal. The pace on the street is fast. The stream of people seem to read each other, walking in pace and never bumping. I try to concentrate so I won't be the odd man out. Their faces are very solemn. There is no acknowledgment of each other. I'm not a smiler, like I said. But I'm not a robot, either. It's hard for me not to express something when I'm standing shoulder to shoulder with someone.

Finally I arrive at 352 East 4th Street. I stand there gazing at the building. It doesn't seem to fit with the rest of the business district. It looks more like a doctor's office than a greeting card company. The sign reads *C.A.T.S.*

"Huh?" I say this because I'm sensing a theme.

I look down at the address on the Heaven Sent Card. 352. Check. West 4th Street. Oh . . . I'm at East. Dang.

I trudge back from where I came, my head hanging in slight defeat. But the second I glance up, I spot it . . . the purple jacket. The same one that I remember from my wedding day. The person who . . . who what? Stole the car? It's so . . . vague.

I hurry through the crowd. Apparently I've hit a doctors' convention because a bunch of people in scrubs are in my way. Once I move past them and am in the clear, the jacket is nowhere to be seen. My eyes dart everywhere, but whoever it was has been swallowed up by the crowd.

Stay on task. That's what I must do. I march forward, toward *West* 4th Street. When I arrive, I'm thankful to see the logo hanging outside. A cat meows nearby, sending me dashing through the front door.

Chimes that sound like heavenly harps greet me. Little cherubs hang from the door handle. Artwork from previous greeting cards hangs on the walls in the lobby. Behind a beautiful, ornate desk sits a young woman who looks like she just stepped out of an Ann Taylor catalog. Or an audition for *The Stepford Wives.*

She's on the phone and I study her suit . . . it's highlighter yellow. Her scarf is yellow too, but it's more the shade of Pine-Sol. I can't see her shoes. I'm guessing mustard. Her earrings are two little sunshine balls.

"Heaven Sent. Sent by Heaven. Where may I send you today?" Her tone smacks of lemon meringue . . . sweet with just a tease of sour. "Sure thing, please hold."

As she's transferring the call, the harp chime goes off again. I turn to see a man walk in, business suit, tie, confident enough to wear both. He's not a GQ model or anything, but he's got the kind of swagger that can grow on a girl. I'm trying not to notice but he's walking right toward me.

"May I help you?"

I step toward the desk, ready to introduce myself to the receptionist. And right as I do, I feel an incredibly sharp pain stab right through the bottom of my foot, *again,* as if I'd decided to wear my stiletto upside down. Except slightly more piercing.

I yelp. I reactively grab my foot and in doing so, drop everything I own, including what little self-worth I have left. The pain is gone, but my cards, my pencils, my sketchpad are all scattered across the floor. I drop to my knees, fumbling to gather it all, trying to keep myself from crying. I can't rent an apartment. And now I can't even properly introduce myself to a company I'm dying to work for.

"Oopsie," the receptionist says. "Did that hurt?"

The question was, *what* hurt me? I hadn't turned my ankle. I didn't step on glass. What *was* that? Probably some mutant heel spur gene that runs in my family.

"I'm fine. Really." We can't see each other. She's on the other side of the desk. I'm on my hands and knees, fishing for my red pencil that has rolled into a shadow.

"Fine, huh?"

I look up. The shadow has a source. It's the guy in the suit.

He squats beside me. "I'd like to hear how you define great."

"The view from here is . . . it's . . . well, breathtaking." I don't get to finish my witty punch line about the aesthetics of the linoleum because he's holding the Heaven Sent card that I brought in for the address. I stand up, brushing myself off, trying to hold the gigantic mess of papers in my hands. "I'm hoping to meet the ladies who wrote that card."

"Looking for an autograph?"

"Well, um . . ." If it gets me in the door, sure. "My mother, actually, she got the card for this . . . occasion. An occasion where people get cards. So, if you could introduce me to the ladies . . ."

"You're looking at them." He smiles, opens his hands in a "ta-da" motion. "Jake Sentinel. I didn't realize I had such a lovely fan."

"I'm Landon." It's the first sign that I'm shedding my old life. New town. New job. New name. Hope always seemed so . . . overly expectant. I shake his hand. "Flattery will get you everywhere. I would even work for you."

He keeps his eyes on me but addresses the receptionist. "Heather, can you make sure the children's home received the new Christmas line? I promised them five hundred."

"Sure thing, Jake."

"I need a job." He lets go of my hand, gives me a polite smile, and walks toward the elevators. I quickly follow. "I just moved here. And besides my stellar talent for embarrassing myself, I've always wanted to write greeting cards. If you'll let me show my samples . . ." They're clutched in my hands at the moment.

"People don't just come here and start writing cards." He pushes the button.

"Oh, I'm all about blazing a trail."

"Seriously, they don't just commit pen to the papyrus and start writing."

"But I'm mad with a pen. And papyrus. If you'll look at these . . ." I hold up both of my hands. It's a grand mess of cards and papers and pencils, any one of which could fall to the ground at any second.

He glances hopefully at the elevator but the doors don't open yet. "Look, I worked under my father for six years before he let me write a single card. When he retired, he left me to do the writing because he trusts me to continue our message."

"I kind of don't have six years. I have rent. But no cats. I illustrate too."

"My dad's sisters, Pearl and Ruby, do that."

"And how they've mastered those puppies and kittens."

He doesn't catch the sarcasm in my voice. His face actually brightens. "Haven't they? The kids, they love Pearl's tabby cat. There's nothing like coming up with cards that make a child smile."

The elevator doors open. With one step, he is inside. They are closing.

"I'd be a devoted employee!" I have no idea why I'm shouting, but that's how it's coming out. "I have no life right now! Literally!"

"It was nice to see you . . . Landon."

Swoosh. They are closed.

I just stand there staring at the door. I can feel Heather's yellowishness burning my backside like the actual sun is sitting there.

To my surprise, the bell *dings* and the doors open right back up like I've said the magic word. Perhaps it took pity on me.

Jake is standing there.

"This is all I can do." He puts a wad of cash in my palm, stuffing it between one of my cards and my drawing pad. "I *hope* you can find the best job, you know, where you can use those talents. Let me know how you weather."

Then, like he was swallowed up by the elevator, he is gone.

Where did *that* come from? Let me know how you weather? Saying *hope* like it's got some magic power?

Well, it doesn't.

6

Praying you are resting peacefully in the arms of our Heavenly Father. May He carry you through this stormy time.'" He closed the card. On the back of the card was a small sunset.

Jake glanced up. Well, she *was* resting peacefully. Of course, that was just observation from the outside. Maybe she was frantically trying to climb out of the coma. Now, though, she just looked peaceful.

He opened the next card. They were coming in by the dozens. For the past four days, he'd made it his job to come and read them to her. There was no way of telling when her mother would be here, and he tried to avoid her as much as possible. But mother or no mother, he felt compelled to be with Hope, even if she didn't know he was there.

He slid the card out of the envelope. It was a picture of a cross on a hill. Green grass rolled in the distance. The sun was setting directly behind it, spraying light in all directions. "'It is in the most difficult of times that we rely on and pray to Jesus. Through His stripes we are healed. Cling to Him in all things.'" He laughed a little. "Well, you don't appear to be able to pray or cling, but we have to cut them some slack." He set the card aside.

He was about to start a third card—it had a little lamb on it—when the nurse walked in. Her name was Bette ("like a gamble," she'd said) and they'd met two days ago. If he was sick, she was the kind of nurse he'd want. Like many in the health-care profession, she seemed not to have the time or energy to take care of her own health. Her scrubs fit tight in all the wrong places and she nursed some sort of energy/sugar/coffee/spiked water drink throughout her whole shift. All her features were sunken, but most of all her eyes. Sometimes Jake sensed when she came to check on Hope that she was a little envious of the sleep she was getting.

"Hi there, Jake." Her voice was always cheery even while her eyes looked swollen with fatigue. "How's our girl today?"

It was this kind of response that caused him to believe that he really shouldn't speak very much. "She's not mine. I mean, she's not . . . we're not . . . you know, together, unplatonically speaking. Speaking of speaking, we haven't really. Not in a long time. But I was delivering flowers for her wedding—I mean, the one that didn't—and then I found her, so . . ."

Bette raised an eyebrow at him as she took Hope's blood pressure. "You're trying to say you're just friends?"

"Of course, yes, that's a much easier way to say it."

Bette patted her hand lightly. "Hope, when are you going to wake up, girl? If I had a hot guy sitting next to my bedside, I'd sure as heck wake up."

Jake actually glanced behind himself.

"Yeah, you," she said with a smirk.

"Oh, um . . . thanks?"

She shook her head. "Sweetie, I believe in divine intervention. You know what that is?"

Jake nodded. "Yeah. I write about that a lot."

"Oh? You're a writer?"

"Not really a . . . per se . . . greeting cards, I write the little . . . inside where you sign . . . you know?"

"I'm going to have to teach you to speak in complete sentences, but I think I'm following. You write greeting cards."

"Not a lot. Just a few to keep in my store. We send a lot of bouquets for funerals and things, so I try to write something hopeful in each card, something that will give them strength."

"That's very sweet, Jake. And you're very sweet to sit in here and read these cards to her."

Jake shrugged. "I don't know if it's doing much."

"Oh, come now. I don't want to hear that from you. We can't give up hope. On Hope."

Jake laughed. "I guess her name requires that we don't, huh?"

From a nearby tray, she took what looked like large needles from a plastic sheath. She walked to the end of the bed and untucked the sheets and blanket, exposing her feet.

"They give shots in the feet now?" Jake cringed. He wasn't sure if he could watch.

"It's called Coma Arousal Therapy. We just call it CAT." She held up a needle. "The bottoms of the feet are extremely sensitive. So we gently stick needles, pricking her here and there, to try to get her to wake up."

She pricked the bottoms of her feet, but Hope remained motionless.

"Several times a day I will come in and do this. Sometimes I put a smell near her nose, like peppermint oil or eucalyptus oil. I've done ammonia too. I'll play music." She looked at Jake as she pricked her feet again. "But I've found that talking to patients who are unconscious is the best therapy around. Studies show that loved ones are the most influential."

"Well, um . . . again, I'm not even part of the—"

"Hope, dear God! Hope!"

Bette sighed before CiCi even got in the room. "That woman . . ."

CiCi rushed in, her eyes frantic, her face splotchy. "I got a word from the Lord!"

Bette was swiping the needles with alcohol and putting them back in their case. "Well, I got a word from the doctor, who sometimes mistakes himself for the Lord. He continues to maintain that you should keep a positive attitude around the patient at all times and not say things that are—"

"Stuck! That's the word the Lord gave me! Hope, you're stuck! You're stuck!"

"Okay, listen . . ." Bette took CiCi by the shoulders and sat her down in a chair behind Jake, away from the bed. "CiCi, right?"

"Yes. Yes." She was nodding, her hands trembling, her lips pressed together so tight they couldn't even be seen. It looked like she'd lost all her teeth.

"I know it feels like she's up against a wall here." Bette was trying to use a hushed voice.

"And no way to get out. No way at all . . ."

"There's always a way. It just might not come like we expect it to. Jake, why don't you hand CiCi some of those cards you've been reading."

Jake gathered ten or so, stacked them, and gave them to her. CiCi opened the first one and seemed to settle a bit, nodding at whatever words she was reading. "Oh, yes. Oh, yes," she kept saying over and over.

As CiCi absorbed herself in the cards, Bette grabbed his attention as she stood by the side of Hope's bed. Her voice was very low. "Jake, listen to me. I understand you're a little uncomfortable here. But the way I see it—and I've been a nurse for twenty-three years—you need to be here. As much as possible. She needs to hear positive reinforcement, over and over. She needs to hear good things about her life. She was knocked unconscious with a broken heart. Somewhere deep inside of her, she believes that she has nothing good to come back to. Be her good. Okay?"

Bette walked out and Jake sat motionless by the side of the bed. Behind him CiCi was talking to herself, but apparently gaining some hope as she read the Scriptures and poems inside the cards.

Jake, on the other hand, was desperate.

How could this all be laid on him? Hope couldn't possibly remember him from years ago. He just happened to be there and now he's here, and she was probably wondering whose strange voice kept reading her all those sympathy and get well cards.

"Well," Jake said, his voice low and a notch below a whisper. "I should say something right now. I should say something that will cause you to want to come back."

Silence crawled into the room. Even CiCi had stopped talking. The monitors didn't beep. The hospital page didn't blare through the speaker. The only noise came from the buzz of the fluorescent lights overhead.

If there was a time when she might tune into his voice, it would be right now.

His mind was totally blank.

He grabbed another card off the shelf and opened it up. "I'm sorry. This is all I can do."

GREETINGS FROM MY LIFE

The door to my room is so thin it won't even slam. I walk in, throw it against its frame and it just makes a little *swooshy* sound. I am fed up. Mostly fed up with myself. I had my chance and I blew it. I'm crawling on my hands and knees like a dog in front of the guy I want to hire me. I don't even get a chance to show him my cards. He hands me a wad of cash. Tells me that's all he can do for me.

Moron.

Me, not him.

He doesn't know me very well. And that's got to change.

As I sit on my Murphy bed, making sure my weight is evenly distributed, I notice the plastic bride and groom I'd tossed in the wastebasket is back on my desk. I stare at it for a long time. What did it do, crawl out of there by itself? I sigh, flicking it with my fingers back into the trash. Maybe I never put it in there at all.

Then I hear noises. Childlike noises. What is going on right outside my window? I decide to pull the shades up. Light would probably do me some good. I raise the window too. Fresh air and all that. Too soon to tell if that exists in NYC.

Right as I open the window, I feel something wet and sticky splatter across my face. I take my hand and swipe it across my forehead. I don't know why I was expecting red, but it's yellow. I glance up to see the girl who was previously in my room now outside in the small, weed-infested atrium, splatter painting. A few other kids are there as well. They're all covered in paint. So are the sidewalks, trees, and plants around them.

She smiles at me. "How's that dream coming along?"

The idea strikes me just then, the way the best ideas always do. "Hey, stay right there. I'm coming to you. I need your help."

An hour later, she and I sit at one of the rusted iron tables in the atrium. I am working on a card. She pulls one out of my bag and I let her. She's a curious girl, as was I when I was young.

"'Do you want to break up?'" she reads out loud.

I glance up at her, wanting to see her expression when she opens it.

"Yes. No. I didn't know we were boyfriend-girlfriend." A pause. Then a roar of laughter. "That is hilarious!"

"Cool. You think it's funny?"

"Funny. And so true. This is sooo my life. Sadly, I relate." She jabs her thumb over her shoulder to a blond kid, around twelve, standing at one of the easels. "David. Is that hair killer or what?"

Well, in my estimation it seems he needs a haircut. But he has a nice smile.

I glance at her. "Aren't you a little young to be looking for romance, kiddo?"

"I'm eleven, Room Eleven, in case you haven't noticed. And by the way, it's Mikaela."

"Trust me," I say, pointing at her with my black sketch pencil. "You love someone, they'll hurt you. Save your heart the trouble and get a pet lizard." I put the final touches on my card and hand it to Mikaela. "If you like it, the Heaven Sent guy will like it, because you're a kid and he likes kids."

She looks over the front picture. I've sketched a cute girl holding a variety of plucked flowers. She is eagerly batting her eyes. Underneath it reads *Will you pick me?*

Mikaela opens the card. Inside there are three choices: *(1) Yes. (2) I need you in my life. (3) I can't say no.* All three boxes are checked.

Mikaela smiles. "Clever. So this guy . . . he must be a hottie."

"The card is for a job, not a man."

"Right. Oooh, wait. If this is Heaven Sent cards, don't you need something about God or angels or fluffy clouds? A lamb? A rainbow? A sparkling body of water?"

"Good thinking. I've got an idea." I stuff my pencils into my bag. "You up for some fun?"

Before I tell you what I'm doing, you must understand something—I am not a rule-breaker. I've never tipped a cow. I've never climbed a water tower while drunk. I don't even have a traffic ticket on my record. I say this because you really must understand that under normal circumstances, I'm not some crazy hooligan from Poughkeepsie. I'm not saying we haven't supplied our share to the world. I'm just not one of them.

"Now!"

As the receptionist leaves to refill her coffee, Mikaela and I dart to the elevators. My thumb punches the up button ferociously, like it's some sort of life-saving procedure. I frantically search the directory to see what floor he might be on.

Three.

"Come on, come on!" Mikaela whispers to the doors.

The doors open and we slip inside just as the receptionist returns, focused on not spilling her coffee as she sips it. She never even sees us.

The doors open on the third floor. As we step off the elevator, there is a large, expansive, open kind of space. There are a few cubicles. Some of the space is divided off like there are different departments. A variety of desks sit here and there. And in the middle of all of it is a crying woman.

The young woman, maybe an assistant of some sort, is wailing at her desk, her hands covering her face. Two older ladies, both gray-haired and looking like twins, are leaning over trying to console her. They're wearing the exact same sweater but in different colors, patting her shoulders, rubbing her back.

I grab Mikaela quickly and we duck behind a cubicle wall.

"Any guesses to which way we should go?" Mikaela's chest is heaving up and down but her cheeks are bright.

I point and we begin sliding, backs to the cubicle walls, toward the area that looks like it has a few different departments. I'm right. We pass ART DEPARTMENT signs. I'm no sleuth, but by the way it's decorated—fruit, flowers, stuffed animals—I'm betting that's where the two elderly sisters work.

If I hadn't seen the banner over the next department, I would've guessed it's where they wrote their Halloween cards. It's dark and abandoned. The banner that is falling off on one side reads HUMOR DEPARTMENT. Mikaela slides on, but I pause to glance inside. It's like a ghost town.

Then I see Mikaela eagerly waving me on. I slide up next to her.

"Is that him?" she whispers, pointing around the corner. I take a peek. He's in his office, at his desk, diligently working. There are Bibles, dictionaries, thesauruses stacked around his desk. Greeting cards hang on his walls.

"That's him. You got this?"

"I got this."

Weirdly, I believe her. The girl seems in total control.

I'm about to give her some specific directions, some "what if" scenarios, but she is gone. I watch her walk straight into his office and plop down in his chair. I thought I'd have to strain to hear the conversation, but it turns out they are easily heard.

I glance around, pretty sure I'm safe since I'm near the dead-as-a-doornail Humor Department that doesn't seem to be frequented by anybody.

"Mister Heaven Sent," she says, boldly and charmingly, reaching to shake his hand, "it's such an honor to meet you. Thank you for carving this block out of your hectic, *hectic* schedule."

He's simultaneously reaching for his Blackberry, his desk calendar, his phone, trying to be cordial but he is thoroughly confused.

"Do we have an appointment?"

"It's not very often important company men, such as yourself, care about the opinions of my generation."

He freezes, right as he's about to dial his assistant, I'm assuming. Awkward. Now he has to care or he looks like a jerk. She's kind of playing this like a genius. He slowly puts the phone down, trying to engage. It's making me laugh.

"And my opinion is, you'd be making a huge mistake if you didn't hire the woman who made this card." She hands him the card across the desk. "She's talented *and* available."

I roll my eyes. She didn't have to add that.

I watch as Jake reads it. He isn't smiling. Mikaela clears her throat. "Get it? Will you pick me—I can't say no because God said so."

He's still not smiling. Mikaela acknowledges this by saying, "You're not smiling."

"Who wrote this card?"

"Room Eleven." Mikaela pauses. "I'm sorry, I don't even know her real name. Did I mention she's available?"

Jake stands. I quickly duck behind the cubicle wall.

"For work, I mean."

I hear footsteps. I squeeze my eyes shut, like that will help.

And then, I hear him breathing. I glance up and he's standing over me, arms folded.

Behind him Mikaela stands, looking apologetic.

I slowly rise, stretching a professional smile across my face. I'm about to offer my hand like this is some kind of usual job interview when he says, "So. Using your daughter to get a job. How avant-garde."

"She's not my—"

"—daughter," Mikaela finishes.

Jake raises a suspicious eyebrow as he glances back and forth at us.

"But if it means I can have the job, then yes, she's my daughter."

"And Mom here," Mikaela says, "she needs to spring for a new pair of ice skates. You'd be doing us both a favor. You look like a guy who likes to do favors. Except you're not smiling."

He doesn't look the least bit happy. "I'm sorry. To you and your Rent-A-Kid. I can't hire you, Landon."

"Landon! Cool name!" Mikaela says.

Jake then turns to Mikaela. "But I'll buy you ice skates if you need them."

Guilt slaps me. The guy seems genuinely concerned about our fake scenario. Ugh.

Sobs, louder and heavier, come from the area where the woman was crying earlier.

Mikaela leans in to me and whispers, "Are you sure you want to work here?"

I look at Jake. "Is she okay?"

Jake looks reluctant to spill the beans, but the wailing is not boding well for a company that writes greeting cards. "My cousin. She's just gone through a broken engagement."

"I've written many cards for her. I'm an unfortunate expert on broken things."

"You are?" Mikaela looks completely dumbfounded. "I'm always the last to know." She sighs.

I slide closer to Jake. I pitch a thumb over my shoulder. "Listen. Your humor department. It's looking code blue. I could revive it with my line of break-up cards and my shining wittiness."

He eyes me. "Landon, the cards we write here use the Bible to *encourage* people."

I slump the way your mom always told you not to. "I guess I can give that a try."

"We do it because we believe it."

"It's so important to believe what you write. My cards also come from the heart. Please. Don't say no."

"But—"

"Don't say no. I need you, Jake."

He bites his lip. I get it, instantly . . . he can't resist helping people. I meant to say "I need this, Jake," but you know, I guess we're just rolling with it. I look as desperate as I know how without test-driving the expression in a mirror first.

"Why do you want to work in the greeting card industry?"

"Do you know the impact that just one card can have on a person?"

"Yes. It's why I do what I do every day of my life. In two lines, I affect people. When I sit down and words come to me, I never know in what way those words will change someone's life."

"My dad always liked my cards."

"That's your credential?"

"I'm just saying, we have something in common, with this family business of yours. Just give me a chance."

Another wail, long and high-pitched, causes each of us to snap our attention toward the sound.

Jake clears his throat. "I think my cousin will be needing some time off. How would you feel being my assistant until she comes back?"

"Your assistant."

"Is that a problem? I need someone I can trust, someone who's here to help me."

I nod. "You can count on me."

"Stop by H.R. It's that way. Fill out the paperwork."

"Thank you. We'll leave you alone now—" I glance around, don't see Mikaela. "Seen my Rent-A-Kid?"

But Jake walks off. I'm left there standing alone. I walk toward where he pointed and find the H.R. department. Did I seriously just get a job? Things like this don't happen to me.

I spot the Human Resources sign. As I take a step toward it, that same sharp shooting pain in the bottom of my foot causes me to yelp. That's more like it—I get a job and a heel spur all at the same time.

I regain my balance and turn the corner into the office. A woman, dressed from head to toe in Pepto-Bismol, smiles as wide as her collagen lips will let her. She's got a tiny, squeaky voice as she introduces herself as Candy. "Jake just called over to let me know you were coming. Welcome to the team."

"Thank you."

"How are your startle reflexes today?"

I sit down, slip off my shoe, rub the bottom of my foot. I was assuming we'd start with my Social Security number. "Um, I don't know . . . but it feels like someone is sticking needles in my foot."

She giggles like I'm making some metaphorical joke.

I wish I were.

My mind is reeling. Really reeling. *Assistant* is doable, but I want more. I've got to get his attention, snap him out of this idea that these sappy cards are what everyone wants. It's what everyone buys because that's all there is. I mean, think of his cousin, right? What kind of card do you send when someone breaks your heart? Something about a deer panting for water? I don't think so.

I'm juggling groceries and my key as I make my way down the hallway at the YMCA, my cell phone pressed to my ear.

"Gertie . . . no . . . Gertie, can you hear me? Turn your hearing aid on . . . no, in the other ear . . . no, turn it the other way, you're . . . what? . . . Okay. Yes! Now, can you hear me?"

"I hear you, Hope. Now what were you saying? Something about Heaven?"

I get to my room. There is a colored piece of paper that is cut in the shape of a W. It's taped to my door. "I've got to convince Heaven Sent, the greeting card company, there's a new way to write cards. Do you think you can get the ladies to write letters to them? Tell them you want a new kind of card?"

I take the *W* off, then fumble with the key to my room three times before I get the door open. Inside, I drop the sack of groceries to the desk and collapse into the chair.

"Oooh, like complaint mail. You think they'll send us free cards if we complain? I love their cards."

I roll my eyes. I think Gertie is missing the point. "Just ask them to acknowledge people's real pain. That's all I want, Gertie. But tell the girls not to be too mean because the writer, well, he's not the worst guy in the world."

"Oh! A man's involved. You didn't tell me that. Then we must help you out!"

I notice just then that the bride and groom that I know I tossed in the trash can is back on my desk. I take it fully into my hand, stare at it for a moment, squeeze it like I'm juicing a lemon, and then throw it into the trash can with a good measure of annoyance.

"Tell the ladies to send at least ten of them."

"Send one?"

"Ten! Ten, Miss Gertie."

I start unpacking my groceries, stuffing them in the tiny closet in my room. The refrigerated stuff has to go in the community fridge. Ugh. I cradle the phone between my ear and shoulder. "Suggest they use humor to help people deal with pain, like breakups. Deaths. Ask them to be more real."

"Muriel? Honey, she died years ago."

"More real! More. Real."

"The proper term is realer."

I sigh. "Let me just give you the address."

I articulate it slowly as I grab my grocery sack and go to the fridge. As Gertie writes down the address on the other end of the phone, I peer into the community fridge in the kitchen down the hallway from me. There are various paper bags labeled with room numbers. Nice and organized, but what's going to keep someone from stealing my stuff?

"Okay, got it," Gertie said.

"Also, don't tell them how old you are. In fact, it will help if they think you're young. So don't use the nursing home address." I grab a Sharpie on the counter and start labeling my bag of food. I write *Room Eleven!!!* four different times. Should I try to draw the Hazardous Material sign on it? Couldn't hurt.

"The nursing home address. Okay. So, our Hope found a man?"

I say my good-byes to Gertie and turn in for the night. I sleep fitfully, barely able to contain all my ideas, going through mock conversations with Jake to try to convince him of the direction he needs to go with his cards.

The next morning, my food is still in the fridge in the community kitchen. I guess that hazardous waste symbol worked. I grab some yogurt and head in to work. I definitely don't want to be late for my first day. But just as I'm entering the building, my cell phone rings. It's Mom—spilling out a dozen questions before I even have a chance to respond. When she takes a breath, I say, "It's so great here. I found this awesome new apartment. So chic. I mean, you wouldn't believe this place. And I landed a job too."

"Have you found a man?"

"Is he lost?"

"You lost him already?"

I sigh. My mom doesn't really catch humor. "No, Mom."

"I've had seven calls responding to my ad in the paper."

"Mom, I got the job at the greeting card company."

There is a pause. I am on the elevators.

"Mom? Hello? You there?"

"They actually hired you to write greeting cards?"

The doors *ding* open on the third floor. I grin like there is a crowd awaiting as I step out. First, a trip to the bathroom is in order, to check my hair and makeup. I walk in, still with the phone to my ear, and stand in front of the mirror. "Not exactly writing cards yet. But I will. I'm going to show them how their sappy cards can be so much better."

I fluff my bangs and turn—and smack into a wall. No, wait. Not a wall. Solid, definitely. But it's a man . . . in the women's bathroom. I drop the phone from my ear and am about to scream for help when I glance over at the . . . urinals. Oh . . . no . . .

I can hear my mom from my phone. "Hope? Hope?"

This is the part that's a little unclear, but in my horror and embarrassment, I shriek and run, only glimpsing a part of his face. Somewhere in there I say it out loud: "Sam?"

I stand, heaving against the wall outside the bathroom. It couldn't have been. But he looked just like Sam. At least the chin and the nostrils. That's about all I saw.

The door to the men's bathroom opens and Sam walks out. Except . . . it's not Sam. Very similar, though. It's just, this guy couldn't be a musician. He's far too clean-cut. He's tall. Solid, as I said before. And dressed kind of casual. But in a way that makes me think he understands fashion.

"I'm Everett. Do you want me to be Sam?" He's grinning at me. It's the kind of grin that melts you right on the spot. In my new life mantra, I'm determined not to be melted by anything a man does, so I stand a little taller, less melty-ish.

"No. Um, no. Really."

"You can call me Sam. Sam's a nice name." He reaches for a handshake, but it's not the kind that business people do to seal a deal. It's the kind where a guy pretends he's shaking your hand, but then he holds it a little longer than necessary. I retrieve my hand quickly.

"Sorry. You just remind me of this guy I knew."

"Is this a good reminder?"

I take a breath. "Let's start over. I'm Landon. New employee."

"In the 'sap' department?"

Oh dear. He heard that. Okay, damage control time. I turn on my best flirtatious smile. And listen, I'm not claiming it's got any power. I haven't really tried one in a long time. But I give it my best shot. "Could you forget you heard that? I wouldn't want my new boss . . . you know . . ."

"No worries," he says smoothly. I am getting a sense about this guy—he's the kind that flirts with everyone but makes you feel you're the only one. Currently, it's working. "I heard this place is going down anyway."

My smile drops. "What? Really?"

"Your new job in the Sap Department will be over by Christmas."

He seals this proclamation with a wink then strolls off. I'm left standing there feeling like I need hand sanitizer.

I find my new desk, right outside Jake's office, and organize it the way I like it. I tape a picture of my father to my computer monitor. This is more for effect than anything, but I have to admit I do like seeing him staring back at me. It's like he's resting on my shoulder, telling me I can do this.

Jake walks out of his office. "Morning." He hands me a stack of papers. He is holding a small dish with a small fork and a heaping mound of tuna fish. "Type these into PowerPoint for our next product presentation." He's talking fast. "When Pearl and Ruby are done with their illustrations, you'll scan those in, mount the words for the front of the card on top of them. Page two words go on the second slide."

"Okay."

He smiles. The tuna smell is engulfing me. "So, your first day."

"Yep."

"Welcome."

"Thanks."

"Okay. Any questions, just holler."

"Literally? Or should I use the phone?" His office is a stone's throw away, but this doesn't seem like the place where shouting happens. Shouting scares puppies and kittens.

He pauses. "The phone's fine. Dial four."

"Got it." I grin while trying to hold my breath. Tuna? Really?

He leaves and closes his office door. I can now only see his shoulder through the window. The tuna smell lingers.

I pull up the PowerPoint program and open the folder that contains the papers. The first one reads: *Be strong. Be courageous. Have faith.* I turn the page to see what the inside of the card is supposed to read: *This too shall pass.*

"Oh, brother." It can only go up from here. I turn to the next page. Jake's handwriting, I notice, is nice, very legible. I read this one out loud: "'I know you think there is no way that you can carry on. Yet don't lose heart. You'll be okay—despite the one who's gone.'" I can barely get myself to turn the page.

"'Our God has a plan, a future and a hope. Let this truth help you cope.'"

"You've got to be *kidding* me!!"

I shout this actually. I don't mean to. It's just some things barrel right through my filter and straight out my mouth. Luckily, nobody is around to hear me. I see Jake sort of lean to his left and peek out the window. I give a friendly wave and pretend not to know what's going on. But I know. Really bad greeting cards. *That's* what's going on.

I feel a surge of renewed purpose. I've got to stop this madness, somehow, someway.

But for now, I have to enter all this bad text for a slideshow, so I do my thing.

Just before lunch, I hear arguing. Jake left around ten, citing a meeting, and I hadn't seen him since. Now I hear his voice, and someone else's too. They're down a hallway but they might as well be standing right at my desk. It's not quite shouting, but voices are raised.

The other voice says, "Sales have dropped twenty percent since last year. Our investors are going to exercise their option to buy us by the end of the year if we don't turn a profit this quarter."

Jake's voice is softer but less calm. "We can't sell. They're not illumined to our audience. You never should have let them buy into us!"

Illumined?

"We need the operating capital. If you wouldn't give away so much of our profits to every bleeding-heart cause—"

"This place is my life!" The words are full of emotion, fueled by what sounds like complete and true conviction.

There is a slight pause in the conversation.

Then the other man says, "Hey, that's your choice."

Suddenly they round the corner. I can't even begin to pretend I wasn't eavesdropping. And I immediately recognize the other voice as the guy I ran into in the men's bathroom. Everett. His frustrated expression brightens as he sees me.

"Well, well, well. Who do have we here?"

"This is Landon. My new temporary assistant," Jake says, introducing me as enthusiastically as one might mention an upcoming colon screening.

Everett grins at me. "L-l-l-andon."

Eck. Not liking what he's doing with the *L*s there.

Jake continues. "This is my brother, Everett, C.E.O. of Heaven Sent."

"C.E. . . . oh . . ." I probably would've gulped except I'm frozen with embarrassment. "Good to meet you, Everett." It's really more of a squeak.

"Some people call me Sam."

I glance at Jake and he is glancing at Everett like, *No they don't . . .*

I clear my throat, stand at my desk, press my palms against it. "Boys, what's it going to take for you guys not to sell?"

"Simple. How about cards people want to buy?" Everett says.

"People *are* buying our cards," Jake says.

"Not like they used to. What do you think of our cards, Landon?"

Sometimes sudden bursts of sweat also come with painful prickles. I feel like I'm being stabbed by my own sweat beads. "Ah, um . . . I . . ." I glance at Jake. He looks like one of those puppy dogs on the cover of their cards.

"Honestly. Gut reaction," Everett says.

Gut. Okay. I measure each word that comes out. "One thing I noticed . . . they're great, you know. Kittens. So cute. Rock on, kittens. But what if we looked at adding a little . . . humor?"

Like "Pop Goes the Weasel," Ruby's head shoots up over her cubicle at the word *kitten*. Pearl's follows. They're the sisters. They have plaques of themselves on four different walls.

I glance at Jake. He looks wounded. Uncomfortable. He's staring at the ground. But I recognize my moment—I mean, it's practically begging me to pitch. I turn to Everett. "A lot of these cards talk about the future, but it's a place people haven't made it to yet. What if we write a card line that addresses the now? Where someone is at this moment? But use humor to help them through it?"

Everett has dropped the "I'm cool" shtick and looks genuinely interested. "Not the worst idea I've heard . . ."

Jake's voice has an edge to it. "I know you want to help, Landon. But we're okay here."

"It's your coffin, Jake," Everett says. "But this next round of cards, make them count. Or they could be your last." He winks at me and clicks his tongue—I'm baffled at the motivation behind the clicking noise—and walks off.

Jake stares at me as I return my attention to him. "Here's what you can help me with. I need love quotes."

For a second I think he's issuing a pickup line. Then I realize he's giving me a job. "You want me to write love poems?"

"No. I want you to compile verses from the Bible about love." He points to the Bible sitting on my desk. "You do know how to reference topics in a Bible, don't you?"

"Of course. I'm well-versed in the accumulation of, um, love verses."

"Now that our Christmas line is out, our next campaign needs to include Valentines."

"Ohhh, *that* kind of love. I thought you meant like 'Love thy neighbor.'" I glance at the Bible. "There's lovey-dovey kind of stuff in there? Maybe I'm reading the wrong parts. The last time I read the Bible the earth was destroyed by a flood. I don't remember anything in there that would go good with chocolate and flowers."

Jake smirks. "Look hard. I bet you can find something." And he leaves it at that.

I stare at the Bible. It must be three inches thick. I'm baffled as to how I'm going to extract meaningful love verses out of a book that I'm sure was very opposed to sex.

I'm pondering this when Candy arrives at my desk. She is still wearing pink, but a different shade. "Ms. Landon, we have a problem. Your background check revealed some . . . how shall I say this . . . irregular test results."

"Is it cancer?"

She doesn't smile.

"What do you mean?"

"When we ran your social, you appear to be dead."

"Not again."

Candy's eyebrows rise. "This is a reoccurring problem for you?" Oddly, she looks hopeful. "I'm a huge fan of *Twilight*. You're not a . . ."

"Vampire? No." I sigh, gesturing to myself. "Do I look dead to you?"

"According to the U.S. government, you're dead. You are claiming to be Hope Landon, are you not?"

"Not claiming. I am."

"Well, honey, we need to clear this up for me to sign you up for health and life insurance. They don't pay for people who are code blue to noxious stimuli."

Candy has the weirdest way of saying things. Oh, wait! Noxious stimuli—does she mean the tuna fish? "I am not dead, Candy."

"I don't know if I can even cut a paycheck for a dead person. We have a strict policy that our employees must have a pulse. Don't we, Jakester?"

I quickly turn. Jake is standing there, listening. "So, Hope Landon. I like that name. Any reason you go by Landon?"

"Sometimes my first name gives people a false sense of who I am." I'm only half kidding and I think he gets that. He looks a little sad for me.

"Anyway, can you get this cleared up?" Candy asks me.

"Yeah. No problem."

Jake returns to his office, not saying another word. I stare at the Bible and wonder which book of the Bible I should start with to try to find verses on love. I decide to just randomly pick. I land in Nehemiah.

I remind myself, this too shall pass.

7

Visiting hours were almost over. He hated leaving Hope's side. He pictured her alone in the dark. What if she woke up? What if no one was here? The evening nurse that took over from Bette didn't seem as nice. But he knew he had to go, so he savored the last hour with her, even if she didn't know he was there.

Nurse Bette came in, looking tired from a long shift, but as always, she wore a smile. "How's our girl doing?"

"About the same."

"Where's the mother?" She always whispered this like just the mention of the woman might cause her to appear.

Jake laughed. "She's not here. Her church was holding a prayer revival for Hope. I promised CiCi I would stay here with her until visiting hours were over."

Bette was holding something in the palm of her hand, but suddenly waved her hand in front of her nose. "Goodness! What is that smell?"

"Oh, sorry," Jake said sheepishly. "Just a can of tuna fish I brought for dinner."

"Goodness, gracious me. I brought in some smelling salts for some aromatherapy tonight. Thought I'd try it before I got off my shift, but I mean to tell you, I think that tuna might do the job a little better!"

"Sorry . . . won't happen again."

"I say bring it on, Jake. Whatever we have to do to get this girl awake. I say bring tuna every single day until she wakes up!"

Jake laughed. "Maybe. I forget how bad it smells. I eat it every day so it doesn't bother me."

"What's that you got there in your lap?"

Jake looked down. It was a sketchpad he took with him any time he thought he might have some time to think . . . the park, a doctor's office. It had traveled the world with him.

"It's just kind of a hobby."

"You draw?"

"No . . . I write greeting cards."

"Is that so?"

"Yeah. I try to find encouraging words and verses in the Bible. And then I also dabble in photography, so I like to match it with a picture I've taken. I turn it into a card and sell it at my floral shop."

"How lovely," Bette said, but seemed to mean it. Most people didn't care much about well-crafted, carefully thought-out cards these days.

"A couple of my cards are over there," Jake said, nodding toward the shelf where all the cards were sent.

"Which ones?"

"The one with the storm and the sun behind it. Took that picture on the plains of Kansas, and then I wrote a poem."

Bette set everything down and went right to the shelf. Jake turned, biting his lip. Bette opened it right up. "Behind every storm in life is a rainbow full of promise and hope. May God's comfort and love be with you."

Bette patted her chest. "Just beautiful, Jake. And so true."

"I'm not sure everyone really believes that. But I do."

Bette smiled at him. "I do too. And I believe this girl is going to wake up. There's a rainbow coming, Jake."

She walked to the door. "What about the smelling salts you were going to give her?"

"Honestly, I think the tuna is doing a fine job."

"Get some rest, Bette."

"See you tomorrow, Jake."

GREETINGS FROM MY LIFE

When I am aggravated, I have an extremely hard time not showing it. I clench my teeth together and then move them back and forth slightly. That's very bad for the enamel. And for the person who has to hear them squeak. But it's the only way I can keep myself from exploding.

It's after work and I've been on hold with the Social Security office for forty minutes. I've been transferred twice by two different operators. Now I'm listening to music that was never good enough to hit a radio station. My head is throbbing. So I walk outside the YMCA and pace the sidewalk across the street. I am in desperate need of getting undead and receiving a paycheck.

I hear a little beep. I grow excited, imagining that someone is going to be on the line with me any second. But then I realize it's my phone, warning me of a low battery. Then, suddenly, a chipper voice greets me with, "You've reached the U.S. Government Vital Records office. How may I assist you?"

My body relaxes like a rag doll. *Finally*. "Hi! Yes. So glad to finally get someone."

"Glad to assist. What can I do for you?"

"You see, my mother applied for my death certificate, so my Social Security number keeps reporting my death. I need to get that fixed."

"Oooh. How unusual." I'm about to rattle off my SSN when she says, "But you've reached the wrong department."

Rag doll goes stiff. "What do you mean? I've been on hold for forty minutes!"

"You've been on hold for the wrong department."

That chipperness in her voice is really starting to tick me off. "Who do I have to talk to, then?"

"Not to worry, ma'am. I can transfer you directly to the correct department and I will see to it that you can talk to someone—"

Click.

"Hello? Hello???" I shake the phone like I can rattle it back to life. But my battery has gone dead.

First my life. Now my battery. There is death all around me. There's almost a third as I step into the street and nearly get run over by a taxi. He honks his aggravation.

"Yeah? Well honk you too, mister!"

I drag myself back across the street toward the YMCA, where I'm apparently going to be a permanent resident. As I start to walk in, I spot Mikaela. She is sitting against the brick wall, drawing something.

She doesn't even look up as I approach. "So, Room Eleven. You revolutionize the greeting card world yet?"

I decide to slide down against the wall beside her. I can't really face my room right now. It's small. Cold. Small.

"Not quite. What are you writing?"

"My own set of greeting cards."

"Really?"

"No. My Christmas list."

"Where did you disappear to yesterday? You helped me get the job and then bam . . . gone."

"We got the job?"

"I was going to buy you a hot dog."

"Things couldn't very well get romantic with me in the way, could it?"

I glance at her. "You mean with . . ."

"Jake. You see the way you look at him, don't you?"

"I, uh . . ." Trick question? Or am I that transparent?

"So, what's next on our plan?"

"You know if they've got any Bibles around here? I have to find verses on love."

Mikaela raises an eyebrow.

"Long story."

I follow Mikaela in and out of some rooms until we land in the kids' area. She goes straight to the shelf and finds a children's Bible. She lays on her stomach, the Bible wide open, scanning verses with her fingers. I catch her up to speed.

"We have one last chance to come out with a set of cards that will sell really well or the company could close. So we're working on the Valentines line."

"Jake's already letting you write? You must be charming."

"Not exactly. On the writing. Or on the charm. I've managed to fail at both so far. I think I actually offended him. He's got this brother who is . . ."

But she's not listening. She's beckoning me over with a hand. "Check this out." Her voice changes, and she sounds like a mature woman. "'Kiss me with the kisses of your mouth! Your love is better than wine.'" Then she puts on a deep voice. "'You are the most beautiful of women, your cheeks with ornaments, your neck with jewels.'"

"Is that right before God kills all the Egyptian babies?"

Mikaela glances at me. "You don't know your Bible very well, do you?"

"I'm familiar with . . . you know . . . the important parts."

"They're all important." She starts reading again. "'My lover is like a bag of myrrh, that lies all night between my breasts."

I snatch the Bible from her hands and clamp it closed. "You can't say *lover*! You can't say *breasts*! Isn't this a children's Bible? We're in the YMCA! Where was this again?"

Mikaela is expressionless as she watches me mildly overreact. Okay, mildly is too mild of a word.

"It's from the Song of Solomon." This girl's tone of wisdom strikes me as too mature for her age. "Steamiest part of the Bible."

I tuck the Bible under my armpit, but not before noticing the lamb and rainbow on the front cover. "Okay, no more Bible for you, kiddo."

"I can handle talking about breasts. I'm not ten. I have a trainer bra."

I grab her by the neck and steer her away from the children's area.

She is grinning at me as I guide us toward a small sitting area near the front of the building. "So, didn't you find Jake heavenly?"

"No." I plop down in one of the old chairs, duct-taped on one side. Mikaela sits across from me. I begin flipping through the Bible, hoping to come across something between mass murder and breasts. There's got to be something that shouts Valentine's

Day in here. It's just a guess but I don't think Jake is going to go for a card about wine and ornaments and breasts.

Mikaela is still grinning at me. "I could pick up a bag of myrrh for him. Help boost his love factor."

"What do you know about love, anyway?"

She sighs and in a dreamy voice says, "It makes me sick to my stomach."

"You must have inherited my low tolerance for risk."

"Love . . . one thing you're missing is—"

I turn to her. "Mikaela, listen. Let me break it down for you. Love means—"

"Loss. Yeah. And loss means pain."

She says this with such conviction in her eyes I am momentarily distracted. I regain my focus. "I don't need either. Perfectly happy without those."

"Landon, Landon . . . you don't have to lie to me."

Am I that pathetic that even an eleven-year-old can read me like a book? Except I don't think I'm lying. I don't need those things in my life. Not even a bit.

I grab the Bible. "You know what? No eleven-year-old is going to tell me what I need. Go play with your Barbies."

I head out the door with the Bible, immediately regretting my anger. I mean, who knows if this kid even owns a Barbie. And honestly, she doesn't seem like she'd play with one if she did. But I keep walking.

"Funny," she calls after me. I round the corner but I still hear her. "Find out what happened to Jake's humor department!"

Yeah. Real funny. That's the whole problem. Jake sees no value in humor. I walk across the street and buy the cheapest deli sandwich I can find because I'm running out of money. The cats have returned but keep their distance.

Back at the YMCA, I don't see Mikaela. I clutch my sandwich and my Bible and head down the hallway.

That old woman, the janitor, is near my door, sliding her mop elegantly across the floor, stroke by stroke. She clutches it tightly, like it might be the only thing that is keeping her from falling over. There is something familiar about her, like I've known her for a long time, but I am certain we've never met. Maybe she just has one of those faces.

I'm so consumed with watching her that I don't at first notice the A taped to my door. When I spot it, I grow angry. I rip it off my door. It really just needed a gentle pull. It was only held on there with a small piece of Scotch tape, but it's just annoying me. What does it mean? Am I supposed to know what it means? Why are people pasting the alphabet on my door? Nobody else has the alphabet posted on their door.

The janitor lady is staring at me. I try a congenial smile as I unlock the door. I slide in and shut it quickly. I wad the A up and toss it in the trash just as I notice the plastic bride and groom are back on the desk.

It's got to be Mikaela. She's found some way to get in my room. I grab the little plastic piece, ball it up in my fist, and throw it straight down into the trash. Then I take my hands and cover it up with the other trash.

After a while, I calm down. I am tired and I still haven't compiled the verses Jake wants. He didn't give me a deadline but I want to make a good impression, have them done sooner than he expected.

I get as comfortable as possible on the bed and crack the book open.

I take my midmorning break thirty minutes after I arrive. I'm stressed. I am struggling to find a way to convince Jake that his card line needs an overhaul. He doesn't seem receptive to change, as was evident when I witnessed his conversation with Everett.

I stand in the break room and stir my black coffee even though I've forgotten to even add the cream. I know I have the answer to his dilemma. I know how to save his company. But how do I convince him?

In a corner, I spot a stack of canned tuna fish. Good grief! Is that what this man eats every day of his life for lunch? How am I going to endure the stench every day? I barely have time to think about that problem when Everett comes in, hands in his pockets, grin on his face, casually observing me as he walks by.

"So, new girl . . ." He pours himself a cup of coffee into a mug he's chosen from the cabinet.

"Everett." I turn to him, still mindlessly stirring my coffee. "I was thinking, maybe we could talk about a new approach to Valentines."

He looks very receptive to the idea and I'm about to pitch him a punch line for a card when he says, "How about we discuss it on my boat?"

Like a flash fire, my whole face heats in an instant. From experience I know that my neck is soon to follow. Also from experience, I know that a wave of nausea is about to trigger a gag reflex over which I have no control. This happens when I get to a level of discomfort that my soul does not want to deal with. Sam's breakup has brought an entirely new dynamic to my just-below-normal tolerance for pain.

"Yeah . . . ah . . . no."

"Was that a yes or a no?"

"A no."

I back up. I don't know why. It's just instinct. Maybe I want to make sure that if I upchuck he's a safe distance away. Or maybe I just want him a safe distance away. He's smiling at me like Sam used to. There is amusement in his eyes, like this is some sort of fun game. I hate to break it to him, but only one of us is playing.

"With a yeah in front of it."

"What?"

"A no, but first a yeah."

"Oh. Yes."

"So yeah?"

"No." I bite my lip because although I don't want to be on a boat, I do want to pitch him my ideas. I know I can help this company! I am certain of it. "I mean, we could talk here." To my shock and horror, this comes out sultry. I'm not meaning it to. I'm kind of keeping my tongue close to the back of my throat to keep breakfast down, and I'm blinking rapidly—not batting my eyelashes—because I'm nervous. "Later," I say with a weird mix of emphasis and breathiness. By the way he raises one eyebrow like I've just seduced him, I realize I'm giving off all kinds of false signals. "Would you excuse me?"

I turn, about to skedaddle right out the door when I run smack-dab into Jake, who is reaching for a can of tuna. He's looking very relaxed today. As I back up and apologize for nearly knocking him over, he opens the tuna with the electric opener. It makes a small buzzing sound, so slight that it gives no hint of what is about to come—tuna odor wafting through the air like we're out at sea in a fishing boat. I can almost hear the slapping sounds of their fins as they're brought up by a net.

He grins at me, oblivious to it all. "Hey Hope. I can't wait to see the love verses you've compiled."

"It's Landon. They're on my desk." I didn't know it was possible, but you can actually speak while holding your breath.

"I didn't doubt it," he says with a wink. He dumps the tuna on a plate, slides it into the microwave. My gag reflex cannot handle this smell heated.

I don't know which way to turn. Everett says, "Did he just call you Hope?"

It's nuked for ten seconds and already the smell is overwhelming. Hot tuna? Can this get any worse?

I mumble something about getting back to work, smile and nod on my way out, and rush to the bathroom.

Luckily, Pine-Sol fills my nostrils as soon as I hit the bathroom tile. I breathe it in deeply, encouraging the chemicals into my lungs. It's better than fresh mountain air. Soon the tuna smell is gone and I'm grateful. I make a mental note to buy some kind of scented candle for my desk and return to work.

Lunch finally arrives. Jake, Everett, and everybody disappear from the office. I don't have money to go shop or do anything like that, so I decide now is the time to go investigate the Humor Department, otherwise known as the Dungeon of Doom.

There is a small desk, nothing on it but a lamp, in the center of the department. There are three cubicles. The corkboard has some outdated company announcements on it and an ad for free puppies. Other than that, it's cold and dark.

I sit down at the desk, trying to get my mojo on. A lamp provides one, small, circle of light from which I can work. And work, I do. I'm on a mission. I've got to produce a whole line of cards that will show Everett and convince Jake that humor needs to return to their company.

I don't realize it, but a lot of time has passed. All of a sudden I hear my name being called. "Hope? Hope, I need you. Where are you?"

I scoop up my pad and pencils and yank open the drawer of the desk I'm sitting at and shove everything in there. I figured it would be empty, but my hand hits something. I pull out a picture frame. It's a photo of Jake with his hands wrapped around a very pretty woman. He looks happy—and in love.

"Hope?"

I rush to my desk and practically jump over it to get to my chair. Jake has walked down a short hallway looking for me and is returning when he spots me at my desk.

"There you are."

"Sorry about that. What can I do for you?" I'm out of breath, trying not to show it, grabbing some sticky notes like I'd just gone to the supply closet.

"I just need those verses."

"Right away!" The overly enthusiastic reply is punctuated by how he pauses at the doorway of his office to glance at me. My chest is about to explode with guilt and wonder. Who was the woman in that picture?

He walks into his office and I also wonder why he keeps calling me Hope. I've specifically asked him to call me Landon. Even if he's seen my real name, he should call me what I want to be called. I'm going to have to address the issue but now is not the time.

I grab the list I've typed up and hurry into his office. Then I'm slammed with the smell of tuna. Again. I assumed he went out to eat, but no—there is that ominous small dish with the cheap metal fork. The tuna has been consumed yet it lingers like a jealous lover. A jealous lover who needs to bathe in something less oceanic.

"Tuna for breakfast and lunch . . . wow . . . some people prefer peanut butter and jelly . . ."

"Some people, when coming to work for a new boss, tend not to galvanize him within the first week. Hope."

"Yes, about that. Not the galvanizing—interesting and ancient word choice there—but Hope. Hope with a capital *H.* I prefer to be called Landon."

"Not a hope kind of girl?"

"Not lately, no."

Just then Everett swings in. I wish I could say he's a breath of fresh air, but I've found that not to be the case.

"It seems," he says, acknowledging me with another wink, "that we've been making enemies. Our first set of hate mail." He throws part of the stack in his hands onto Jake's neatly arranged desk. The letters slide into a line, stopping right at the edge. Everett holds a couple in his hand. He reads the one on top out loud:

> *"'Dear Heaven Sent People. Your cards are far from heaven sent. After my marriage ended, I received a card that said life will get better. It hasn't. If you're going to lie to me, you could at least make me laugh. Sincerely, the Former Mrs. Teasley.'"*

My eyes widen so much my eyeballs start to hurt. Wow. I didn't know Mrs. Teasley had it in her. I glance at Jake. He looks genuinely pained. I'm kind of regretting the plan now, but Everett begins the second letter:

> *"'Your cards make me mad. When the love of my life left me, people gave me your generic sympathy cards, as though they would help. They didn't. Miss Lonely.'"*

Jake is thumbing through the envelopes. Everett continues with a third. I've bitten every single nail off every single finger on my hand. Now I'm about to bite through my lip as I watch Jake, his eyes dark with worry.

"'When my husband died, my family sent me cards saying everything would get better. That I'd find love again. I haven't and I'm still a spring chicken! I should sue you for your empty promises!'"

I didn't have to guess who that was.

"'Signed, Miss Gertie.'"

There's no way for me to leave. Everett is blocking the doorway. The room grows very quiet, so quiet that I wonder if guilt is audible, because if it is, I'm toast. But then I calm myself down, realizing there is no way they can know my plan or figure out who sent these. I remind myself this is a gentle nudge—though it turned out to be a bit assaulting—to help Jake see the light.

"We've never received feedback like this before." Jake's voice is quiet.

"Oh, well, you know . . . I mean, take the constructive parts, see what you can do with it . . ." My hands are clasped behind me, pressed forcefully into my butt.

"It's interesting, they're all about lost love."

There is something lost in his expression just then, something that dwells deeper than what I have access to. He's been hunched over his desk but suddenly stands up, a couple of envelopes in his hand. I think he's about to declare the humor department reopened when he says, "Hey . . . these are all from the same address." He looks closer at them. "From Poughkeepsie."

Turns out *guilt* is audible—it wheezes. Didn't I tell Gertie *not* to put the addresses on them?

Everett laughs. "Seriously? Poughkeepsie? What good thing ever came from Poughkeepsie?" Everett turns his attention to me. The tuna smell is now masked by the musky stench of my own guilt. "I'd ask you what you think, Lan, but I already know Jake won't listen."

Lan? Seriously?

But Jake is looking at me like he might listen. So I try to seize the moment. "Maybe we should help people through the pain of lost love with humor, you know, instead of telling them they'll get over it. You guys have an entirely vacant department over there. Nice, roomy desks. Firm chairs." I smile like I've just struck gold with the best idea ever.

I notice Jake glance at Everett and Everett glance at Jake. Something passes between them, something I'm not privy to, but sense nevertheless. "What?"

Jake ignores the question. "People who receive our cards already know they're in pain. They need encouragement to get past it, a reminder that even in the midst of trouble, they're not alone. That things will get better."

Everett smirks. "Yeah. That'll save us. Your best intentions are going to sink us. Don't blame me when this fails." Everett walks off, but his words still hang in the air.

Jake sits down in his chair, gazing at all the mail. There's at least a dozen letters there. I feel shame for what I've done. It's hurt him and I'm sorry for it. I take a few steps toward his desk.

"Have you ever received a card and gotten past your pain?"

A flash of pain temporarily freezes his expression but is gone as fast as it came. Then he grabs one of the envelopes and taps the return address with his finger. "I want to get these ladies on the phone."

"Whh . . . . at? I'm sure a letter that lets them know you heard them would surely be . . ."

He's not listening to me. He's Googling the address. His hands drop from the keyboard. "A nursing home? Old ladies are complaining about lost relationships?"

"It's probably some kind of exercise they're doing to help improve memory. Like bingo."

"I've got to talk to these ladies."

"I am your assistant," I say hastily. "Right? Let me take care of this. I'll reach them."

"Okay, make initial contact and we'll go from there."

For the second time today, I rush to the bathroom.

8

He'd gained a lot of favor from Bette, and was allowed to stay past visiting hours now. She felt strongly that the Coma Arousal Therapy would work for Hope, but she needed help. Jake was encouraged to talk to her, squeeze her hand, even eat his tuna fish. It all felt a little preposterous but here he was, despite it all.

It was getting harder and harder to leave her side.

At exactly 8:19 p.m., Jake took her hand into his, scooted the chair closer to her bedside and whispered, "Hope, where are you?" He was shaking as he said it. But she needed to know that nobody really knew where she was.

He looked down at his feet. No. What she needed to know was that, no matter where she was, she had something to come back to.

But he needed a moment to collect his thoughts. He popped open a can of tuna and stood, stretching his legs. With a plastic fork, he ate it bite by bite.

The door opened and CiCi slid in, glancing behind her like her life was in danger, and then she shut the door as carefully as if it were made of paper. She yelped as she noticed Jake.

"What are you doing here?" Then she smiled, pointing a finger at him. "You snuck in too, didn't you?" She plopped down in the chair at the end of Hope's bed. "That nurse . . . Bette? . . . she is something else. Real strict about those visiting hours. Always lecturing me about how to get Hope out of this horrible mess she's in."

"It's not a mess, it's just what—"

"It's all a mess! Her whole life's a mess!"

Jake set his tuna aside and sat down. "CiCi . . . yes, something bad happened, but we can't let Hope believe that her life is a mess. She has a lot to live for. She's very . . . driven. Very . . ." The words were stuck in his throat but she needed to hear it. ". . . pretty."

CiCi glanced at her daughter. "She could use a hair washing."

"I think what Bette is trying to say is that we need to be encouraging."

Suddenly tears streamed down CiCi's face. "But look at her . . . she's so . . . lifeless."

Jake tried to find the right words. He was so bad with speaking words and so much more comfortable when he could write them down. "It's not true. She's in there. We just have to figure out a way to get her back here."

CiCi wiped the tears with a tissue that looked like it'd been through a war. "Do you know where she was planning on going after she was married? To New York City. She wanted a career writing greeting cards. Who has heard of such a thing?"

Jake's gaze snapped to Hope. For real? Sure, he remembered how much she liked to write cards, but he never imagined she wanted to do it for a living.

"She's got real talent," Jake offered, his attention back on CiCi. "She has to believe in herself."

CiCi blotted her face. "The truth is, Jake, that I didn't believe in her. I thought the whole idea of moving to New York City was a huge mistake." Her hands shot in the air and she shouted out a hallelujah. She looked at the ceiling, waving her hands. "Oh, Lord, Lord! How I wish now that she was there! Oh how I wish she was there right now!"

The door opened to the room and Bette stood there like a mad bull. CiCi's arms dropped to her side and she mumbled to Jake, "We're caught."

Bette's finger pointed straight at CiCi. "You, missy, come here right now."

CiCi obeyed, sheepishly shuffling toward Bette.

Bette looked like she could beat an elephant into oblivion. "As I told you before, we have strict rules about visiting hours. And here you are, making all kinds of racket. What are you trying to do, wake our patients?"

CiCi looked genuinely confused as she glanced back at Hope. "Yes . . . yes, I am . . ."

Bette realized her mistake as she glanced at Jake. "Yes, well, we must contain the efforts to visiting hours." She spoke more softly as she guided CiCi out of the room. She glanced back at Jake. "And you, sir, I'll be back for you in a second." But she winked at him like she had no such intentions.

The door shut and the room was quiet again. Hope never moved, just breathed shallowly and softly, like she had since the day she got here.

Jake clasped his hands together, trying to come up with a plan. "Greeting cards, huh? Why am I not surprised?" He stood and touched her shoulder, very slightly, as if he were afraid she might break. "The thing is . . . Hope . . ." Why could he not say these words? "The thing is . . . I need you."

It sounded so ridiculous. He'd only reconnected with her a few weeks ago, and she was unconscious at the time. How could he need her? More importantly, why would she need him? But he'd written a lot of cards over the years, written cards that spoke of divine moments, divine intervention, of God coming down and working something amazing out.

He had more to say, but for now, that was all that would come out. So he sat back down and took her hand into his.

GREETINGS FROM MY LIFE

I know so far it seems as if I spend a lot of time in the bathroom for things other than what a bathroom is typically used for, but my predicament is that I don't want Jake to hear, and Everett literally seems to appear out of nowhere. So I'm in a stall, sitting on a toilet with the seat down, whispering into my cell phone to Becca, trying not to echo.

"If you could call, tell Jake your grandmother wrote the letter but her hearing aid won't let her chat by phone—"

"You want me to lie."

My whispers are all hissy because I'm tense and trying to get my point across. "It's either that or I end up back home on a hide-a-bed, searching want ads for the next Bed Pan Queen job, while every dork in Poughkeepsie waits on my front lawn!"

"Oh yeah, that."

"So will you call?"

"Have you met that special guy on top of the Empire State Building yet?"

My whisper drops completely and now I'm just two levels below shouting. "Becca, not you!"

"At least tell me you're closer to getting your cards published. If I can't have you here, at least one of our dreams for you should be progressing."

"I'm working on it." I think I hear someone come in, but it's a false alarm . . . the automatic paper towel dispenser went off by itself as it sometimes does. "We have a big presentation in two days. I'm getting my samples ready."

"I'm so glad your boss sees your talent."

I don't have the heart to tell her that my scheme continues far beyond the nursing home fiasco.

After Becca and I hang up, I notice Jake is out of his office, probably for a meeting, so I hurry to the dark Humor Department and begin pulling out my pad and pencils.

"Hope?" My name is called distantly.

I literally growl—so glad no one was walking by at the moment. A growl coming from a dark room could send Pearl and Ruby into early retirement via death. I rush around the corner and hurry to my desk.

Jake is in his office, grabbing his jacket off the back of his chair. He is excited about something, I can tell. He's grinning before he even sees me and he's not a grinner. When he turns, he says, "Come on, we've got work to do."

I follow behind him as we head for the elevators. He is talking fast.

"Let's forget all the cards I had you type up for the presentation. We're going to do something new."

"Okay. Cool." I say this way more calmly than I'm feeling. Maybe the nursing home ladies pulled off a miracle. "I'll be right back. Hold the elevator for me."

I burst to my desk like my butt's on fire and grab my portfolio bag, which contains a few of the cards I didn't put in the desk. I manage my way back to the elevator just in time, slightly out of breath. Ruby and Pearl walk by, staring at us.

He says to them, "We're going out to do some writing."

I nod, but I really have no idea what's going on.

"You?" Pearl asks. "Out?"

"As in out-out?" Ruby asks.

He holds the door open as it starts to shut. "While we're gone, draw whatever you can think of that ties to love. Hearts. Flowers. Sunsets."

"Regrettable tattoos," I add, accidentally out loud.

Suddenly Candy steps right in front of Pearl and Ruby. Pink again. I'm guessing it's a thing with her.

"You're still dead, girl."

"I'm working on it."

"No paycheck until then."

"What does a dead person need money for?" I try a laugh but it comes out sounding like a small critter dying.

Jake looks at me as we ride down. "Dead?"

"Small mix-up at the Social Security office."

"Ah. I had my identity stolen once."

"Oh?"

"Yep. By a florist."

We step into the lobby and outdoors. The autumn sun feels good, just warm enough to be comfortable. And then I hear it. It feels like claws against a chalkboard.

Meow.

Below me, the same four cats I couldn't shake a few days ago are back, moving in and out of my stride as I try to walk. Jake notices and smiles. "I love cats."

"Must be a family thing," I say.

"You don't?"

"Oh . . . they're so . . . loyal." I trip over one of them and Jake catches me.

"They seem to like you." He watches over his shoulder as they continue to trail us.

I change the subject. "So. You've never been out of the office?"

"They exaggerate. Of course I go out."

We walk by a homeless man I hardly notice. But Jake stops. I watch him pull out a card and hand it to the man. As the cats circle me (and not the homeless dude? seriously?), I vow to hold my tongue, but this is my point. A card? To a homeless man? I mean, what good is that going to do him? I mean, *The Lord will keep you and make His face shine upon you?*

The dude needs a place to eat and sleep and an acknowledgment that—

The man opens the card and a ten-dollar bill falls out. Jake smiles warmly at him and continues walking. I do, too, but I can't help but glance over my shoulder. The man has the money in one hand and is reading the card in the other. He smiles at something. I think there is a rainbow on the outside of the card, as best as I can tell. He closes it and stares at it.

"We are going to come up with something fresh for Valentine's Day."

"To go with hearts, flowers, sunsets . . ."

"I don't know what I've been doing wrong." He walks fast when he talks. I try to keep up. The cats even look drained. "Maybe I've been forgetting to connect with people."

Ah hah! "I think you're on to something, Jake."

He stops, turns to me. The cats come to a screeching halt, watching us. "We'll hit every romantic hot spot in the city."

"Oh, uh . . ." It all comes back to me at once, every romantic place Sam and I ever went. I blink, trying to shake all the images. Restaurants. The river. The barbecue pit (a risky one but it was so fun). Jazz concerts. A balloon ride.

"And we're starting with the Empire State Building!"

He hands me a note pad and pen.

If we weren't outside, I'd rush to the bathroom.

I realize I have no scientific evidence for this, but I think mothers have a special power over daughters. It comes in a lot of different forms, but perhaps the root of it stems from the same place—regret from their own lives.

It's like they can will things on their daughters that they wished for themselves. My mother—as strange as she is—is no exception. She and my father met on a farm, but I always suspected she wished she had a better story to tell.

Jake is asking me if I'm afraid of heights. Apparently I'm turning white and making tiny gasping noises that sound as if air is leaking from my belly button. No, it's not the height I'm afraid of.

It's the irony.

Listen, I'm a fan of irony. And it comes in many forms. Verbal irony is sarcasm. I've got hundreds of cards based solely on verbal irony. It's probably way overused in my life.

There's dramatic irony, when a reader understands more about the events of a story than a character. Obviously that has nothing to do with me, but thought I'd throw it in there.

Then there is situational irony. That's what I'm knee-deep in right now. Situational irony is when what actually happens is the opposite of what is expected. To be blunt, I was not expecting to be at the Empire State Building writing love cards.

There's also a lesser-known irony—let's call it the crazy-cousin-nobody-invites-to-the-dinner-parties: cosmic irony. For me, that's the line between human desires and the harsh realities of real life. It's when you feel like you have control over your life when in fact you really don't. Call it God or Fate or whatever you will, but the fact of the matter is, there's an influence far beyond what you can perceive.

That's the kind of irony to avoid. When it comes knocking, lock the doors and windows and hide.

It's also generally helpful to avoid expectations at all costs.

I have learned this the hard way.

We board the elevator and zoom to the top of the Empire State Building. The elevator doors open. Everyone exits but me. I peek out. I'm not sure what I'm looking for or hoping not to see. Well, I guess I'm partly hoping against a cute guy looking for a girl to ask out. But I notice nothing but couples. Lots of them. I quickly follow Jake.

"Let's watch these people, imagine what they'd like to hear through a card."

We both spot a couple nearby holding hands and gazing out at New York City.

"What do they need to hear?" I ask him.

"Write this down," he says. And then he kind of slips into a weird trance. He stares forward, his eyes a little more open than normal, and he goes monotone on me. "'Your hand is mine to hold for years. I'll never leave, through smiles or tears. And when mountains move our way—together we'll climb each step, each day.'" He turns to me, wistfully. His expression drops. "You're not writing."

"You're not serious," I say, but instantly I know otherwise. "You're serious? You want me to use precious and limited company ink in the midst of unpredictable finances to write that down?"

I bite down on the pen because instantly I know I have hurt him. Ugh. Why do I have to open my mouth so much, say exactly what's on my mind?

"You really don't like it, do you?" He gazes at me with eyes so vulnerable I'm afraid that they might fall right out of their sockets. I've already got a bloody emotional mess on my hands. I don't need this.

"Jake, no . . . seriously, I do . . . I love mountains . . . it's just—"

"You don't have to feign."

But I can't help it, I continue to gush out a heck of a backpedal. "Not many people can rhyme on cue. And you . . . you have the biggest heart. It's the clue department that needs a defibrillator." Wow. That didn't come out right. "Look, not every guy is ready to climb that mountain with a girl. Even if he buys her the card that says he will."

I've said too much. I know he can see it in my eyes. There is a place deep in my heart where that is true and it's just come right out in my words. I'm forced to divert. "Ah . . . yeah, see that couple over there?"

Jake looks.

A girl and a guy, in their twenties, stand nearby. They appear to be feuding. I try a playful approach. "Go recite what you think they need to hear in a card. See how they respond. If it works, I'll give you a dollar."

He smiled a little. "A whole dollar?" He pretends to think. "Hmm. You're on."

Wow. Didn't see that coming. I was just trying to avoid a conversation about who didn't climb what mountain in my life. But I like the bet. Jake needs to see in real time what happens when he spouts off one of his poems, one of his grand proclamations of love.

He strolls over. I can hear the guy's voice rising as the couple argues. "I'm not trying to be insensitive. I just can't win with you!"

Jake approaches. I want to duck and hide behind something, but the only thing available is an elderly couple I'm bound to spook if I huddle at their legs.

"Excuse me," Jake says.

The couple stops arguing, looks at him, both with sour and pinched expressions.

Jake is very casual, not the least bit nervous. "If there were a card shop up here, he'd buy one for you that expresses his love."

They glance at each other. I know they're probably expecting him to pull out flowers to sell.

"This place symbolizes your love," Jake continues.

"Oh brother . . ." I grumble. This is going to be disastrous.

"Its height. Its strength." Jake is gesturing like this is Shakespeare. "Its firm structure to draw on in times of trouble." He looks at them both. "Because the value of your love is worth the pain of challenging times."

I hang my head. Half of that didn't even make sense. Besides, where was the rhyme? I glance up, just in time to see the guy say, "Yeah. What he said."

The girl gazes at him. "Really?" She reaches out and embraces him. They hold each other—and right behind them is Jake, smiling at me.

I grab him while we have a chance and whisk him to the other side of the deck. Jake is still smiling. He sticks out his hand.

"Fine," I grumble. I dig in my pocket for a buck, probably close to my last, and slap it in his hand. "I think it was a lucky break. I mean, I can't believe they fell for that. Height? Structure? It sounded like an architectural tour."

Jake continues walking. I catch up with him. We stroll along the side of the deck where we can see the view. "I'll admit . . . I can be resistant to change. But that back there, it's shown me something. It's shown me what we need for Valentine's Day."

"Break-up cards," I say.

"Exactly," he says.

"Really?"

"Yes! Yes! Make-up cards!"

"I said *break-up* cards."

"I thought you said make-up."

I sigh. I thought for a moment we were on the same wavelength but we weren't even on the right frequency.

"Make-up cards . . . ?"

"Because people do fight. Case in point back there."

"No kidding. But you're overlooking someone."

"Who?"

"The one without a valentine. The one whose idiot boyfriend chose to end their relationship."

"I can see this is personal," he says, stopping to look at me.

"It's an example. I don't even have a boyfriend." Ugh. I think I've just made his point.

"I like where you're going with this . . . we can write cards for them about how their true love is on the way!"

"That's exactly what I *wasn't* thinking." Oh my goodness, this guy is totally not getting it.

Suddenly we hear a burst of emotion. We turn and there is a woman, maybe thirty, by herself. She is tearing a photograph. Ripping it to shreds. Letting the paper fly into the wind, tossing the rest off the edge. Tears are streaming down her face.

Jake glances at me and I shrug. "I dare you."

He doesn't even hesitate. He walks next to her. This time I don't even try to hide. I want to see this whole thing play out.

Jake gently pats her shoulder. She looks at him, embarrassed but seemingly comforted that someone sees her pain. She smiles a little, shakes her head, wipes away the tears.

"There's another out there for you. Do not lose hope, the future will bring a love that's real. Because God sets the lonely in families."

"Huh?" she says.

Wait, that was me.

The woman's expression drops right there in front of him. It's so dramatic that Jake actually takes a step back. I think that's probably a good idea.

"The *last* thing I need is someone shoving me toward someone new! If I didn't think he was the best, I wouldn't have been with him in the first place! Jerk!"

It's unclear who the jerk is here . . . Jake or the boyfriend . . . but she's made her point and she stalks off.

Five seconds later Jake is slapping the dollar bill back into my hand.

"One to one." I smile.

"This isn't over."

We walk again. "Jake, do you seriously believe what you told her? That it's really as simple as someone better coming along?"

"The foundation of our company, when my father built it, was for the purpose of encouraging people . . . that in times of pain, something good will come of it."

I glance at him. "Do your cards come with a money-back guarantee?"

"It's not like we came up with that message on our own. It's in the Bible."

"And you believe the Bible?"

"I do. My dad, he never wavered, no matter what was going on in our lives or with the company. He always believed something good would come, even in the midst of some tough circumstances. It's been hard since he retired because my brother doesn't exactly . . . believe. But Dad put him at the helm. My dad sees the good in everything and everyone . . ."

I stop. Something gets me, kind of strikes right into my heart. I'm taken by surprise. I hadn't really felt my heart do much of anything lately.

"What? Did I say something wrong?"

"No, it's just . . . I don't know. I wish I could be like you, trusting that everything will be okay."

He touches my arm. "What's not okay for you right now, Hope?"

I look up at him. I know my eyes are shiny with emotion. But I'm tempted . . . so tempted to spill everything.

And then, suddenly, I can't.

I start walking again. "Well, for one thing, you heard Candy. I'm still dead according to the government. Until I'm alive, you can't pay me." I glance at my watch. "I need to get to the Social Security office."

"Give me a couple of more hours. I have a few more places I want us to go."

I follow him, but I'm dragging my feet.

9

"I brought you a little something to eat," Bette said, carrying a food tray into the room.

"Bette, that is so kind. You didn't have to do that. I brought some tuna."

"I know you did. And trust me, I want you to keep on using it. The guy next door woke up from a traumatic brain injury yesterday and I'm halfway convinced it was your tuna."

Jake laughed. "That smelly, huh?"

"That's what we need. We can't make loud noises so we're forced to keep the needles and the tuna up. But I figured you'd like something else." She set the tray down on the ledge with the cards. "Not promising it's any good, but there's some Jell-O and a nice, buttery roll there."

"You seriously don't have to bring me food. I feel like I'm in the way half the time."

Bette's expression turned serious. "Jake, I don't mean to get personal here, but I think you're the only thing keeping this girl from sinking so far away that we lose her. A mother's love can go far, but this mother's love is far out. Lovely lady, otherwise, but if she screams "hallelujah!" with no forewarning one more time, I'm going to be moving some people to the cardiac unit, if you know what I mean."

Jake laughed. He watched her take Hope's pulse and blood pressure, writing down her vitals in a chart that was getting thicker by the day.

"Bette?"

"Yeah?"

"You look tired."

She glanced at him, tried a quick attempt to smooth out the ponytail that seemed like it probably never even came down. Two mismatched clippies held a few stray hairs, but mostly everything fell in her face anyway.

"I don't mean to pry, but you take care of everyone around here. I see you helping the patients, other nurses, and now patient visitors." Jake glanced at the food tray she brought in. "Who takes care of you?"

Bette didn't answer for a long time. She tightened some tubes, used a syringe to put medicine into Hope's IV. Jake looked down. Maybe he'd said too much.

"My mother."

"Your mother takes care of you?"

"No. I take care of my mother." She didn't look up. It was like she felt ashamed to even mention it. She kept busy, changing the bed pan and tucking the sheets, as she spoke. "She's got the beginning signs of dementia. Not sick enough for twenty-four-hour care, but sick enough that she can't live alone anymore."

"What a noble thing to do."

Bette looked at him. "Honey, it's not noble. She's my mother. How could I not? And this is my job. How could I not care about this sweet woman in this bed?"

"Not everyone has a Bette in their lives, but I know they wish they did."

She went to the sink to wash her hands. "It's been hard. I'm a single mom. My son is sixteen. I worry about him all the time. And now I've got my mom living with us. Sometimes it's hard to find time to just go to the store or the money to buy the extra things we need."

"I'm really sorry. My dad once told me to try to look at everything in terms of seasons . . . that it won't always be this way. And it's been true. The good seasons don't last forever. But neither do the bad."

Bette grabbed two paper towels and looked at him. "That's very wise."

"Nah. Just life."

"I have to go check on Mr. Warren, but I have a favor to ask of you, Jake."

"Anything. I'll start eating anchovies if that will help."

She laughed. "It's actually for me."

"Sure. Anything at all."

"Would you make me a card?"

"What?"

"A card. For me. Whatever you feel like you should write. I want a card, something to encourage me, something to get me through the day that I can go back to and look at when the day seems like it'll never end."

Jake was so touched he didn't know what to say. "Of course. Yes. Sure, I would love to."

She smiled. "Thanks. Now I must go. Compacted bowel in Room 4. It's going to be a long night."

She left and Jake couldn't stop smiling. He grabbed a pen and one of the envelopes that a card had come in and began jotting down ideas.

Then the door burst open and CiCi came in, wailing with her arms in the air. She flung herself over the bed, her head resting on Hope's shins. "My baby girl, my baby girl. You are in the fiery furnace! It is scorching your soul! But believe! Believe that you will be delivered!!"

Jake sighed. Bette was right.

It was going to be a long night.

GREETINGS FROM MY LIFE

I'm literally biting my tongue and having quite a heated conversation with myself on the inside. I'm following Jake all over the city . . . Central Park, Times Square . . . every place he thinks a romantic moment might spur him into free verse or a limerick or something. I'm jotting down every idea, every word. He'll spontaneously shout "butterfly!" or "star gazing!" and then we move on.

I'm biting my tongue because I'm a smart girl and I realize this is a job that, if I can ever prove myself alive, is going to pay the bills. But if Everett is right, and the business is going to tank, then it's not going to pay the bills for long. I know I can save it. I know I've got the right kind of card, the card that nobody is printing but everyone wants to read.

Jake enjoys pointing out all the love around us . . . old couples holding hands. Young couples dreaming of futures that have endless possibilities. Even dogs look to be canoodling.

Sure, I think. It's easy to love and dream when you're in the greatest city in the world. It's real life that makes everyone trip and fall. That's what I want to try to convey to Jake. Rainbows and mountains and butterflies, sure. But what about cliffs and flash floods and dungeons. Dark, certainly. But am I lying?

By the time Jake finally runs out of ideas, I'm exhausted. My calves are killing me. We're sitting on a bench and I'm packing up my notepad and pencil. "I'll get these typed up for you and have them ready in the morning." I smile like the good assistant I'm trying to be.

"Thank you," he says, grinning. "I really think we're on to something here. I'm excited. I should've done this years ago." He gives me a playful punch in the arm. "Thank you."

"Sure . . . whatever I can do to help . . ." All sarcasm must stay in my head as much as possible. "Well, I should probably go get in the Social Security line before they close. You don't mind if I take off a little early?"

"Not at all. I understand you've got to get that resolved."

"Thanks."

"See you tomorrow." He walks off with a little bounce in his step.

I grab my bag and head the other direction, feeling a little bad. I feel I'm like the person that tells a little kid there aren't real unicorns. He really feels triumphant. He feels like he's nailing it. He wants to write make-up cards. I want to write break-up cards. We're the yin and yang of the greeting-card world.

I walk a few blocks to the Social Security office and am dumbfounded to a standstill. A line. And as far as I can tell, it actually wraps around at least a block. I check my watch. It's four. The office closes at six. Is there any chance I can get in before it closes?

The truth is, what choice do I really have?

It's already a little chilly. Now gray clouds are gathering atop the skyscrapers and it looks like rain. But I take my place in line, sit with my back against the wall of the building I'm standing next to, and pull out my sketchbook. Like clockwork, the cats appear. They sit near a pole, watching me.

It is an hour and a half before I check my watch again, but in the meantime I have designed and written ten new cards. Some of them are super darn funny too, if I do say so myself.

I've covered a lot of topics . . . breakups, stupid men, lousy relationships that are stuck and going nowhere. My favorite joke comes with a little play on words, where the dude loses his e and becomes a dud. You have to see the picture to get the full effect, but let's just say I'm envisioning a catfight in the card aisle if this is the last one left—women are going to eat this up.

I chuckle reading it for the fourth time. Above, the faint sound of thunder gets my attention. I look up and it's the first time I notice the old man. He is watching me with interest.

"Whatcha been working on, woman? I seen you sitting here for a while now, barely lookin' up once."

"I'm a card designer."

He blinks. Blankly.

"A greeting card designer."

A small nod of slight recognition as to what I'm talking about.

My ten cards lay on the concrete and I smile at a job well done. "I'm working on a plan to save the card company I'm working for." I gesture broadly to my pile of cards. Inside my head, a loud, angelic chorus proclaims its greatness.

"Never heard of saving anything through a card."

I'm about to explain, very thoroughly to this old man, the power of a greeting card when a woman wearing a navy suit steps near our line and yells, "We'll be closing in thirty. Anyone behind this point, come back tomorrow." I'm at least twenty people from where the woman's cutoff line is. A loud, collective groan comes from the crowd.

Then, as if God spoke his displeasure at the situation, thunder rumbles loudly overhead, rattling the nearby windows. In unison, everyone looks up. And as we do, a torrent of rain the likes of which nobody has seen since the movie *The Perfect Storm*, pours out of the sky, drenching everything in its path. People are actually screaming, running this way and that. I quickly reach for my cards, but a boot smashes into one, and then someone's tennis shoe runs right over my hand. I look up, hoping the old man sees my plight and might be willing to help, but he is gone. By the time I manage to gather my cards and stuff them in my bag, I'm drenched and so are they.

The cats sit there, unmoved, their eyes taunting me. I wish I knew something insulting in the cat world. I would totally use it right now. Instead, I stalk off toward the YMCA. If I had cat ears, they'd be flat.

In the pouring rain with no umbrella, I walk. The day is as gray as Stonehenge and if you could see me, you'd think me pathetic. And I am. I'm slouched, trying to protect myself from the rain. I'm wet. Angry. Fed up. I just want to get home . . . or wherever it is I'm staying. I want dry clothes and I want that stupid Murphy bed. This rain reminds me of my wedding day and so yes, my heart is a soggy mess of sorrow at the moment. It is, dare I say, a bleeding one.

I arrive at the YMCA. I stand under the small stoop, letting myself drip-dry a little bit. I don't want to track water all the way to my room. Some old person might slip and fall. I listen to the rain and decide it's rather soothing if I'm not standing in it. I try to think of a plan to get Jake to notice my cards. What can I do to wake this guy out of his creative coma?

Finally, I stop dripping. I head to my room. I pass the old lady janitor, who never seems to acknowledge I exist. Sitting on top of one of her buckets, though, is a tabby cat, who stares me down as we pass each other. I stare it down too. Bring it on, I say. Bring it on.

I reach for my key but before I get to it, I notice a note stuck to my door. It simply says *"Rent overdue"* and my gaze drops to the door knob. There is a padlock on it.

A minute later, I'm sitting across from Morris, the guy I met the first day I arrived. I figure Morris has seen plenty of people on hard times in his line of work, but I must look like a culmination of them all. He isn't meaning to, but his head is tilted to the side like I'm quite the spectacle.

I slap a credit card onto the desk in front of him. It is my last resort. I vowed I wouldn't go into debt making my dream come true, but at this point, I'm just trying to find dry clothes and a bed, so I figure this would be considered an emergency.

"Can you put the next couple of weeks on my credit card?"

"I already tried. Wouldn't go through."

This is the kind of desperation you don't really expect in life. This and being left at the altar. I'm sitting in this chair, across from a guy with no neck, and I'm realizing I'm homeless. For real, homeless.

Homeless. Spouse-less. And also dead. I might as well jump feet first into the fiery furnace of hopelessness, because I'm not seeing a way out of this.

"I'll get cash from my boss tomorrow." I know Jake will do this for me. He hands ten bucks out to homeless people. And I'm his assistant. I'm sure the loan will come with a card encouraging me through my homelessness, but at this point, I'm desperate enough to take it and read the thing. I look at Morris. "Will that work?"

"Yep. And as soon as I see that cash, I'll let you back in. Tomorrow."

An hour or so passes. Maybe five. I'm not sure. All I know is that I'm against the wall next to my padlocked door, still wet. I'm cold. I'm hungry. And I'm the kind of person that takes my hunger out on other people. When my blood sugar drops, you better get me a carb and fast.

I rest my head between my knees, trying to keep a headache at bay. I realize I'm about as low as I can go. I mean, probably to encourage me you'd say, "Well at least you're alive." But technically, according to the government, I'm really not. I wonder what kind of card Jake would send to someone like me? How do you comfort someone by greeting card who doesn't have a postal address? What serene nature picture is going to keep me from jumping off the proverbial cliff?

I hear a sound and look up. On the other side of my closed door, sitting against the wall just like me, is Mikaela. When she slipped into the picture, I don't know. But she's beginning to grow on me.

I get up off the ground. I'm vaguely aware there's a prominent wet spot on my rear.

"How was your date?"

I sling my bag over my shoulder. "Does your mother know you sneak out and harass me all the time?"

"I'm too charming to fall under the harassment category."

"Right. What room are you in again?"

"You never asked me the first time."

"Does it have floor space I can borrow?"

Mikaela also stands and she produces a padlock key from her pocket and hands it to me. "I'm in tight with the janitor lady. Room Eleven, can I ask you something?"

"Don't you always?"

I've known Mikaela only for a short time, but I've never seen her face cloud over until now. She is pondering something deeply.

"How do I get a boy to like me?"

Oh brother. I do not want to deal with this question. My advice would be to stay away from boys for the majority of life, until you are both about seventy and they're finally tame enough to enjoy and nearly dead enough to collect Social Security benefits.

As I stand there trying to figure out a way to explain all this to Mikaela, there is an overwhelming antiseptic smell, like the girl bathed in it. It's not going to attract any boys, that's for sure, although I suspect she's totally safe from the West Nile virus.

"Take a shower, first of all. You smell like antiseptic."

"I was hoping for something a little more existential."

What eleven-year-old uses that word? "Well, sorry to disappoint you. I'm of the philosophy that a good shower is never going to fail you. After that, you're on your own."

I unlock the padlock and throw my stuff on the bed, then dig through my bag looking for dry clothes. When I turn around, Mikaela is already digging through my other bag, holding up the soggy cards one by one.

"What are these for?"

I put a towel down and sit on the bed, gazing at the sopping mess. "Tomorrow, Jake and I present to the team the next set of cards. Only Jake's cards"—his face pops into my mind, as does the expression of complete fulfillment he had when we were at the park—"will sink us for sure. So I'm writing my own set. Except I'm going to have to start over, but I'll have them done by tomorrow."

"Wait." Mikaela hands them to me one by one as I set them on the desk. "Jake doesn't know about these?"

"Of course not. If he did, he wouldn't let me present."

I reach out for another card, but Mikaela pulls it to her chest, looking at me just like those cats do. "Wait a minute. I helped you get that job. And now you're going to stab Jake in the back?"

"It's not like that. I'm trying to help him save his company."

She crosses her arms. "Is he going to see it that way?"

Now I don't know about you, but I have some pet peeves. I don't like when people younger than me call me *honey* or *sweetheart*. I also don't like eleven-year-olds crossing their arms and lecturing me on ethical issues.

"Mikaela, give me the drawings."

"Then give me back that key!" I'm surprised by this. She's typically pretty calm . . . incorrigible, yes . . . but I've never seen her face red.

I cross my arms, holding the key in my hand. Oh yeah, it's a standoff and I'm in the kind of mood where this is somehow making sense in the moment. I understand that you're probably having second thoughts about me and an eleven-year-old throwing down, but you have to try to be in my perspective. See it through my eyes. See it through the day I've had. Remember that I was having to write down rhymes about deer bounding over prairie grass.

Suddenly, Mikaela throws all the cards at me. It's like confetti popping from the ceiling. But there's no big prize and no winner. I watch them float to the ground, then I look at Mikaela. Her hands are on her hips. She suddenly looks like the little girl she is.

"It's not supposed to be like this! I'm changing my Christmas list!"

She storms off. I grab all my cards off the ground, trying to neatly stack them. I don't know where Mikaela has gone, and frankly, I don't have time to care.

I sit at my desk and pull out my pencils.

The next time I glance at the clock, it is 4:30 a.m.

* * * *

It's morning. And by morning, I mean the time most people get up. I fell asleep somewhere around five and awoke around seven, still at my desk, drooling on a card that had half the punch line written.

I shower, trying to wake myself up. I look dreadful. Maybe I should present a line of zombie cards.

I decide I need some breakfast. But as I open the fridge in the community kitchen and dig around sacks, I realize almost immediately my food is gone. Someone has stolen it. I glance at my watch. I'm already late.

So I go.

Once in the office, I quickly type up everything Jake requested and have it on his desk by the time he arrives. He still has that bounce in his step . . . like a deer bounding over fields of optimism.

I see him in his office, reviewing the printout. He's talking to himself, making mental notes, I guess. While he's distracted, I take the cards I worked on all night and slide them into a folder. Jake walks out, looking at his watch.

"Okay, it's time to go to the board roo—you okay? You look a little . . ."

"Just tired." I stretch a grin so wide across my face that he leans back a little, like he's afraid it might bite. I dial it back a notch. "Yeah, you know, just so much excitement about our big presentation and all that. Hard to sleep. This is what we live for, right? Greeting cards." He smiles helplessly, if I had to describe it, and it kind of stings my heart. "This new love line will make those nursing home ladies swoon. Thanks for typing everything up this morning." He shoves his hands in his pockets and smiles at me in one of those moments where you feel like something is passing between the two of you but you don't really know what. "I, um . . . I had a lot of fun yesterday."

We walk together to the boardroom, my legs shaky underneath me. Jake seems as calm and cool as I've seen him. Pearl, Ruby, Everett, and a couple of the accountants file into the boardroom as we do. Everyone gets situated, a couple pour coffee. Everett checks his phone. I swallow. Guilt is kind of strangling me at the moment. But at the same time, I know what I must do . . . for Jake, for Everett, for greeting cards everywhere.

Everett calls the meeting to order and then says, "All right. What do we got?"

Jake's face lights. He gives me a knowing look before he says, "Everett, this new line . . . I'm sure these cards will sell. Hope?" He gestures toward me and nods toward the computer where we've put all of his notes into a PowerPoint.

I stand, adjust my pants and my shirt and my hair. I adjust my watch. I adjust my pants again. And then, with resolve, I adjust my expression and head away from the computer toward the easel in the corner, where I'd put my cards earlier and draped a sheet to hide them.

I can see Jake out of the corner of my eye. He's pointing to the computer, sort of frozen mid-gesture, watching me walk. Everyone is.

"Good morning," I say very formally, but my voice shakes a little. "Today, I want to present to you a new idea." I glance at Jake. Slowly, his arm is lowering. "People who are together, they don't need our cards. They should be writing their own words to each other. So I propose we do a new thing this Valentine's Day, something that's never been done in the history of greeting card companies. For those who feel it's time to end a relationship, or those who are grieving a lost love . . . let's target them. They need us to say the right words for them. That's why I propose we develop"—I can almost hear the drum roll. Almost—"a line of break-up cards."

"Now *that's* what I'm talking about!" Everett says and claps . . . all by himself.

"Hope," Jake says, "what are you doing?"

I look at him, hoping he sees the wisdom I'm offering. "Jake, just listen. It's marketable. More people break up than make up, right? If we want to talk numbers, right?" I glance over at the two accountants, who don't seem to speak "relationship" but whose eyes light up when I say numbers. With the flare of a magician, I pull the sheet off the easel and unveil my very first card. I pick the first one up and show the outside: "'God never closes a door on a relationship without opening a window.'" I open the card. "'Feel free to jump. I'll wait for you at the bottom.'"

I still crack up at that one. I look around the room. Only Everett is smiling and nodding.

I clear my throat and unveil the second card. "'It was God who said man is not meant to be alone.'" I open it. "'I hope God wasn't talking about your ex. That schmuck deserves to be alone for the rest of his life. You are too good for him.'"

Everett howls with laughter. But Jake stands and moves to the computer.

"Excuse me," he says in a tone I've not heard him use before. "These are not the cards we prepared for today. I appreciate your efforts," he says, casting me a look that says otherwise, "and I'm sure you worked hard, but—"

"I want to hear them," Everett says. "Landon, go on."

It's tense in the room, which does not seem ripe for the receiving of punch lines, so I try to explain the vision. "We could also develop a set for that moment when you realize you're with the wrong person . . . and who can't relate to that, right?" I say with a kind of snorty, awkwardly whistling laugh. "Um, how about this one? 'The Lord said seek and ye shall find . . . when I found you, I should've kept looking.'"

Everett is rolling. Pearl and Ruby look at each other as I unveil the fourth card.

"Where are we supposed to add the puppies?" Pearl asks.

"Do you have kitten jokes? We love kittens," says Ruby.

"I'm working on that," I say to them, "but let's think about the woman whose man cheated on her. How about quoting

Numbers 6:24: 'The Lord bless thee and keep thee . . .'" I open the card. "'Because I don't want thee anymore, you cheater."

Everett rubs his hands together. "Awesome."

"We can't use the Bible this way," Jake says, throwing up his hands. "I know this is your dream and you think these are good ideas. But my father left me in charge for a reason." His gaze is bouncing between Everett and me.

"Correction, Jake. You're just the writer. I get to approve what goes to market." Everett points to the next card I'd unveiled. "What's this one?"

I look at it. It's a drawing of a woman buried in wedding gifts. She's not looking happy. I'm sure you can imagine.

"It's a 'No Thank You Card' for right after a busted wedding."

Ruby and Pearl look completely lost. "I've never heard of those," Pearl whispers to Ruby.

"Me neither," Ruby whispers back.

Few have, I assume. So I explain. "They come in handy when your betrothed"—I use this word to try to help Ruby and Pearl along in their understanding—"leaves you at the altar, feeling stupid, because you thought he'd stick around. And he was the only one you ever loved and you have all those gifts to return."

I have to be honest, everyone looks confused and stumped. Even Everett.

I clear my throat. "Jake, if we mix the Bible with humor, maybe it will save your company!" I'm sure you can picture it—I'm frozen in excitement, waiting for him to come along beside me.

He doesn't. "I have my own new cards," he says to Everett, completely ignoring me.

"Lan, you got anything else?"

Lan . . . ugh. Why is he calling me that? It's so . . . Sam. And I didn't even like it that much when *he* called me that, but it was his pet name for me and it had a certain amount of charm to it because I thought he was in love with me.

I glance at Jake, suddenly convicted by my scheme. He stands there looking totally wounded. He shrugs his shoulders, like I might as well continue.

"Well, um, I'm also working on some Anti-versary Cards, for those dates on the calendar that are painful. Or for divorcees, Newly Unwed cards."

Admittedly, there is a certain dark cloud hanging over the conference room, but this is reality . . . this is what people go through. I try to brighten the mood. "Of course, we can't ignore congratulations for those few who do find love."

Pearl and Ruby sit up straighter, nodding and smiling. I unveil the final card. On the front is someone praying. "'I know you've waited so long to find God's best.'" I open the card. "'I see you got impatient. Congratulations on your engagement." Pearl and Ruby are back to looking confused, but Everett leaps from his seat.

The next thing I know, he's grabbed my head, pulled me forward, kissed my forehead, and let me go. I stumble back, breathless and disoriented.

"You are just what we needed!" Everett says.

"We can't print these." Jake steps forward. His face is a shade of red that's somewhere between ripe tomato and blood. "Sales are not that bad. Our inventory is moving . . ." His voice is high and thin and desperate.

"Because you give half of it away! Since these aren't specific only to Valentine's Day, let's get them out there, see if they boost sales."

I glance at the accountants, then at Ruby and Pearl. Everyone is watching this verbal Ping-Pong match with a lot of interest.

"These can't be our last-chance cards." He looks at me, but there is a wall so high and wide in his eyes that I'm not even sure if he's seeing me. "I need our notes."

"Jake," Everett continues, "it's either we try this or we sell. Your choice. What do you want?"

At that moment, I feel complete regret for what I've done. Yes, I believe in my cards. Yes, I think the company needs an update. But I realize now I've done this in the most horrible way imaginable. I've embarrassed Jake in front of his coworkers, his brother. I've made him look stupid and backed him into a corner.

"Jake, I'm—"

But he storms out.

The accountants slip out, happy, I'm sure, to return to their predictable world of numbers. Everett leaves, but not before lightly tapping his hands together in what I guess is a congratulatory clap. Pearl and Ruby move slower, pushing themselves away from the table, helping each other stand.

I hear Pearl whisper to Ruby as they walk out, "I haven't seen him that upset since he lost his wife . . ."

They continue to chat but I can't hear what else they are saying as they leave.

I'm left alone standing by my cards and only one question occupies my mind . . .

Jake had a wife?

10

Jake watched silently as Bette unsealed the envelope. She pulled the card out, looking over the picture he'd affixed to the front. It was a picture he took in Kansas . . . a sun rising over a field of golden wheat. An old wooden, one-room church sat in the foreground, long-ago abandoned but still holding strong the steeple that pointed to the heavens. She paused at the picture, a serene expression softening her features. Jake watched her eyes move back and forth across the text as she opened the card.

"'I look up to the mountains—does my help come from there? My help comes from the Lord, who made heaven and earth! He will not let you stumble; the one who watches over you will not slumber.'" Bette gazed at him over the top of the card, tears shiny in her eyes. "Jake, this is exactly what I needed to hear. How did you know?"

Jake just smiled and shrugged.

She closed the card and held it to her heart. "Well, I am keeping this forever, I will tell you that. Thank you."

"You're welcome."

"Now, what about this girl?"

"What about her?"

"Why don't you write her a card?"

"Oh . . . I don't . . . I mean, nothing has come to me . . . and plus, she can't really read a card . . ."

Bette laughed, tossing him a look that said she wasn't buying any of his excuses. "I bet you can think of something." Jake looked at the floor. "It can't ever be wrong if it comes from the heart. Read that in a card once."

Jake laughed a little. "I'll see what I can do."

"You eating enough, honey? Man can't live on tuna alone, you know."

"It used to be ramen noodles. I'm moving up in the world."

"Let me know if I can bring you anything. We've got stashes of cookies and juice like you wouldn't believe."

"Okay. Thanks, Bette."

Bette left and Jake checked his watch. CiCi would be arriving soon, as she always did around six or seven in the evening. He dreaded it. The poor woman just couldn't get a grip and tended to ramble about crazy things, like Hope's father. He didn't know the story behind that one, but it didn't seem likely that he would return soon, whatever the history was. If a daughter in a coma wasn't going to get him home, there wasn't much else that would.

Jake studied her, still sleeping peacefully, but she didn't look as healthy anymore. Her skin was sallow, the color gone from her now gaunt cheeks. He'd overheard the doctor talking to the nurse that they'd soon have to begin looking at putting a feeding tube in. Her vitals, he'd noticed, were not as strong as they once were.

"Hope," he said, his finger tracing the metal safety bar that seemed useless, "you've got a lot to come back to. A lot to live for. Just . . . just open your eyes. I promise, everything is going to be okay."

A quiet and slight knock came at the door. He wasn't sure who it would be. Becca and CiCi normally came right in when they visited. A few other friends had stopped by for visits, but nobody stayed long. It was, he thought, probably too painful to look at her like this.

It wasn't his room and he felt a little awkward saying "come in" but he did anyway and the door opened a little. It was Mindy, his assistant at the shop. She carried a beautiful vase of flowers.

"Mindy, hi! What are you doing—I'm so sorry, I know I haven't been at the shop very much and you've been having to work extra hours and—"

Mindy set the vase down. It was one of her finest works. "Jake, please. Don't apologize. This is a difficult time and I completely understand why you need to be here."

Jake smiled, but honestly, he didn't really understand it himself. "The flowers are beautiful."

"Thanks," she said, touching the petals. "I've been studying a new technique I saw on Pinterest."

"It's working."

"Listen, Jake, I can't stay. I wanted to come by and tell you I'm thinking about you and Hope and praying that she will wake up. I also wanted to tell you to take as much time as you need. The sisters and I have everything under control at the shop. Everyone has been able to come in and work more hours so we're good."

"Thank you."

"But there's one more thing I need to tell you. And I . . . I hesitated about this . . . I wasn't sure if this was the right time, or if you needed to know this now . . . it's just so . . ."

"What is it?"

Mindy drew a deep breath. "Maybe you should sit down."

"I am sitting down." By Mindy's increasingly startled expression, he decided she was the one who needed to sit down. He stood and grabbed the chair nearby, pulling it closer. "Here, sit."

Keeping her attention on him, she sat, then reached into the bag she carried on her shoulder.

She pulled out a stack of greeting cards.

GREETINGS FROM MY LIFE

"Thank you. When the guys can cut my first paycheck, I'll pay it back, I promise."

"No worries," Everett says as he slides a wad of cash across his desk toward me. His office is unusually playful, like a twelve-year-old set up shop. Basketball hoops hang off the doorways and closets and candy jars, rubber toys, marbles, and a slingshot line his desk. "So weird how you can't prove you're not dead."

"If I could just get through that stupid Social Security line. It's like a living nightmare down there."

"Well, it'll get sorted out eventually. For now, we've got to focus. But first, I need lunch." He stands, grabbing his jacket off his chair. "Want to come? I'm buying."

I squeeze the roll of cash in my hand while trying to casually dismiss the invitation. "I better not . . . got lots of . . . need to prepare and start to work on . . . get the ball rolling—"

"So that's a no." He smiles briefly.

"Yeah, I mean . . . it's a—"

"So, he's paying you to take down the company?"

I whip around and Jake is standing in the doorway. Looming, really. He seems taller. His shadow stretches long and lean against the office floor. He is eyeing the wad of cash in my hand.

"No, no . . . gosh, no . . ." I'm laughing the kind of laugh that is drenched in guilt. You're hoping it sounds like a giggle but really it sounds like a witch's cackle with hints of psychopath.

Everett is standing near me. Too near. I want to step away but there's nowhere to go. "You should be thanking God you might have this final opportunity to keep your precious card company. Because of her." He points right at me, though there's not another "her" in the room, so it's redundant. Everett looks at me with the warm smile of decade-long friends. "After lunch, we've got work to do, Landon."

I look at Jake, trying to squeeze out some kind of genuine expression but I don't know what to do or say. I'm feeling genuinely guilty, that's for sure. But I'm also feeling sure that I have his answer, if he only wouldn't be so blind to my ideas.

"I have a question for you."

I brace myself. My mind neatly forms five bullet-points to counter his stance, whatever it is. "What?"

"What size skate does that little girl wear?"

"Little . . . who?"

"The little girl with you the day we met."

"Oh, uh, Mikaela."

"Yeah, what size does she wear? I saw a pair of skates at Macy's she might like."

Admittedly, I'm thrown. I vaguely remember hearing her mention skates or skating or something like that. I hadn't thought about it since that day. He'd obviously been putting a lot of thought into it.

"I'm sorry, I don't really know." I step toward him. "Listen, Jake, I—"

"I'm happy for you." He takes two steps back. Then another for good measure. "I'm sure this is what you wanted."

He turns and leaves.

Yeah . . . this is what I wanted. I just didn't picture it feeling this way.

I SPEND SOME time walking. New York City is made for walking. Lots to see and do, but lots of noise to drown out thoughts you don't want to think about. So I walk until the sun sets, absorbed in pretend conversations justifying my actions.

When I arrive back at the YMCA, I'm cold and hungry. My appetite suddenly returns with a vengeance. Even though I know my food is gone, I decide to check the community fridge anyway. Sometimes people will put a sign on a box of yogurt that says, "Please take one." As I round the corner into the kitchen, I immediately spot Mikaela. She's on her tiptoes peeking inside the freezer that is above the refrigerator. I'm about to call her name when I see what she pulls from the freezer.

A blue Popsicle.

She pulls the cellophane off and the imaginary flavor bursts into my mouth. I slowly back away, shivering at the weird coincidence and all the memories that the Popsicle brings to the surface. I hurry to Morris's office, drop an envelope of cash through his mail slot, and rush to my room.

But before I can even unlock the door, there is another alphabet letter stuck to my door. *K.* I rip it off and get in my room as fast as possible. Instinctively, I look for the bride and groom that pops up on my desk every time I throw it away. But it isn't there.

I drop the K in the trash and dig around a little for the statue, but it is gone.

"Well that's a relief!" I say to my Murphy bed. We're on a first-name basis now.

I sit and dwell on the day. I sleep fitfully that night, but in the morning I feel strangely energized, ready to tackle the tasks at hand, hoping I can prove to Jake that my cards will win back his company.

I arrive before anyone else and begin to clean and tidy the Humor Department. I dust. I vacuum. I change lightbulbs. Basically, I resuscitate it. It looks pretty good. It needs some colorful decor, but I can work on that. For now, I have a desk, I have my drawing pad and pencils, and nothing—finally, nothing!—to stop me.

It's around ten a.m. and I'm in the middle of sketching a bride behind the bars of a jail cell when Pearl and Ruby walk into the Humor Department. I feel uneasy because their expressions are serious. They are probably very fond of Jake—who wouldn't be? And this is their family business, now infiltrated with an outsider.

They stand in front of my desk for a moment, gazing down at my drawing. I hate for them to see the sketch without the punch line—it feels a little like it's being observed in its underwear.

Then Pearl says, "Can we try?"

"Try?"

Ruby's shoulders drop along with her voice, which is now very low and barely audible. "We're so sick of drawing puppies."

"And kittens," Pearl adds.

"Truly, how many puppies can you draw in a lifetime? I mean, I've covered every breed with every expression known to the canine world. But each year I'm expected to make them cuter and cuter, so I keep making the eyes bigger and bigger." Behind her thick glasses, her eyes widen.

"It's true," says Pearl. "Same for the cats. Pretty soon their eyes are so big that you think something has gone terribly wrong in the breeding cycle."

"They look deformed. How large can a pupil get before you begin to suspect you're dealing with alien life?"

"I agree," Pearl says. "Listen, I'm eighty-four years old. I got material. I got lots of material."

Ruby nods. "You should've met her husband, Dick. Enough said."

"Do you two mind sharing that drafting table over there? There's two stools and a really good light."

By the way they break into a grin, I assume it's fine. And for the next two hours, we work in focused silence, except for a few times when one of us laughs out loud at one of our punch lines.

It's at the exact moment when Ruby cackles, "Dick is rolling over in his grave right now!" that Jake manages to walk by. He stops and looks at the three of us. Pearl and Ruby don't even notice, but my desk is right at the entrance of the department, so if I pretend I don't see him it's going to be a hard sell.

He observes Ruby and Pearl, frowning, tilting his head to the side like he can't really process what's going on. Pretty soon he moves along, never really acknowledging me.

Outside: *For everything there is a season. A time for every purpose under the sun.*

Inside: *Sorry to hear it's breakup time. Where shall I deliver the chocolate?*

Behind me Pearl and Ruby are cracking up again.

"You gotta see this, Landon!" Ruby squeals. "She's all skinny on the outside of the card and then you open it and she's fat as a potbellied pig. Pearl is drawing chocolate drooling down her face!"

We work for a solid week on the first batch of cards to go out. It is the most fun I've had in a long time. I feel like my dreams are finally coming true and that this is what I'm made to do. It's like I've seen the mountain, I've climbed the mountain, and I've conquered the mountain. And there's not even a punch line that needs to go with it!

It's Monday morning when Everett comes to my desk. "Come with me, for about thirty minutes."

There's not a hint that the intentions include a date, so I follow him to his car. He does open the door for me, like a gentleman would, and I watch him hurry around to the driver's seat. "I've got a surprise for you," he says. Dread washes over me. I'm hoping it's not a romantic helicopter ride over the city. Or a lunch in a cozy booth. Oh boy, what have I gotten myself into?

"What is it?" I ask.

"You'll have to wait and see!" He's looking and grinning at me more than the road, but within ten minutes, he's pulling into a parking garage next what looks like a large warehouse. We enter through the back door and I suddenly realize where we are.

The manufacturing plant. It's the printing press.

I stand in the doorway in awe. The machines roar and every second or two make a precise chopping noise. The paper is going by so fast it's blurry.

Everett takes my hand. I'm so thrilled that I don't really care. I just want to see what's going on. We walk to the end of one of the large printers.

Everett shouts over the noise. "Hey Ralph!"

"Hey there, Everett!"

Everett reaches for a stack of cards, sealed in cellophane. He hands it to me.

"My cards . . ." I am as breathless as I've imagined I might be on my wedding day, when it was time to kiss the groom. There must be a hundred of my cards in this one stack. "They're . . . beautiful." I look at Everett, tears in my eyes.

"They're genius, that's what they are!"

We watch the whole process, how they're packaged, sealed, and then put into shipment boxes. It's a wonder to watch.

I stand there in the midst of all the noise with the realization that I'm finally a published greeting card writer.

I tackle Everett with a hug.

I come home for the evening, thankful I can afford a deli sandwich. I'm mentally and emotionally exhausted, but still on quite a high from the excitement of the week. I lay on my bed for a while, picturing all my cards being printed, bound, shipped. I imagine them arriving at card stores, to the delight of all that work there. I imagine them flying off the shelves as women roar with laughter in the card aisle, throwing their heads back, clutching their hearts or stomachs or the lady next to them.

Time passes, maybe an hour, and I decide I should go find Mikaela. I should find out her shoe size, find out what she might want for Christmas. Jake has a kind heart, to remember a little girl he only met once, and to somehow know what she wants for Christmas.

I walk out of my room and go to Room 12. I knock and the door barely cracks open. The woman on the other side is old and hunched, a weary life etched into the deep crevices of her face. Everything on her face is turned down . . . her eyes, her hook nose, a mouth with no teeth to hold it in place.

"Hi. I'm Room Eleven . . . I mean, from Room Eleven. I'm looking for Mikaela. Does she live here?"

The door shuts in my face. Maybe when she said neighbor she meant two doors down. I knock but there is no answer. I try another, but the man grunts and huffs and closes the door.

Then I notice the janitor. She is walking, as she always does, pushing her cleaning cart down the hallway. She is about to pass me.

"Hey! Hi! Um, do you know what room Mikaela lives in? She's eleven years old, about this high, has eyes that . . . they're kind of like mine?"

The janitor only stares me down, but it's after she passes me that I notice it: a Columbine flower tucked behind her ear.

I stop, pondering this, suddenly missing my grandmother very much and wishing she could see me in my element. But I refocus—I need to find Mikaela. I haven't seen her in a couple of days.

I wander the YMCA to no avail, asking people if they've seen her or know her. Nobody seems to know anything about her.

I am passing the front door of the YMCA when I hear noise, the sounds of children. I hurry outside and see a group of them on the sidewalk. And then I spot Mikaela, at the back of a disorganized and rowdy line.

A woman is clapping her hands, raising her voice above the noise. "Kids! Kids! One line, please. You know the drill. The bus will be here in a moment to take us back."

Mikaela is busy writing in her journal. She glances up and the cute boy she likes is passing her by. She smiles shyly at him. "Hi there, David."

She's so cute! The perfect amount of flirt in that smile. But the boy bumps her shoulder and walks by without even a glance or an acknowledgment. I watch the joy in her eyes fade and she turns her attention back to her journal, her face nothing but a sad mess of emotions.

I'm going to cry.

I hurry to her, like she needs rescuing or something. As I come up beside her, she looks up, startled. Then she looks toward the crowd of kids, her expression a little sheepish.

I cast my attention toward the line of kids. "So, you're not my neighbor?"

"I merely live down the street with 112 brothers and sisters, minus one crush. Can't call him a brother, citing the ick factor."

I suddenly realize it. She lives in a group home, the one I walk by every day on my way to the subway.

I swipe hair out of her face. "Are you still mad at me?"

"Is Jake?"

"Yes."

"Then yes. Yes, I am."

As you've probably gathered so far, I'm impulsive. I snatch her journal out of her hand like I'm the little kid.

"Hey!" she says, reaching for it.

"Then what can I buy off your Christmas list?" That's right, now I'm buying a kid's love. I quickly scan her list titled MY CHRISTMAS LIST. "True love. Pencil set of all colors. More time." I look at her, holding the pad away from her as she tries to snatch it back. "More time? What does that mean?"

She crosses her arms. "You'll figure it out. If it's not too late."

The bus lumbers to the side of the curb and the kids burst with excitement as they load in the exact opposite way the lady in charge is instructing.

I look at Mikaela. "Don't tell me you're one of those kids who's sick and going to die on me."

"I'm not sick."

"Then what does this mean?"

"Come on, kids! Load up! Mikaela, that means you!" The lady is waving her hands, trying to corral the masses.

While I'm looking at the woman, Mikaela snatches the journal back. She hurries into line and disappears into the sea of kids. I watch the bus roar to life and leave.

More time. What could she possibly mean by that?

More time for what?

11

Mindy sat there for a moment and then slung her bag over her shoulder. "Listen, Jake, I'm going to leave you with that, okay? If you need me, let me know. Take all the time you need."

"Oh um . . . thank you . . ." Jake said but he couldn't tear his eyes away from the cards.

The room became very quiet and he held them in his hands for a long time. But it still felt like a mirage.

The envelopes were addressed to him and sent to the shop's address. The handwriting was barely legible, like there was hardly a hand attached to write it. In the return address was the word *Hope*, and under that, only the words *Poughkeepsie, New York*.

Inside the envelopes were typical greeting cards, with beautiful pictures of mountains and streams and rainbows. Inside the cards were messages of hope, offering Scriptures about God's strength and love. But most of the text on the inside was scratched out and rewritten into some kind of punch line. And strangely, each card was signed . . .

By Hope.

But how? How could she possibly send him cards, five of them to be exact, while she's in a coma? He clutched them and closed his eyes, praying to the Father that he sometimes—most of the time—didn't understand. He loved the Father's promises and hoped very much they were true, but deep in his heart he wasn't always sure. All he knew was that he wanted people to have hope and the best chance of hope he ever knew was in God.

And only God knew how a woman in a coma could send him greeting cards.

"Oh, God!!!"

Jake's head jerked up as CiCi rushed into the room.

"Oh dear God!!"

"CiCi . . . shhhh, there are other patients—"

"I'm not talking to you!" Her eyes were fierce, which surprised him, because she didn't really seem capable of fierceness. "Oh dear, dear God . . ."

Jake hurried to shut the door. He turned around, his back against it, trying to figure out what in the world was going on. He cautiously approached the bed where CiCi was splayed out over her daughter, her arms trying to reach the width of the bed in what looked like a gigantic hug.

"CiCi . . . are you okay?"

She turned her head to look at him, still resting on top of her daughter. "I was in the chapel and I was praying and I got a message from the Lord."

Jake felt equally alarmed and curious. "Uh huh . . .?"

CiCi stroked Hope's face. "She is about to do something that is going to cost her everything."

Jake cautiously stepped forward. "CiCi, what could she possibly do? She's in a coma."

"Do you think I understand this?" CiCi snapped. "Of *course* she's in a coma. But I specifically heard from the Lord, that I was to pray that her path is set right."

"You're not making any . . ." But his words trailed off as he glanced at the stack of cards sitting in the chair. He swiped them up and put them behind his back before CiCi noticed them.

"Something very strange is going on," CiCi said, her voice low and cryptic. "Some things that can't be explained." She was standing over her daughter now, both hands spread wide over Hope like cat claws.

Jake didn't know what to say. She was right, of course. But CiCi was crazy . . . wasn't she?

"I can't lose her too. No . . . no, I can't lose her too . . ." CiCi was wiping tears.

"CiCi, I'm not really one for, um, openly expressing my, um . . . you know . . . God and all that, but I know he hears our prayers. I know he is working in this situation. We just can't see it."

"I must pray, I must pray, I must pray," she said, squeezing Hope's arm. "I must pray for her to be set on the right path. She's on the wrong path. She's on the wrong path." She turned to Jake. "If you have the kind of faith that's going to move a mountain, then put your hands right here on my daughter and together we'll pray. Yes, together we'll pray as the Lord has instructed."

"Um . . . I just . . ."

Her eyes narrowed ever so slightly. "But if your mustard seed isn't cutting it, then get out. Hope needs the Lord to come down into this room and move in one mighty miracle, just like a strike of lightning. *Boom*!"

"I . . . I'm kind of . . ."

But CiCi had returned her attention to Hope, crying and wailing over her daughter, quoting obscure Scriptures that didn't even seem to apply to the situation.

Something very strange is going on.

And CiCi was the only one who had said it out loud.

GREETINGS FROM MY LIFE

I discovered over the past couple of days that I'm not hard-nosed. Stubborn, yes. Passionate, most definitely. But putting it to Jake has not brought me the least bit of satisfaction and cost me a lot of sleep. Everett, on the other hand, seems unaffected, which is strange considering this is his brother.

I decide I must make things right with Jake. I must set him at ease, show him with gentleness and care that the switch to a more modern greeting card is only going to help him keep the company he and his father love so much.

It's midmorning when he walks by.

"Jake!"

He stops, looks at me, says nothing. There's not even an expression on his face. Blank hurts. I'd feel better if there was at least a scowl.

"Hey, look, if the cards do well, we'll need our next set. I want your help."

He stands there for a moment, then shrugs. "I can't help you, Landon. What you write—it makes fun of what I believe."

I can't help but notice he's given up calling me Hope.

"There are people out there in pain because of love. Love smacks them over the head, leaves them for dead." I'm gesturing with my black and white pencils. "They could use humor."

Suddenly, he's standing at the edge of my desk, having charged up to it like an angry bull. His nostrils are even flaring. He leans across my desk now, his hands flat against it, his face glowing with radioactive anger.

"Your *humor*, it just covers up the pain. There are many who lose love and find it again."

I'm frozen, one pencil pointing to the sky, the other having rolled out of my hand, onto my desk, and then to the floor. It's hard to describe how close he is to my face, but let's just say I'm regretting the everything bagel this morning.

His hand moves. He's reaching for one of my cards. He doesn't take his eyes off me as he picks it up. He stands erect now and reads the card out loud. "'The Bible says, God is not a man that he should lie. Sorry your man is not God. What a liar he turned out to be.'"

"Happens all the time. It'll be a best-seller. But this one won't be." I snatch my notepad from the Central Park brainwashing session. "'Love is patient, love is kind. Our lives will always be entwined.'"

He grabs another one of my cards. "'The Bible says God keeps your tears in a bottle. That's a bottle. One. Don't fill it up on one ex. Trust me. There will be more.'" He stares at me. "You really think this helps? This isn't even funny."

He was right. Not one of my best, but it was a first draft.

He tosses it and it lands on the floor.

Now it's on.

Instantly I remember the card I used to find the address of Heaven Sent. It's still in my bag. I plunge my hand in and pull it out. I use a breathy voice, just for effect. "'In this time through the valley, you struggle to go on. God's hand will sustain, as you mourn one who's gone. Memories will help this pain in your heart. Mountaintops will return as God does his part.'"

"That's the truth," he says.

"Yeah? Well someone gave this to my mother when she . . ." Filters fly up. Not the time to mention wedding fiasco, rumored suicide, death certificate. ". . . when she lost someone. Do you think that's what she needed to hear?"

Dang. He's got another of mine in his hands. "'The best way to dull the pain from your breakup is for something really bad to happen next. I'll pray for that.'"

I crack up. Now *that* one rocks. It actually doesn't, but I have to hold my ground here with a grin that says how awesome I think it's not. He tosses it in the air. The forced smile snaps right off my face. Now I'm gritting my teeth.

"These are mean-spirited," he says, pointing his finger at me. "Anyone going through pain won't be ameliorated."

"Ameliorated?" I'm standing now. And it could be argued that I'm shouting too. Nearby I hear Ruby's hearing aid sound off with a high whine. "Jake, do you live with your nose in a dictionary? A thesaurus? Nobody uses that word. Nobody even knows what that word *means*! Try the real world, where real people live."

"Oh, so now you're not just revising my cards, you're rewriting my conversations?"

And then I yelp loudly, that high kind of pitch that kids describe as a girl scream. But that sharp pain is going through my heel again. "Look," I say, trying to hold my foot and keep from crying at the same time. I grab the dictionary off my desk, but my heel still feels like it's being poked. "Ouch!!" I wobble, off balance, and instinctively grab his arm. I squeeze.

All muscle.

But then I'm back to my heel, which continues to feel like it's being stabbed by something, but upon inspection, there's nothing there. I open the dictionary, flipping through the pages quickly, trying to find *ameliorate.*

My finger is halfway down the page when I find it. *"Ameliorate. Mend. Help. Improve."* I'm about to use this word against him, explaining that I am *ameliorating* his company, when he puts his hands on my desk again. This time more gently.

"What's the word when you want to kiss someone you're really mad at?"

"Passion." I blurt it out right as I begin to think it's not the definition he's interested in. I'm guessing this by the way he's staring at me. Our eyes are locked. "Also, crazy. Cracked. Demented." Each word gets softer because his face is moving closer to mine. I don't get the word *insane* out because our lips are now pressed together.

I can't breathe.

And right at this moment, I don't want to.

But then I come to my senses. I pull away. "Don't *do* that! I don't kiss—I mean, I kiss, of course, but I don't . . . what I mean is, I don't . . ." I've got an entire dictionary at my fingertips and I can't find a single appropriate word.

"You don't risk? Chance? Gamble?"

"If you love someone, they go away. That's life. You know it, better than anyone. And you can't even talk about it. About her."

The words are out before I know it. Yet again, my filter has failed. Big time.

My words hang between us and slowly he backs away, his expression wounded, his eyes filled with pain. He turns and rushes out of the room.

Behind me, I hear Ruby and Pearl gasp.

I'm quickly putting on lipstick. It's more like lip balm. It's actually got no color at all. It's the best I can do. What can I say, I'm not a makeup girl. But according to Everett, I'm about to be on camera.

Seconds after Jake stormed out of my office, Everett was calling me on the phone, telling me I needed to come with him immediately. He rambled in the car about the press release, about the phone calls, about the interest. He said his company has never seen anything like it.

"Our publicity department was overwhelmed!" Everett says as we round the corner on to 8th Street.

"We have a publicity department?"

"Just one lady. Denise. She's also our marketing director."

"Oh."

"Landon, listen to me. You've got to exude confidence, okay? Stand tall. Be the persona of these cards, okay?" He is very wound up, his eyes large and focused, his grip on my arm squeezing tighter with every word.

"I got it."

"You can do this." He smiles warmly at me and I feel myself gaining confidence.

The car sweeps to the side of the street. Everett exits effortlessly. I'm a little clunky getting out, but I manage. Everett is instantly by my side, guiding me at the elbow. I look up and notice we're at a card and gift shop. And then I see the camera crew.

The reporter, trailed by her husky camera operator, greets us on the sidewalk.

"What are we doing?" I whisper to Everett. I wasn't prepared for reporters.

But Everett doesn't answer. He's too busy shaking the hand of the reporter and introducing me to "Starla."

Starla seems fully enamored with Everett, even as she politely shakes my hand. Her eyes don't leave him.

"Thanks for covering this for me, Starla."

"Anything for a ride on that boat." You have to see this—she's stroking the microphone like it's a toy poodle. Her voice purrs. "So this is your writer."

"This is Landon."

Starla regards me for a moment. With her four-inch heels she's a good six inches taller than I am. I hate standing next to tall women. They always make me feel small. She flips her finger in the air, makes a circular motion, and the camera operator suddenly comes to life, moving toward me. Starla steps in front of Everett, giving him a coy smile, and then is standing beside me.

"Heaven Sent cards just unveiled a new kind of card, something you wouldn't expect from them. You heard it here first, a line of breakup cards. If you haven't seen these, rush out to your nearest card shop and take a look."

It's like they spontaneously appear but I realize they're drawn by the news truck, and the flashy guy in the suit—that would be

Everett—directing them into the store. Before we know it, the little card shop is overwhelmed with customers. The cameraman is wandering the aisles, taking shots and sound bites as Starla leads the way.

"I'm buying this breakup card and I don't even have a boyfriend!" says one customer to the camera. "It just made me laugh!"

"I tell ya," says another lady, right behind her, "if my guy broke up with me, I'd want one of these cards. They're hilarious! These cards tell it like it is!"

Starla manages to find the only guy browsing the cards.

"I just found out my girl cheated on me. They have the perfect card for me to end it."

Everett smiles and winks at me from across the floor, pitching a thumbs-up. I'm enjoying the moment, there is no doubt. I'm a greeting card writer so I hardly ever get to see people's reactions to what I write. I just have to imagine it. But here it is, right in front of me.

And then, so is Starla, with the microphone shoved in my face, asking me a question about my feelings.

I look at her. "I hope they'll be a hit. I was so tired of the normal cards out there that promise a better life to come, especially after a breakup. Pain hurts. Might as well make it funny."

Starla grins as she turns toward the camera. I see Everett off to the side, watching us, glee beaming off his face like moonlight.

"And make it funny she has!" Starla's giving the camera her mega-watt smile. "Heaven Sent may have struck gold on this one, folks. Perhaps these cards—and this writer—are a gift sent from heaven. Time will tell."

~ ~ ~ ~

I'm actually asked to sign autographs. If my dad could see me now. On the way back to the office, Everett is fielding phone calls, one after another. I sit in the car silently, staring out the window, the buzz from the attention wearing off like lipstick at the end of the day. I decide I must find Jake when we return, set some things straight. First of all, no kissing. Second of all, I respect him. I want him to know that. We just have different views, that's all.

Everett puts his hand by the small of my back and guides me into the Heaven Sent office building. The news is indeed spreading fast. Heather waves excitedly and I'm finally not annoyed by her undying optimism expressed daily through the color yellow.

"The public is going to love your humor," Everett says as we step onto the elevator.

"Thank you. Thank you for giving me a—"

"I want you to take over being the voice of this place. Replace Jake."

"Wait . . . what? Jake, he's your brother, and he's still—"

"Forget Jake. Let's head out on my boat this afternoon and talk about you." His hand caresses the small of my back as he steps closer.

"Everett," I say as smoothly as possible in a situation like this, "guys like you . . . they don't like girls like me." Just a casual observation, but Starla has fire-red lips. I'm the lip balm girl. Things aren't adding up. "What's your game?"

"I don't have one," he says, charm sizzling like a 4th of July sparkler.

"I won't go out with you."

"Why? Because of Jake?"

"No. Not Jake."

The elevator doors open. I practically dive out—and right into the path of Candy. Today, it's intense fuchsia, the kind proven to trigger migraines.

"There you are! I've been looking everywhere for you." Candy sighs, putting her hands on her hips. "Here's the deal, sweetheart. We're going to have to ask you to leave."

"What?" Everett says.

"If I don't get the U.S. government the proper paperwork on you by one week from Thursday, you will no longer be employed by Heaven Sent."

"Candy, she's our potential gold mine. She's not going anywhere."

"We don't have a choice, Everett. I'm sorry."

"One week from Thursday?" Realization hits me. "That's Thanksgiving."

"I don't make the rules, Ms. Landon. Just fix it."

"I'm trying! It's just that I can't seem to . . . the Social Security office is always—"

"Prove you are who you say you are, or your life here is over."

Candy walks away. I turn to Everett, but he is walking away too, his hands thrown into the air. I'm left by myself.

The one who can't prove she's alive.

It feels like I'm living in one of those nightmares you can't get out of. Everett tells me to leave immediately and go get this taken care of. "You should have plenty of time to get through the line today," he said. And he's right. Usually, I'm there in the late afternoon and the line is always wrapped around the block. But if I leave now, I've got four hours. So I grab my things, rush out of the building, and power walk straight to the Social Security office.

Now, if you were a total stranger and you walked by, observing this scene, you'd think I'd lost my mind. But since you know the whole story, you'll understand why I'm clinging to the glass of the front window, my left cheek pressed against it, pounding and wailing. "No! No! You can't be closed!"

But a sign on the front door clearly says *Closed*. "Why? Why?? How??"

A mounted police officer rides by, the horse's hooves clacking loudly against the concrete. "Ma'am?"

I turn, my back and palms now against the glass. I look like an oversized window decal.

"Are you okay?"

I'm aware of the tears streaking down the side of my face and the fact that my hair is clinging to my cheeks the same way I'm clinging to this glass window. "They're closed." I manage to get the words out like a normal person, but then I sob.

He remains expressionless. "Yes, they are."

"Why?" I wail. "I mean, why would they be closed on the one day I can get here on time?"

"It's a federal holiday."

"What?"

"They'll open again tomorrow, ma'am."

"What federal holiday? There's no federal holiday!"

"Move along."

I notice his hand has moved to his taser. Awesome. Yes, please taser me. That would be the perfect end to my day.

He waits. I sigh, grab my bag, and walk away. I don't even bother going back to work. Not looking like the mess that I am. I wander the New York City streets for a while, hoping to be inspired by the vibe. I'm not. I'm hopeless. I'm going to end up losing my job because I'm dead. And then I'll die, for real, from a broken heart.

Speaking of broken hearts, I find myself thinking of Jake a lot. Especially . . .

The kiss.

Why would he kiss me? As surprising as it was, I don't regret it at all. And that surprises me even more. My life has been plagued with regret, so it just seems like that would be natural order of things now.

I *must* make things right with Jake. But before I do that, I have to get my life back. Literally. I decide I'm going to get up at the crack of dawn and arrive first thing at the Social Security office. That will ensure me a spot. Then my life can go on.

I'm in bed and the hopelessness returns. I've tried not to think of my wedding day. The busyness of the new job has helped. But alone in the darkness, atop lumpy old Murphy, I find myself dwelling on it. Then crying about it. I can't sleep. But I must.

Then there's a knock at the door. I almost don't answer it, but there's a little optimism in my heart that says this could be opportunity knocking. Silly things like that pop into your head when you're mourning your pathetic life.

"Hi." It's Mikaela.

The fluorescent lights in the hallway nearly blind me. I put my hand over my eyes to shade them.

"Mikaela, what . . . what are you doing here?"

"I need to talk to you."

"Kiddo, it's late."

"It's 8:30 p.m."

"I . . . look, I've had a really hard day. I'm sorry, I just can't . . . maybe tomorrow? Okay?"

She doesn't say okay, but I smile and nod as if she did, and I shut the door.

It seems weird that being in the dark sparks thoughts of God, but this seems to be the place that I begin to remember him. Despite the nonsense that my mom brings to the table in the religious realm, I've always sensed God and known he loves me. It's just that more often than not, I don't pray. And I can't really think of a good reason why that is so. It just is.

Maybe I'm a little mad at him that I got dumped at the altar. But then again, he wasn't the one who dumped me. Maybe I'm a little mad at him that my dad disappeared. But then again, he isn't my dad. I run out of excuses at some point and as I stare up into the dark, trying to find the ceiling. I say the first prayer I've uttered since coming to New York City. I ask for help proving I'm alive. He parted the Red Sea. Surely he can get me to the front desk of the Social Security office.

The next thing I know, it's morning and my alarm is sounding. I shut it off, dress quickly, and forego breakfast. I grab my bag and hurry, walking faster than the already frenetic crowd of the NYC sidewalks.

I round the corner, bracing myself for a long line at the Social Security offices. I gasp.

There's one person in line. The door hasn't opened yet. It opens in five minutes.

I hurry to check to see if there's a sign declaring a federal holiday. There doesn't seem to be. The man in front of me is old, using a cane. I don't stand too closely for fear of knocking him over, but I'm about to burst with excitement. Finally!

I remember my little prayer to God and I silently thank him for making a way.

A woman walks to the door and unlocks it from the inside, opening it for the old man. I follow closely behind, flashing her a wide grin. I don't really expect her to smile back, but she does.

Wow, this day is getting better. I glance behind me. There's not even a line forming! Please tell me this isn't a dream!

I expect to stand and wait, as the old man was there before me, but there are two windows and a friendly looking woman beckons me over to her window. I slide past the old man and quickly take a seat. There is a lump of happiness and relief in my throat.

"Hi," I say.

"What can I do for you today?"

I explain my dilemma. By the look on her face, I can tell this isn't something she sees every day. I take my passport and driver's license out of my bag and slide it toward her. "So, as you can see," I conclude, "it's very important that I get this resolved today."

"Oh yes. What an ordeal." She's looking at me with some pity, so ordeal might be referring to being dumped at the altar, but no matter, I'm just happy this horrible nightmare is almost over.

"Yes, it has been." I nod. "It really has been."

She picks up my passport and driver's license, examining them both. Then she looks at me. "Unfortunately, we have a problem."

12

Jake didn't know what to do. CiCi continued to pray, though not as loudly and boisterously as before. She was praying about Hope not being fooled. It was absurd. How could a woman in a coma be fooled? He wanted to leave because it was all making him feel uncomfortable, but it also felt wrong to leave Hope with her mother draped over her body praying prayers that didn't make any sense.

There was not a seed tinier than the mustard seed, so was it a trick question? The next level after faith as big as a mustard seed was no faith at all. And that certainly wasn't him. He had faith. He'd written dozens and dozens of cards about faith during the dark times, faith that the sun would rise tomorrow, that God is good, that God has a plan. He'd written about all of it. So why couldn't he join CiCi at Hope's bedside, lay his hands on Hope's arm, and try to pray her out of this coma?

Instead, he sat glued to his chair, staring at a woman who believed with all her might that her prayers were working and moving mountains. There was no such thing as faith by proxy. You either had it or you didn't.

The door opened. Jake shot out of his seat, for no particular reason except he was being caught off guard in so many respects it just felt like he should be ready for anything.

Relief flooded him as Becca walked in carrying a teddy bear. She noticed CiCi flung across Hope and shot Jake a questioning look. Jake quickly took the bear, tucked it at the end of the hospital mattress, and guided Becca outside. CiCi never looked up. She was still praying.

He closed the door behind them as Becca whispered, "What is going on in there?"

"You don't want to know. It's the kind of thing that can send a woman into early labor."

Becca smiled, patting her big belly. "At this point I wouldn't mind. Four more weeks." She glanced toward the room. "Is CiCi going nuts?"

Jake cleared his throat. "Well, um, she's been very . . . what's the word . . . *enthusiastic* about praying Hope out of this coma. But honestly, most of the time, I don't think she's making sense. Today she was rambling on about Hope taking the wrong path. I just think the stress is getting to her."

Becca nodded. "That is very strange."

"The thing is, Becca . . ."

"What is it?"

Behind them a flurry of chaos erupted. Someone was coding behind a curtain. Doctors and nurses rushed by them with a crash cart. It was a grim reminder of how serious Hope's condition was, no matter how peaceful she looked. He didn't know how much time she had. Nobody did. And here he was, dragging his feet, trying to come up with a way to express what he was feeling in a way that felt safe. He glanced over to the room where all the staff had flooded. Maybe they didn't have time for safe.

"Jake, what's wrong?"

He looked down at the cards he was still clutching in his hand. "It's just that . . . things are getting kind of strange."

"What do you mean? Hope? Is she not doing well?"

"I got these . . ." How could he even explain this? He was getting cards from someone in a coma. He was going to sound as crazy as CiCi.

"Yes? You got what?"

And then it came tumbling out of his mouth, partly because it was time to say it out loud and partly because it was easier to say than trying to explain the cards: "I love her."

Becca's mouth parted slightly. It didn't drop clear to the ground, but there was shock there. Her expression backed that up. Her eyes were enlarged like she'd just seen some sort of meteorological phenomenon.

"I . . . I know that sounds crazy, doesn't it? I mean, we hardly know each other. We *know* each other. Gosh, we've known each other since we were kids, but . . . sometimes she'd come into the shop and order those flowers and she was just so . . . and I couldn't ever say anything to her. I could barely say hello. I thought about writing her a card once, but that's all it was. Just a thought. And now she's here, and I was there on that day, and I'm just thinking that . . . well . . ."

"It's not a coincidence?"

Jake looked up at her, catching his breath after a long-winded explanation that tried to capture what Becca said in four words. "Right. Maybe we're meant to . . ." He shook his head. "It sounds so stupid. I get that."

Becca placed a gentle hand on his arm. "Jake, you've been here nonstop since this happened to Hope. You've been at her bedside. You've shown total dedication. I think she'd be lucky to have a guy like you."

Jake smiled. It felt good to be affirmed. "The thing is, Becca, I can't . . . I mean, I've sat there and tried to tell her. I even tried to write her a card. I just can't get it to come out. I'm too scared."

"Don't you think she senses you're there?"

"I don't know."

"It's hard expressing feelings. I get that. But there's probably no safer place to try out what you're trying to say than when she's in a coma. I mean, what's she going to do? Laugh at you? Storm off? Tell you you're crazy?"

Jake smiled. "True enough."

"I know one thing about that girl in there—she needs to be loved. She needs the kind of love that transcends from this life into whatever place she's in now. Sometimes I'm afraid she's in this dark, cold place, with nobody there for her. Maybe if she heard you tell her how you feel, she'd somehow find her way back to us."

"But she's just been through the thing with the wedding. Isn't it too soon? Aren't I treading on some kind of timeline boundary or something? Isn't there a rule that you can't go for the girl who gets dumped at the altar for six months or something?"

Becca laughed. "You and Hope . . . you two kind of think alike. I don't know what the rules are, but I think we're under special circumstances here."

Suddenly the door to Hope's room flew open. CiCi stood there for a moment, breathing hard, glancing between the two of them, her knuckles ghost white as she gripped the doorknob.

"We must pray she doesn't go with him!" CiCi said.

Jake and Becca exchanged glances. Jake asked, "Who, God?"

"No!"

"The devil?"

"Stop making this spiritual!" CiCi barked.

If this wasn't spiritual, then what was it? Who in the world would Hope go with?

Becca stepped forward, her face the picture of calmness, her voice smooth and low. "CiCi, maybe you should walk around the building."

"What?" CiCi's attention snapped to Becca.

"Around the hospital building. Isn't there something in the Bible about walking around a building seven times?"

CiCi's expression indicated this was registering.

"Is it seven?" Jake asked. "I thought it was seventy?"

"Oh, gosh, maybe you're right. I think it is seventy," Becca said.

CiCi looked to be counting something on her fingers. Then she nodded. "Yes, it's seventy. Seventy. Seventy." She walked away nodding, her hands lifted in the air, completely oblivious to the room down the hallway with all the activity. She walked right past it without even noticing.

Becca had moved into the room to see Hope. Jake let her have some time alone. He stood in the hallway a long time, staring at the cards with Hope's name as the sender, with her handwriting on the inside.

Then he noticed everyone filtering out of the room down the hallway. Doctors pulled off their masks. Nurses peeled off their gloves. Monitors were unplugged. Whoever was in there was gone. Jake closed his eyes. He'd written cards for people who were blindsided by tragedy. He knew firsthand that nobody knows what is waiting around the corner, so everyone should seize every moment.

He took a deep breath, closed his eyes, and prayed for even a half of a mustard seed's faith in himself.

GREETINGS FROM MY LIFE

Remember when I told you that my life is like a poorly timed step on to an escalator? You've probably already seen several examples of that, but here's another. I am on the phone with my mother and, as you already know, this is an exercise in patience. And when I'm impatient and frantic and frustrated out of my everlasting mind, I pace and gesture. Pace and gesture. Pace and gesture.

I'm all of the above times ten, so you can imagine I'm quite a sight to behold. And the mounted police officer confirms this as he pulls his horse to the curb and gets my attention.

"You again," he says.

I cover the mouthpiece of the phone. I don't want him to hear my mother. He's already looking alarmed and she's sort of shouting through the phone.

"I'm fine," I say, before he asks if I am or not.

"You're outside the Social Security office again, behaving . . ."

"Emotionally?"

"Fine. We'll go with that. What seems to be the trouble now? They're open. There's not even a line."

"I know." I nod, my head bobbing up and down so hard that the horse is getting startled. "Yes, it is. I've been in there already. My morning is not working out as I had planned. I prayed for a parting of the Red Sea at the Social Security office and indeed, the sea was parted, but I wasn't specific enough, I guess, and I should've asked that he also raise me from the dead." I know, I know . . . total wrong choice of words and metaphors and, accompanied by my gestures, body language. That statement alone has probably put me on a federal watch list.

"Ma'am"—he uses the kind of tone that makes you realize he has a badge and a gun and the authority to use both—"I am going to need you to leave. Now."

I can hear my mom, she's calling my name, wondering what's going on, thinking we've got a bad connection. There's a metaphor in that, too, but now's not the time for metaphors, obviously.

I sling my bag over my shoulder and walk. I glance back once and he's watching me, so I take the first corner I can to get out of his line of sight.

"Hope? Are you there?"

I sigh and turn my attention back to my mother. "I'm here. Sorry. Listen, what I was saying is that the Social Security office told me a passport and driver's license isn't enough. I need my birth certificate. Can you please overnight it to my work address?"

"Well, um . . ."

"What? What??"

". . . I'm going to have to find which souvenir box that might be in."

"What? You put my birth certificate in a souvenir box? Mom, that belongs in something like the safe-deposit box. Look, never mind. Just please find it, as soon as possible, and overnight it to me, okay?"

"I'm praying, Hope. I'm praying. And I will keep praying until you come back to me."

"Mom! This is important! I am going to lose my job if you don't help me."

"Does that mean you'll come back? That's what I'm praying for. I still got your couch bed."

Tears are stinging my eyes. I cover my eyes as I talk. "Mom! For once in your life, can you listen to me? I know you don't care about my cards, but Dad did." And then I do a despicable thing. I know it's wrong, but I do it anyway. I play to Mom's delusions. "If Dad comes back, don't you want him to know you supported me in this?"

There is silence. Silence is uncomfortable anyway, but when it's coming from my mom it can be utterly terrifying. Silence is usually followed by a shout to the Lord in the most socially unacceptable way possible. I brace myself. At least she's not here in person.

But there is nothing, and suddenly I'm overwhelmed by guilt. I shouldn't have played the Dad card, for her sake or for mine.

"Mom, I'm sorry, I—"

"You're right. I'll find that birth certificate, Hope, and I promise on the grave of Abraham that I will get it to you."

I nod. I've just resurrected the most useless form of hope in my mom and I feel terrible. I thank her and get off the phone. I'm on a side street, leaning against the brick wall of a building that stands eleven stories high. I'm engulfed by emotion. Tears stream down my face. People walk by, taking no notice of me, and I am thankful. You can't cry on a side street in Poughkeepsie and keep it a secret. It's going to be in the town newspaper the next day and in the gossip of half the dinner tables that night.

I wipe my tears with the back of my hands and glance up just in time to see her.

It's hard to describe, but it's like everyone else is a blur and she is in full and complete focus. Nobody else even looks my direction, but she does. As she passes by me, she turns her head and looks straight into my eyes. I recognize her immediately—she's the waitress at the diner that I first arrived at after I left the church. I was still in my wedding dress, and coincidentally probably looking the mess that I am now.

Stranger still, she is not wearing her diner uniform. Instead, she is wearing a nurse's uniform. She smiles at me. Fluorescent pink gum sticks out against shiny silver fillings.

And then, just like that, she disappears into the crowd and is gone.

I stand there, tears now dry, determined, above all else, to make things right with Jake. What good is saving his company if he gets wounded in the crossfire, lost in the jumble of it all? I take my cell phone out of my pocket and dial his number, but there is no answer.

It doesn't surprise me that he won't take my call. I'm going to have to find him in person. I return to the main street and enter the rapid current of the stream of people. I'm aware, suddenly, of how lonely a crowded street can be, and how far away one human can be from another even while our shoulders brush against each other. I stand and wait at a crosswalk and dial the office number. I ask for Ruby.

"Hello?"

"Ruby, it's Landon."

"Hi, dear."

"Listen, I'm trying to find Jake. He's not answering his phone. Do you know where he is?"

"Well"—Ruby's words are as slow and aged as she is—"let's see here." Long pause. I can hear her breathing. I try to be patient. I wonder how scary the world around her must seem, how fast it moves and how different it is from how she grew up. "Oh, that's right . . . what, Pearl? . . . Oh, I thought you were talking to me . . . who is this again?"

"It's me, Hope. Wondering about Jake."

"That's right. Yes, I remember now. Some cute little girl came in crying. She was looking for you."

The crosswalk light glows white and the crowd pours into the street, heading for the other side, but I don't move. My heart sinks at the thought of Mikaela crying. She seems like such a strong kid, but a kid can only take so much. She was obviously upset last night and I dismissed her. Then she sought me out again and I wasn't even there.

"Jake talked to her and I think I heard him say he wanted to take her skating at Rockefeller."

I look to my right. I am a mere five blocks away.

"Thanks, Ruby!"

I hurry, weaving in and out of an already fast moving crowd. A light but hardly cold snow begins to fall. The air is crisp and cool but not unbearable. By the time I hit the skating rink, I am out of breath. My hands are braced on my knees and I'm trying to recover. I realize I must make myself exercise, but that is a task for another day.

When my lungs finally recover, I stand and notice the sign: *Early Season Special Today: $10.* I pull out the wad of cash in my pocket. Wad is not the right word. It's two five-dollar bills. It's the last of my money.

Then I spot Mikaela. She is alone on the ice, spinning in a circle, her arms wide and open, her tongue catching the snowflakes as they come down.

I pay at the window and am issued skates. I sit on the bench, tie them up, and glide onto the ice. It's been a while, but I always liked to skate. It brings back good memories almost instantly. As I skate toward Mikaela, I notice Jake on the other side of the rink. I skate past him, but he doesn't notice me. He's giving money to a mother and a child who look like they've come and watched and never skated themselves. Their faces are filled with delight.

I come along side Mikaela. "Hey, kiddo," I say with a friendly grin.

She scowls at me, her expression a cold mess of anger and sorrow.

"What's the matter?"

From her jacket, she pulls out a crumpled envelope and then what looks like a card. She tosses it to me and I slip a little trying to catch it. She then skates off. I stand there while others skate by me on my left and right. On the envelope is Mikaela's name written in pen and spelled wrong. I turn the card over to the front. I immediately recognize it as one of mine.

The front reads: *Do I like you?*

Inside, there are options with little boxes next to each one: *No, Nada And Never.* All the boxes are pre-checked, but someone has circled them for emphasis. And then the punch line: *the Bible says God works all things together for good. Trust me. This rejection is for your good.* And it's signed *David* . . .

Her crush.

My heart stings with guilt and sadness and anger. She's been nothing but nice to this kid. I've witnessed it firsthand. I turn to find her but she has now skated up right next to me.

"Mikaela, I'm sorry he did this."

"It's not your fault, right? You didn't give it to me." Her cheeks are red from the cold but I suspect that's not the only reason they're glowing.

"Look, it's a joke, okay? It's supposed to be funny. It's . . ." How to explain this to a child? "Trust me, this is for your good. Stay away from boys and especially don't kiss them. It messes up your senses."

"You kissed Jake?"

"What? No? . . . No." The first denial came out as a question, so that never really bodes well for believability. The next one should've been followed by an exclamation point, but it honestly barely deserves any kind of punctuation. It's more of a raspy, unconvincing croak.

"He kissed you?"

"Mikaela!" I am so flustered I'm trying to shush her but I can't even get my finger to my lips. It's sort of waving around like it has no place to go.

"Is he a passionate kisser?"

I almost faint right there on the ice. I've lost sight of Jake. For all I know, he could be standing right behind us. "I am not talking to you about this!" I whisper, managing the exclamatory ending while flashing casual smiles to passers-by.

"So he *is*!" Mikaela says. I notice she is momentarily distracted. I turn to see what she is looking at. It is a father skating with his daughter. "My dad used to take me skating at a lake near our house. We'd go every Saturday."

I'm filled with emotion for my little friend, so much so that it knocks me right on my backside. No, wait. That wasn't emotion. Turns out it was Jake. I'm splayed out on the ice with Jake halfway on top of me. He rolls off and Mikaela is standing over us, laughing, while Jake is profusely apologizing and helping me to my feet.

We all skate together for a while, Jake and me quieter than normal. I watch him with Mikaela. He has a way with her—she seems to drop a lot of her facade and acts like the kid she is when she's with him. It also seems, for now, she has forgotten about David.

After about an hour, we lose Jake again. He's found someone else to help, a young woman sitting alone on a bench, distraught over something. I don't catch much of the conversation, only what I can hear while skating by. But he's in card quoting mode for sure.

". . . never lose hope. You'll find what's missing . . ."

Mikaela and I circle back around. We don't have to admit it to each other—we're both fond of eavesdropping. At our next pass she is talking.

"How can you say I'll find it? This is the fourth time I've been stood up!"

I didn't know it was possible, but she stomps off the ice with skates on her feet. She's wobbly, but she makes it to safe ground. Jake returns and I playfully hold my hand out. He smirks and slaps a one-dollar bill in my hand.

"Best three out of five?" I ask, but he skates on. I don't suppose we'll ever see eye-to-eye on this matter.

As I'm stuffing the dollar in my pocket, Mikaela looks at me. "He's going to lose heart if you're not careful." I sigh and roll my eyes at her. "He's waiting for your cognitive instincts to kick in."

"Cognitive instincts? Who says that? Did Jake slip you that special dictionary he uses?"

"I think he wants to believe what he tells you. But it's hard."

"You guys talked about this?"

But she skates off to join him, giggly and small again.

I go to work later, but my heart is not in it. I have trouble concentrating and nothing I write is coming out funny. I leave early and go buy a candy bar. I am two cents short but the cashier waves off the pennies.

Back in my room, I close the door and collapse with even weight distribution onto my bed. Before I'm able to draw my feet on there as well, there is a knock.

"Mikaela . . . I'm tired."

There is a knock again. I know her. She's going to stand out there and knock until I open the door. I pull a few strands of hair out of my ponytail, just to try to make myself look as ragged as I feel. Maybe she's a visual learner.

I yank open the door, but it's not Mikaela.

It's Jake.

He doesn't wait to be invited in. Instead, he steps right past me into my room. I close the door and stare him down, embarrassed by my situation. I can't even offer him a glass of water. Or a toilet. He stands and looks at the Murphy bed for a moment, his hands in his pockets.

"This is where you live?"

"The Milford Plaza was booked." I cross my arms. I should probably fix my ponytail but right now but I need my body language to make a few things clear. "Why are you here?"

Jake sits down at the desk. The chair creaks beneath him. "Who made you so untrusting?"

"You came all the way over here to ask me that? I don't want to talk about it anymore than you want to discuss how your wife died."

He doesn't flinch but he does pause. "She didn't die. I almost think that would have been easier."

My arms drop to my side. "What?"

"When someone dies, at least you know they loved you. They didn't choose to leave you."

"Then . . . what happened?"

"She left me for my cousin. They both worked in the humor department. They wrote together. She said she wasn't cheating and I believed her. For a long time I believed her. And then one day she told me the truth. And even then I tried to make up with her, tried anything to get her back. But no matter what I said to her, it didn't help." He shrugged as he stared at the ground. "Ironically, I couldn't ever find the right words. I even tried to be funny. She said I wasn't funny like him."

He looked so sad at that moment. My heart broke for him. I stepped closer to where he sat. "That's why you never laugh? Or even crack a smile?"

"I've always been told . . . well, she always told me that my smile looks weird."

I step even closer and sit down on the edge of the bed. "Jake, I'm so sorr—"

It hitches up, throws me on my back, rolls me into the center as it closes up on me. I slide to the bottom and once again, I'm trapped on the other side of this stupid Murphy bed. I pound against the mattress. As you might imagine, it's not making the kind of noise I was hoping for. I try to grab the edges to rattle the thing, get it opened up, but it's locked. "When will I live somewhere besides this Y with this stupid bed that wants to kill me?" My face is smooshed against the sheets so I probably sound all muffled and pathetic. But who are we kidding—it's not the mattress that is making me pathetic.

I can hear him laugh. "I kind of like this. You're a captive audience."

I smile in the darkness. I can hear that his tone is playful. "Is there a card for this?"

"Too much of a niche market."

"I can't be stuck in here while Jake Sentinel is finally laughing."

"Gives us a chance to discuss that kiss." And like that, he's unlatched the bed and it comes crashing open, with me on top of it. There is no way to play this calmly and coolly. My ponytail is definitely not cooperating. I can feel it flipped over the top of my head. I roll over on my back. He's looking down at me as I scrape the hair out of my face.

"You know, the first time you rewrote me, I could deal with it. I mean, your pigtails, they kind of got to me."

"What?"

"Technically, your check-in-the-box cards, you learned those from me."

The realization slams into me like a rogue Murphy bed. "You . . . the 'yes, no, maybe so' boy?" I remember him now. He was small with glasses, hardly noticeable, especially to a girl who had no interest in boys yet. But that was not the only time he was in my life. I remember now, a boy named Jake, sending me cards through the mail every once in a while. I was just a kid, but my grandmother seemed to think he was something special. She sat me down one day after a card arrived, telling me that boys, in general, needed to be watched carefully, but any boy that sends handmade cards in the mail needs special consideration. I thought she was crazy at the time and dismissed the advice. Eventually, sometime during the first year of junior high, the cards stopped coming and I never thought about him again.

He smiles at me, a warm, familiar smile that flushes my cheeks. "Did you really think I'd hire some stranger off the street just because she's dreamed of writing greeting cards? You're practically the only nonfamily member we've ever hired."

"You were the first boy who liked me." I know, I sound like an eleven-year-old little girl and in case you were wondering, yes, I'm kind of gushing as I say it.

I'm still on the bed, on my back, gazing up at him. It feels very black-and-white-movieish so I sit up. The bed starts its slow rise, but I wiggle my rear to the center and then slowly get up. Except now we're very close. Maybe it's not a romantic moment. After all, the room is tiny. There's hardly room for two people to stand and not stand close. So the goose bumps are less about proximity and more about how he's looking into my eyes, like he can see my soul.

"You have to go!" I blurt out. "You can't . . . I mean, we can't . . ." There's nowhere to go. I'm cornered by both Jake and Murphy. My skin tingles and I'm afraid my upper lip is soaked in sweat but I'm not sure. I wipe it with the back of my arm anyway.

The only way to get around him is to squeeze past him, and that means we'll brush against one another but I decide it's worth it to get to the door. I slide on past. He puts a hand out to steady me. I laugh inappropriately, like he's tickled my ribs or something. As you can tell, I'm not a smooth operator. This isn't the kind of scene you're going to see in a movie. Nobody has armpit sweat rings soaking through her shirt at this point in a love story. They're gazing at each other, the romantic tension bursting from the screen. In my case, something's bursting, but it has more to do with my pride exploding by an awkward exit. I fall against the door with a thud. Don't even ask me what my ponytail looks like at this point. You know. I open the door with shaking hands.

"Why are you so afraid?"

"I'm not afraid. Just go." I feel like crying. Maybe I am crying. I can't quite tell. It's sweat or tears. Not sure just yet.

"Okay." He walks past me and leaves. I close the door and clutch my heart. I slide to the floor. This can't be happening. I can't be having feelings for another man. When will I learn my lesson? I've tried to teach it to Mikaela but I can't even learn it myself.

Don't fall in love. Don't believe those mushy, idealistic cards that say the stupidest things.

It's too risky.

Jake is too risky.

13

Jake let out a deep, almost grinding, breath as he leaned back into his chair, watching Hope. It was stupid, but he thought maybe she would move her hand a little or show some sign of life in there. But there was nothing, just the steady, shallow breathing he'd become accustomed to hearing. And watching.

A sudden sadness swept through him. Before he even had a chance to try not to react to it, tears were streaming down his face. He couldn't wipe them away fast enough and tried to laugh it off, but his emotions weren't fooled. He shrugged, glancing up at her.

"So, that's what happened. She left me. Because I wasn't funny enough. Men have been left for not making enough money, for working too hard, for flirting too much. But I think

I'm probably the first guy who got left for not being funny." It ached to even say it. He'd never said it, to a single person, ever. He cited irreconcilable differences, just like the divorce papers said, when anybody asked about it. "Ironic, huh? That's the very thing I always liked about you. You were funny. And not funny in an attention-getting way, you know? Intelligently funny. Your jokes went over most people's heads. But I got them."

It was a ridiculous scene, he knew, sitting there with his tuna fish, pouring out his heart to a woman in a coma about his sad tale of being left because he failed in the humor department. "Hope, I just think . . . I mean, forget about what happened with your wedding. I know it was painful. Believe me, I get that. I promise I do. But life is worth living, you know? And love is worth trying again. Take a risk. Maybe we can take it together."

He felt a strange urge to kiss her and he tried to dismiss it. First of all, there was the tuna. But second, who would kiss a woman in a coma? Only a man so pathetic he thought that might be his only chance to do it.

Still, as he looked at her, it was a *Sleeping Beauty* sort of moment. Could he ever be her prince? It was an inexplicable pull and he stood, backing away from her, right against all the cards, knocking a few of them over. His hand was covering his mouth, like he was guarding it, or her . . . he didn't know which. Someone needed to be guarded.

The door to her room opened and Jake turned away for a moment, pretending to be setting up the cards. If it was Bette, she had a strange way of seeing straight through him and he didn't want her to have to see this. If it was CiCi, he was going to have to make a quick exit—he was afraid there might be a demon or two she would want to pray off of him, and he wasn't so sure he shouldn't be prayed for at this point.

He swallowed down any remnant of emotion and turned, trying to peg an expression somewhere between hysteria and depression. Whatever expression he landed on didn't stay there long.

A guy stood there at the end of her bed, glancing between Jake and Hope. His hands were in his pockets. He wore jeans that drug the ground, dusty flip-flops and a wrinkled shirt, but looked strangely put together. His hair was cut very modern . . . messy with purpose.

It couldn't be . . . ?

"I'm Sam. Who are you?"

"Jake." It came out way stronger than he intended. There was something rising up in him, something like a . . . like a punch to this guy's face! It all seemed surreal. This guy was actually here, after all this time? What was he doing, paying his respects?

"And you are . . . ?"

Jake felt his fingers twitching. It was like he was growing into some sort of greeting-card version of the Incredible Hulk, except this was no greeting-card moment.

"I know who you are. You're the guy who left her at the altar."

Sam's face contorted briefly, like something just slapped him. Yeah, buddy. It's called the truth.

"So who are you?" Sam asked, after his face stopped rolling through a catalog of emotion.

"I'm the guy who—"

But his words were cut short by a shriek. And there was only one person in the world he knew who would shriek like that inside the Neuro Intensive Care ward of a hospital.

"Sam!!!" Her face was so lit with excitement, it was like Sam had risen from the dead.

Jake glanced at Hope. How could she sleep through all this? Come on, have my back here, Hope. But she didn't move.

"Sam, Sam, Sam! You're here! I've been praying for this, praying for it, praying for it!"

"I thought you were praying for her to wake up," Jake said, as flatly as any sentence could be said.

"Oh, yes, that too! Yes! But I thought it would be Sam who might be able to give her the hope she needs to return!"

"Sam? He's the very reason she's in this predicament," Jake said.

Sam glared at him. "You think you know? Who are you? You don't know anything. You have no idea."

Jake sucked air through his nostrils, trying to keep himself calm. "Look, we need to step outside. She doesn't need to hear all this."

"She's in a *coma*," Sam said. "She's dead to the world."

"Shut up!" Jake hissed the words. "Don't say that!"

"Look, dude, I don't know who you think you are," Sam said, stepping away from CiCi's clutching embrace. "But you don't belong here. This is a family matter." He smiled briefly at CiCi, who missed the whole look because she was clutching her hands and praying to the ceiling.

"You don't—"

"No. You don't. You don't need to be here. Hope is *my* fiancé." He glanced over toward the bed. "Yeah. I made a mistake. I get that. But I'm here now and this room is just too crowded as is. You get what I'm saying?"

CiCi's eyes brimmed with tears. "It shows, Jake, that prayers are answered! Look, Sam has come back! Now, perhaps, Hope's father will return as well! It's a sign. I just know it is a sign." CiCi rushed to Hope's bedside, raising a small, black plastic toy in the air. What was that? He looked closer—a wedding cake topper of a bride and groom. "Hope! Hope! Guess who's back!"

Jake couldn't take another second of this. He brushed past Sam and stormed out the door. Bette was behind the nurse's desk. She stood, knocking her Styrofoam cup of coffee over. "Jake? Jake? What's wrong?"

But he couldn't stop. He needed air. He needed to get as far away from this as possible. Why in the world would he ever let himself be this vulnerable? He knew better. He'd learned this lesson once before and he'd vowed to never put himself in this position again.

Love was altogether too risky.

It always would be.

GREETINGS FROM MY LIFE

It's one of those mornings you coast through . . . your thoughts are somewhere else entirely, and you're doing weird things like putting your pants on backwards or pouring coffee in your cereal. I've ruined breakfast and fashion, but I'm out the door and there's a spring in my step that I can't deny. Jake has texted me, asked me to run a few errands before I come in, and I'm glad. I'm dreading seeing him, but only because I want to so badly. You're tracking with me. I'm falling for this guy in the worst of ways. I'm terrified. But not terrified enough to stop thinking about him. It's not sheer terror. I'd equate it to the kind of terror you feel when you've asked the nice lady in the elevator when her baby is due only to find out she's not pregnant. My heart is skipping a lot of beats inside my chest as I think of his smile and his jokes and his declaration that we should talk about our kiss (his kiss, not mine)—but it's more like a dance in my chest rather than a heart attack.

I finally arrive at the office a little after eleven, smearing lip balm over my mouth. What kind of attraction I think this is going to cause I don't know, but there's something about lip balm that soothes me. If I could, I'd smear it all over my face. All over my soul.

I round the corner, drop my bag into my chair, and turn to walk into Jake's office when I see the most horrifying sight I can imagine. And listen, I watch a lot of crime shows, so when I say *horrifying*, I mean it. Obviously not in a murder-plot kind of way, but in the kind of way that stops your heart and you can only hope you're having a heart attack because you don't want to face what is to come.

My *mother*.

She is standing in Jake's office holding what looks like a serving tray, but not really a nice one, more like something you'd see in a hospital. And she's got small little cups of . . . is that soup? Are they eating soup? They don't notice me at first and all I see is Jake laughing and slurping something from a spoon. My mom has that look on her face, that same look she had when she declared my honeymoon on the potato farm.

I brace myself against my desk.

"Mom?" I don't even think the word came out the first time. It sounded more like the wheeze of an asthma attack. "Mom?" I say louder.

They turn. Jake grins. My mom does too. "There she is! I'm so glad to see you! Oh, my baby girl!" I can only be thankful she's holding a soup tray, otherwise her hands would be waving in the air in a shout to glory. "I was just getting acquainted here with Jake, your new friend—"

"Boss."

"You didn't tell me"—Jake sips the soup—"your mother is a soup maker."

I haven't told him anything about my mother. My gosh, where would I start? Definitely not with soup.

"And you didn't tell me your friend here has no plans for Thanksgiving."

"It's true," he says, watching me through the steam of the soup.

It's as if I'm watching tennis the way my head is whipping from one side of the office to the other. Is this really happening? I mean . . . *really?*

I stand there for a moment, and I try to level-head my way into a lucid thought. And I realize suddenly that Jake has taken a risk . . . another one . . . on my behalf. He wants to spend a holiday with me. And what risk have I taken for him? None. Because I'm trying to live a risk-free love life. And what kind of way is that to love?

I walk in as cautiously as a deer on the open plains during hunting season. Mom holds out the tray. There is an envelope beside the little cups of soup. "There's your birth certificate, just like you ordered. Soup?"

"Mom," I say, grinning so hard and stiff my jaw is protruding, "thank you, of course. Yes, so thankful you brought . . . but you could have overnighted it. I hate for you to go to all this trouble to hand-deliver . . . and soup . . . and all that." The fact that I'm not speaking in complete sentences isn't lost on me. It's just that I'm trying for a lot of things here—a subtle message to Mom that she should leave, while also trying to appear grateful in front of Jake because he has no understanding of my mother yet and I don't want to look like a jerk.

"And miss a chance to see my only daughter's new place of employment? And it's a beautiful drive. Oh, so glorious! So divine! Jake, if you come on up for Thanksgiving, you can see. Up there in good ole Poughkeepsie."

I laugh a laugh filled with no joy. "Seriously," I say, batting my hand, "I'm sure Jake's got better—"

"No, I don't. I've been wanting to take a drive up there anyway."

My hand drops. This is just so . . . weird. I can't have this, can I? Jake with me and my mom? On a holiday? What is going on?

"She doesn't serve tuna." I say it. That's all I've got. I can't think of another good reason and obviously, there isn't one, and now I'm looking desperate.

"I can cook tuna." Mom eyes me. "You've lost weight."

"He doesn't cook it, he heats it in the—"

"Maybe you will get to meet Hope's father! In fact, why don't we just agree in prayer right now—"

"Mom, no!"

Jake startles. It's because I'm shouting at my mother. Anybody would be startled by this who doesn't know my mother. She's standing there holding soup. How can I yell at her?

I dial it waaayyy back. "I mean, Mom, please . . . Jake doesn't want to pray here in the office. Isn't there a federal rule against displaying acts of begging God for things that won't happen?"

"Put down your soup, Jake. Come now, come now. Gather round."

Jake looks like this is the most normal thing ever. And my heart kind of softens because there doesn't seem to be a judgmental bone in this guy's body. I like him even more. I step forward and we clasp hands. My knees grow a little weak. His hands are nice and strong. My heart must be extremely healthy because it's been through a lot in the last twelve hours, you know? If I were my heart I would've given up back at the soup tray discovery.

"If we all stand in agreement, the Bible says if two or more agree . . ."

I peek and see Jake looking at me. Mom's the only one with her eyes closed. He smiles and winks at me, like he "gets" her and it's okay, I can relax. He's not going to judge me for it. The humiliation just washes off me like a mudslide.

"You ladies over there, you need to pray, too, for this to work," my mom says.

I glance behind my shoulder. Pearl and Ruby, who are normally way more conspicuous about their eavesdropping, are standing in the doorway gawking. Once caught, they sheepishly join in our prayer circle, taking careful steps, I note, to make sure Jake and I are still holding hands.

"Lord!"

Everyone but me ducks because nobody ever expects someone's first word in a prayer to sound like the shriek of a vulture.

"Lord, please bring Hope's father back to us in time for Thanksgiving. You said we can move mountains with faith like mustard. Lord, move the mountain that stands tall between us and—"

"Amen!" I say.

Ruby and Pearl stare, eyes wide. When old people get shocked you know it's bad, because they've lived a long time and have seen a lot of things.

"So lovely . . ." I'm smiling, nodding, trying to look as serene as possible after having shouted in the presence of old people. "Well, listen, we better get to the Social Security office so we can get this all cleared up." I take Mom's wrist, pull her through the circle, out the door.

"Thanksgiving, my house," she calls out to Jake.

"Mom, he has plans. He was just being polite."

"I don't," Jake says from his office. Pearl and Ruby nod in agreement. "It's true," Pearl says. "We boycott Thanksgiving on account of how they seem to target turkeys for this holiday, which we find to be prejudiced."

"Why not eat peacock?" Ruby says.

I glance at Jake. I'm not the only one who has weird relatives? He smiles helplessly. I run into my desk smiling back at him.

That's going to bruise.

I hurry and usher Mom to the elevator and outside as quickly as possible. I'm walking fast and realize my mom can't catch up. It's the first time I notice her age. She's nearly being swept away by the sidewalk crowds. I hurry after her and try a slower pace, but I'm anxious to get to the Social Security office.

"Have you heard from Sam?"

I strike, and I mean it in the killer-lightning sort of way, a sideways glance at her. "What do you mean?"

"Just wondering if you've heard from him. I've been praying."

I stop right there. People part and go around us. "Mom . . . why would you ask for that?"

"Never lose hope, sweetie, never lose hope."

"The thing is, Mom, typically—and I realize that term doesn't apply to us—but typically, when a girl gets dumped at the altar by a guy, it's the mother who goes all psycho and wants to make him suffer and stuff. It has happened. I watched it on *48 Hours*."

"Sam is just such a nice boy."

I keep walking, not bothering to keep her by my side. She keeps up anyway. I knew she wasn't that old. "If Sam's so nice, why invite Jake to Thanksgiving dinner?"

"He's very nice too!"

Thankfully we arrive at the Social Security office. There is no line. It is so baffling. Inside, a few people mill about, but nothing that keeps us from getting to a window right away.

Immediately I notice the bun, wound so tight that I can already peg the personality. This woman is a rule-follower. It sends a shiver down my spine, but I proceed forward. After all, I have my documentation. All of it. What could go wrong? Besides my mother, of course.

"Mom," I whisper as we sit down. "Just don't talk, okay? I'll do all the talking." We slide into the seats. For the hundredth time, I explain my dilemma. "So as you can see, I've been trying to get this fixed forever. My employer has to hold my wages until I get the certificate proving I'm alive." And then I notice it. It's a bright yellow E taped to this woman's computer monitor. It looks just like the letters I've found on my door.

"No problem. I'm sure we can clear this right up."

I melt into my chair with relief, forgetting that stupid *E*. "I've got my birth certificate, just like you—"

I realize suddenly it's not in my bag. I frantically punch my hand into its depths, feeling around with every finger. ". . . it was here . . ." Did I put it in my bag? I was in such a hurry to leave . . . oh no . . .

"It's right here." My mother smiles and hands it over.

This single moment makes me almost forgive the potato farm.

"Thanks," I whisper softly to her. We have a mom/daughter moment I will always cherish.

We watch the woman unfold the paper and lay it flat against the desk. I see my two tiny ink footprints at the bottom. It makes me a little sad. Nobody knows when they're that little what their life will end up doing to them.

I glance up to see my worst nightmare.

The Bun is frowning.

"This is really all my fault. I had her declared dead," Mom says.

It's true, but that doesn't seem to be why the woman is frowning.

"Hmm . . ." the Bun says.

"Hmmm? Hm? What?"

"Not good . . ." She's slowly shaking her head back and forth. My fingers grip the bottom of the chair because I have this sense that the bottom is getting ready to fall out.

"But, in my defense, she did crash my car into the Hudson. What was I to think?" Mom's voice sounds echo-y. Maybe it's a defense mechanism kicking in. Or maybe I'm about to faint.

"This is the hospital birth certificate."

"They gave it to me after we stamped her feet there. I like souvenirs," Mom says.

"Last time I was here, that's what they told me to bring." The sentence reads way more calmly than I'm saying it. My words are spiking high notes in weird places.

"No. We tell you to bring the county birth certificate."

"It is!" I tap the desk with my finger. "Poughkeepsie County Hospital. See? Right there on top."

"That was a nice hospital. Except for the blood pressure."

I glance sideways at Mom. She is not making sense, more so than usual.

"No dear," the woman says. "The one with the county seal. You order it from vital records."

"The vitals are showing signs of stress," Mom says. I glance *again* at Mom, give her the look that says *please stop talking,* the one that never registers with her.

"You guys never said anything about county or anything else."

The woman looks sympathetic even as she is pushing the certificate toward me. "You'll have to come back when you have the right paperwork and a urinalysis. Next!" She waves to an old man waiting behind me.

"I have to pee in a cup?" I shout. Through the window I notice the police officer and his horse. I can only see their legs. He moves on and I realize I must too.

I walk outside, Mom trailing me.

"I'm sorry, I thought it was the right one."

Her apology is one of the most lucid things she's ever said to me. And the truth is, it isn't her fault. Anybody could've made the mistake.

I smile because moms need to see their daughters smile. "It's fine. I'll get it taken care of. Listen, I have to get back to work. Where did you park your car?"

"I took a taxi."

"To the train station?"

"All the way here."

My throat swells with emotion, so tight and bulbous I can't manage a word. I hug her and that seems to be all she needs. I flag a taxi for her, my heart soft at the idea that she would be so concerned I get the birth certificate she would spend what little money she has to come all this way to deliver it quickly to me. I load her into the taxi and watch as it drives off.

Mom is turned, staring out the back window, with an expression I can't quite pinpoint at first, but it's like she thinks she'll never see me again.

I'm learning some things from Jake, and it's that doing nice things for others keeps you from dwelling on your own pain. I'm dead broke, so I can't do much, but I manage enough change to buy a small box of blue Popsicles for Mikaela. I stash it in the freezer for her.

I find her in the atrium. I watch her for a moment, working hard in her journal, probably her Christmas list. It must be a hard thing to make a Christmas list you know won't ever be fulfilled. I wonder why she works so diligently on it. She doesn't hear me walk up behind her. I manage to glance at her latest entry: *An answer about*

That's all it says.

"Got plans for Thanksgiving?"

She whips around, her hand sliding over her list. "Oh yeah. Turkey. Yams. Cranberry sauce. Four kinds of pies."

I walk around to the chair sitting across from her. "Let me ask you something. Do you think they'll let you get away? My mother, crazy woman that she is, invited Jake, so . . ." I anticipate a squeal of excitement from her.

There is no squeal. Just a slight tilt of the head. "I'm your buffer, eh? Not very romantic, you know."

This girl is good. She can read my mind and my motives now. Don't know how she does it.

I slump. "If you're hoping to get Jake and me to fall in love so you can have a new set of wacked-out parents, then you might want to rethink your plan."

"Don't flatter yourself."

There is an edge to her voice and I realize how insensitive that statement was. My humble offering of blue Popsicles can't erase a self-absorbed heart.

Her tone is serious. "That's not what this is about. I wish you would wake up!"

"I wish you would stop talking nonsense. Stop speaking in silly riddles."

We both stare at each other for a moment, cooling our jets.

I nod toward the journal. "How's that Christmas list coming?"

"I don't know yet," she says, but she's distracted by something. She's looking past me, to the TV in the atrium. "Hey . . . isn't that Heaven Sent?"

I turn and she's right. It's a shot of the front of Heaven Sent, the sign and the logo.

I hurry over and turn up the volume. Mikaela kneels next to me.

Starla is standing in front of the Heaven Sent office, right in front of the window Mikaela and I spied through. Her microphone is in front of her chin as she speaks.

". . . and we can tell you, they're not happy."

A packaged news story rolls. A woman being interviewed is crying. "I seriously think he just bought it because he thought it was funny. But he ended our relationship. Four years of my life went to that jerk."

Then another customer, a guy: "Heaven Sent thinks they're being funny? I don't need to be reminded how much dateless life sucks. I already know."

Starla returns to the screen, staring right at me, like we are face-to-face, mano-a-mano. Or womano-a-womano. "Well, you heard it here, folks. What started as a funny trend for the buyer has turned ugly for the receivers. Some of the customers I talked to have even used the word *liability* and have mentioned they're considering suing for damages. Perhaps," Starla says, leaning in toward the camera, "this is one employee Heaven Sent needs to return to sender." She glances sideways and notices someone. She beckons her cameraman over and suddenly Everett is seen walking out the front door of the office. He glances around and then notices Starla.

She steps up next to him like they're old friends. "Any comment?"

"First and foremost, we'd like to apologize to our customers. It's never our intent to harm anyone. We hear you loud and clear. We're announcing today that the writer of these cards has been terminated from our company. She's done here. That's all, thank you."

"He's talking about you, right?" Mikaela whispers.

I'm too numb to answer. She switches the TV off and helps me into a chair.

"I guess it doesn't matter if I'm alive or dead anymore, does it?"

"What?"

I stand up. My legs are wobbly but I turn and leave.

"Room Eleven, where are you going?"

"Don't call me that."

"You can't give up. You can't!"

I keep walking.

"Hope Landon!"

I turn, looking at her. This little kid, with all this wisdom, all this pain, all this . . . me-ness.

"You're stronger than this. Fight!"

"You'll find someone else to hang out with." My heart feels dead right inside my chest.

"No, I won't!"

I stomp away and can hear her crying, but I don't care.

As I unlock the door to my room, the old lady janitor, with her mopping bucket in tow, brushes by me slowly. Our gazes meet. I realize instantly that I have just seen a glimpse of my future, that I am the old woman whose dreams are nothing but dirty mop water.

They say a new day brings hope. It doesn't. It feels as bad as the day before. And all you can think about is how bad it's going to feel every day from now on. I thought I might feel some relief leaving behind this tiny room with its hazardous bed, but I don't. I guess it's because where I'm headed is far worse.

The tiny trash can in the corner is overflowing with all my cards, which I ripped up last night. I throw one last card away, my favorite. It was the one I always laughed at, no matter how many times I read it.

It doesn't seem the least bit funny anymore.

I zip up my bag. The truth is I want to kick the daylights out of Murphy, because I'm mad and desperate and pathetic and Murphy seems like he could handle it. But I don't. I've already made a scene. No need to make another.

I open the door and he's standing there, leaning against the wall of the hallway, waiting patiently.

"I really appreciate you doing this, Jake. I'm sorry I had to call you. There's just no other way I could afford to get home."

"I don't mind at all. We'd be going anyway, for Thanksgiving, right?"

"You still want to have Thanksgiving dinner with the meanest girl in town?" I shake my head. "I'm so sorry for what I've done to your company."

He starts to say something, then notices my bed. "You left your pencils."

I look at him. I don't have to say anything. He understands instantly it's intentional. He sighs and walks in to get them.

"I don't want them anymore."

"Maybe Mikaela will."

I look at the concrete floor. It's like I can feel its coldness through the bottom of my shoes.

"Thanks for . . . this thing with Mikaela . . . thanks for understanding. She doesn't get that I'm not coming back here, you know? She doesn't quite get the ways of the world. So when it's time for you to return, you will probably have to take her kicking and screaming. I'll try to say my good-byes as best as I can, okay? But I know you'll take care of her. I know she'll be looked after, because that's the kind of guy you are."

"She adores you."

"Don't remind me."

"Hey!"

We turn and Mikaela is making her way toward us, dragging behind her a tiny suitcase she could probably better carry. "Who's ready for a Thanksgiving road trip?"

I try a smile, but it's like the corners of my mouth weigh a hundred pounds each.

Jake picks up the slack and grabs her suitcase. "Come on, let's get this trip going!"

They walk together and I follow along. My suitcase makes a horrible scraping sound along the concrete floor, like a wheel is stuck.

There is a sudden sharp pain, the one that always hits my heel. I don't even flinch. Pain is relative.

We load into Jake's town car and I tell Mikaela to sit in the front. As she buckles her seat belt, I realize she's really too small for up there. The whole seat kind of swallows her. But she is lit with excitement and jabbers all the way out of the city. She finally settles down, decides to work on her journal. I can see Jake glancing at me in the rearview mirror.

"Hope . . ."

I must look really pathetic. "I don't want to talk about it."

About an hour goes by and then Mikaela turns and looks at me from the front seat. "I should have invited Matthew to join us. I want you to meet him before you leave me."

"I'm not leaving—"

"Who's Matthew?" Jake thankfully interrupts what was about to be a lie straight to her face. But somehow I get the feeling Mikaela already knows.

"The new boy, he just moved in. He's got these weird glasses, but I kind of like him."

"You move on fast," I say.

"Lose one, find another. Isn't that how it works?"

"According to Jake's cards, yes." I sigh, wishing I weren't so mean when I get upset. But Jake doesn't seem to be rattled by this defect in my personality. I point ahead. "Turn here, on the right."

But Jake turns left. He glances at a set of directions he has sitting beside him.

"I said *right*." But he ignores me.

I slouch in my seat and stare out the window, a hot mess of grudge.

Just as fast, I slide back up, my spine totally erect as I stare out the window. This can't be happening. We've just pulled into the nursing home parking lot. I roll down the window to make sure I'm seeing this right.

I'm trying to find something to say, some way to get out of this. Jake and Mikaela hop out of the car.

"Uh . . . wait. You know, my mother, she's neurotic. She likes people to be on time." This may be the only time my mother's neuroses save me.

Jake opens the back door, offers his hand. I realize instantly I cannot refuse a chance to put my hand in his. It's probably going to be my undoing.

"Your mom doesn't seem to be the type to get ruffled over time," he says. "Besides, I have a few ladies to apologize to."

I try to keep my pace in front of theirs. I'm walking so fast I look as awkward as those speed walkers you see on the jogging trails. But maybe I can thwart this somehow, get to Gertie before Jake does.

The doors *swoosh* open and a gaggle of residents are gathered in the front commons area, all wearing turkey hats and watching some black and white movie.

Gertie's in the back. She turns and I almost dive behind the front desk, but it's too late. She sees me.

"Hope!"

Jake glances at me. I hurry over to her, but I recognize my problem immediately. I can't whisper a plan to Miss Gertie. She won't hear me.

"My goodness," she says, embracing me. "Oh my goodness, Hope! I didn't expect to see you today!"

"Hi, Miss Gertie."

Jake steps up, offering his hand to Miss Gertie. "Miss Gertie, eh? I'm Jake. And I just wanted to tell you . . ." He glances at me, a wistful smile on his lips. "I just wanted to tell you that in life, we can feel abandoned. Alone. But our Lord above watches each of his own. You belong to him in the palm of his hand. You're never out of reach, like all the grains of sand."

Miss Gertie melts right there in her wheelchair. "You seem like a nice man. Hope, doesn't he seem like a nice man?"

"No bet," I say to him, "I'm completely out of ones. You two get to know each other. Also, the sand line makes no sense."

He looks at Miss Gertie. "But how do you know Hope?"

Miss Teasley rolls up. "Did I write those letters all right for you?"

I bite my lip. I'm caught. Jake's expression says everything. I notice Mikaela. She's hurrying down the hallway. Where is she going?

"I'm sorry . . . how do you all know . . . ?" I don't hear the rest of Jake's question because I race after Mikaela. Last I saw her she was headed to the wing where my grandma is.

At Grandma's door, I spot Mikaela. She is sitting in front of my grandmother, leaning forward in an embrace with her. I notice some of the cards I've left her are gone. In her more lucid moments, she sometimes gave them away to the cleaning ladies, but she hasn't been lucid in a while. Maybe someone is stealing them because they're so incredibly funny.

Maybe *I'm* the one who isn't lucid.

"Oh my child, how I've missed you. I'm so, so sorry about what happened to your daddy."

I step out of their line of sight, my back against the wall just outside the door. How is my grandmother talking? And how does she know about Mikaela's father? I can't imagine any of this and my mind is reeling . . . so much so that I don't see Jake walk up until I spot his shoes next to mine.

"Let's go," he says.

I try a grin. "Ready for my mom's great cooking?"

"I'm not staying. I'll drop you off and come pick Mikaela up when dinner is over."

I touch his arm. "Jake . . . I'm sorry. If I still had my job, I'd quit. I'd tell you to fire me."

He looks me straight in the eyes. "After I did you a favor and gave you a job, it hadn't occurred to me you set this up to get what you wanted."

I sigh. No surprise. It was known around the nursing home that Miss Gertie's pastime was getting in other people's business, matched only by her inability to keep a secret. She'd apparently spilled all the beans. "I never meant to hurt you."

"This isn't just about work, Hope. You won't give me a chance because you're too afraid I'll hurt you. But all you've done since you came in my life is hurt me. Just call me gullible. Stupid. Trusting." His eyes flicker with deep pain.

"But that's what's adorable about you, Jake," I grin. Yeah—I have a habit of throwing in a punch line when I shouldn't. That very defect has cost me my job. And more, I am seeing.

"Why? So people like you can take advantage of me? Let's go."

He walks off. I call Mikaela's name and she appears in the hallway. Her eyes look red and a little swollen. She walks past me, not saying a word. I stand in the doorway of my grandmother's room and observe her. She looks catatonic again, like I've known her to be for some time. I can't explain what is happening. But I'll have to worry about my grandmother later. The car ride is quiet as we drive to Mom's. There's a lot I want to say to him, but not in front of Mikaela. I'm hoping he will change his mind about staying, but we pull up to Mom's house and he keeps the car idling. The gentleman that he is, he steps out of the car and opens my door for me. Mikaela gets out too, observing the house with a strange intensity.

"I'm sorry," I say again.

"Have a good Thanksgiving," he replies. He reaches in and grabs my bag for me. He sets it on the grass.

He's about to step back into the car when my mom comes flying out the front door, racing down the driveway like something's on fire. "Oh, hallelujah!! My daughter is home. Home, home, home!" She pulls me into a one-way hug. "I kicked out the renter in your twin bed. You'll want to wash the sheets." She lets go of me and grabs Jake. "Welcome, welcome! Come in, come in! Jake, I made a tuna casserole, all special, just for you."

She then takes Mikaela by the arm and leads her inside. Jake looks unsure what to do. He's too nice of a guy, I realize, to reject a tuna casserole made especially for him, no matter how mad he is at me.

He shuts off the car and we walk inside, side by side, but not speaking a word.

I am surprised that dinner seems to be ready. My mom is the kind who starts dinner at five and we eat at nine. I have vivid memories of eating carrots and potatoes, and then two hours later, getting the roast that was supposed to go along with it.

I drop my bag at the door, gawking as my mom comes in from the kitchen holding a tray, but it's not a serving tray like you'd see in a Martha Stewart magazine. It's a cafeteria tray, like I had to carry every day of my school life. And on top of it is a plastic plate with little dividers, just like my lunch was served on in school. There's green Jell-O, vanilla pudding, rice, Salisbury steak, and a large helping of tuna casserole.

"Let me help you with that," Jake says. What kind of Thanksgiving dinner is this? It's like I've landed in the hospital and they're bringing in my dinner. I probably nearly cringed to death at some point today.

I watch as Jake puts the tray at the head of the table.

"Don't put it there," Mom says. "We leave that open in case Hope's father shows up. We did pray, remember?" She points to the third chair on the far side of the table. "But you can have Sam's seat."

"Sam?"

"Mom!" I bark.

"Ever since he left Hope stranded at the altar, I haven't invited him back." And she walks off to fetch another tray. Jake follows her to help, but casts me a look. The anger is gone. I look away. I can't stand the pity that's now in his eyes.

That's when I notice Mikaela. She is sitting on the nearby couch, flipping through a photo album. Tears are in her eyes. I sit next to her, realizing she is not unlike me, in so many ways. She is hurting, this little girl with her wise ways about her.

I notice the picture she is looking at. It's one of my favorites: Dad and I are standing out in the snow together, smiling at the camera.

"Holidays are hard, huh?" I say quietly.

"Do you ever worry about what's next?"

"All the time."

Her cheeks flush as a tear rolls down her face. I put a very gentle hand around her shoulder, as if I've never hugged someone before. Mikaela collapses into my embrace, leaning fully into my chest. We sit there for a while as I watch Jake and Mom carry in hospital food for our Thanksgiving dinner. My life is so surreal.

"Come, come! Time to eat!"

Jake smiles slightly at me as he puts the last tray down. I smile back. Could it possibly be my mother's quirkiness might reconcile us to at the very least speaking terms?

We take our places, the three of us staring down at our food like you do when you're in the hospital, unsure you should eat it because it might make you sick. You're in a hospital after all. Surely it's safe. It just doesn't look safe.

Mom claps her hands. "After dinner, I have a surprise for all of us!"

Nobody has to say it, but we're all thinking it: *This isn't it?*

I glance at Mikaela. "This can't be good," I whisper.

She laughs and swipes away a final tear.

14

In the darkness of the shop, Jake stood in the midst of the chaos and destruction he'd caused. Flowers thrown everywhere. All of his cards ripped to shreds. It looked like a tornado had blown through. It's exactly what his soul felt like too. At his feet, he stared at shredded pictures of rainbows and mountains and quiet streams winding into serene forests.

What a crock.

How could he have been so foolish to believe things always work out, somehow and some way? He bought into his own nonsense. He bought into carefully chosen, poetically rhythmic words that held hope up on a pedestal.

He slumped against the small wall of the front counter, sliding to the ground, wishing the darkness would just go ahead and suffocate him.

The problem was . . . he *did* believe it. It was like this thing in him he couldn't shake. Whenever he lost hope or became disgruntled or even when his marriage and life fell completely apart, he knew that everything would, eventually, work for his good. More often than not, there was a peace that superseded all other emotions.

So why now? Why couldn't he see anything good right now?

Somewhere nearby, he didn't know where, he heard his phone buzzing. If he could find it, he'd probably throw it across the room. He couldn't believe he let himself fall for a girl in a coma, of all things. He was so naive to think that was a safe thing to do. What a pathetic loser he was. He only had courage around a woman if she's totally unconscious?

But he knew the truth. He'd had feelings for Hope long before that. He couldn't even explain it himself, but there was just something about her that seemed right for him.

Keys rattled at the front door. Before he could scramble to his feet, it opened and Mindy stood there, her mouth gaping as she flipped on the lights. Then her hand covered her mouth as she saw Jake.

"Mindy, just leave, okay? I'll clean this all up. I just had a . . . moment."

Mindy's eyes darted from crushed flower to broken glass to paper shredded so wildly across the floor it looked like something had exploded. That something was him.

"Jake . . . what's going on?"

"Mindy, please. I just want to be alone."

She eyed him. "No, you don't. And I think that's the whole problem."

Jake sighed and looked away.

"Listen, we've known each other a long time, Jake. And I feel like I can speak forthrightly to you. You love her."

"Mindy, don't. Please."

"No. Now you listen." Her hands were on her hips. She was stepping carefully over all the mess on the ground. "You two belong together. I feel it."

Jake rolled his eyes. "Really? Because I think it's just one of us feeling it. The other one is unconscious and not even feeling needles stabbing into her feet."

Mindy stood for a moment, looking around at the mess. And then she stooped to his level. She picked up one of the cards he'd ripped in half.

"She needs you, Jake."

"Whatever."

"I was just at the hospital. I was bringing up some tuna and bottled water to you. Who was that guy in the room with her?"

"Who knows."

"He was sitting in a corner, typing something on his phone. He wasn't looking at her. Talking to her. He was just sitting there."

"So?"

"So, *you* talk to her, Jake. You're the one who's helping her. You're the one that should be in that room."

"Look, Mindy, I appreciate the sentiment here, but it's just not going to work out, okay? Even if there wasn't another guy in the picture, how am I supposed to have a relationship with a comatose woman? Granted, that's probably the only kind that can love me, because I'm so . . ."

"So what?"

"So . . . delusional. I write delusion, don't I?"

"No. You write hope."

"Well this isn't looking too hopeful. And my life has never looked too hopeful. So I think I'll get out of the card writing business and just stick to selling flowers to people who believe that romance and goodness and hope are still alive."

"Don't let this one roadblock keep you from the woman you love."

"I don't love her. I love the idea of her, that's all." Jake looked at Mindy. "I want to be alone. Just leave me alone."

Mindy sighed and stood up. "Okay, Jake. I'll leave you alone. But you need to know something."

Jake looked up at her.

"When I was leaving Hope's room, I heard two doctors and that nice nurse talking. And they said it wasn't looking good for her."

"What do you mean?"

"Something about her vitals not holding steady. I didn't catch all of it, but they looked worried."

Jake dropped his gaze, focused on the floor. What else could he do? What was he supposed to do? He wasn't her doctor. He wasn't her fiancé. He was nothing. He was the boy she always ignored.

"Don't worry about coming in tomorrow morning," Jake said. "I'll be here. I'm coming back to the shop. I can't miss any more work. I appreciate your being here when I needed it. I'll see you after lunch."

Mindy hesitated, then left, turning off the lights and locking the shop behind her.

GREETINGS FROM MY LIFE

You just never know where you're going to have a complete meltdown. It's never where you expect. And I can tell you one thing, I wasn't expecting it here, of all places.

Snow is drifting down in the most romantic of ways—big and soft though it hardly seems cold enough to snow. Jake is standing on my left. Mikaela on my right. And we're all just frozen, but not from the temperatures—from shock.

"Isn't that hilarious?" my mom says.

That phrase has probably never been uttered at a cemetery, but it has now. We're all gazing down at a dark gray headstone. I can't peel my eyes off my name, which is etched deeply into the stone. So is my birthday. And the other date.

"See? I forgot to cancel it!" My mother cackles. Nobody is laughing.

Mikaela starts to point. "But—"

"Bet you never thought you'd visit your own gravestone. Who can say they've visited their own gravestone!" More laughing by just the one.

I can feel Jake watching me, almost like he senses what is getting ready to happen.

I look at my mom. "You think this is funny?"

"It's like being dead without being dead!" Mom's hands pop up like she's produced some sort of magic trick.

"You have *no idea* what it's been like to have everyone tell me I no longer have an identity!" I'm yelling now.

Mom's arms drop to her sides. "What? It's not that big of a deal, dear. It was a mistake."

"Not a big deal? I'm the one who's still here, Mom. Trying to *live*. Trying to make something of the shambles my life has turned into! And you keep making it harder! You should have put up a stone for *Dad* so we could move on! Dad is dead, not me!"

It is a swift and stinging slap that I never saw coming. My head jerks sideways. I hear the gasps around me, the loudest one coming from my mom, who covers her mouth. Remorseful tears burst from her eyes just as I start to feel the sting.

I glare at her. "He's the one who is gone, Mom. Not me. I'm still here. You keep saying he's on his way home. Well, he isn't!"

Mom's expression hardens. Her lips stiffen into a tight line across her face. I've never once in my whole life seen this expression on her face.

"Well"—her voice is almost a whisper—"then maybe I should try to find him." Her eyes are so wounded that it's like her soul is spilling from her pupils. She turns and rushes off, toward the car.

"Mom!" I yell after her, but she doesn't stop. I have to stop her. There is no telling what she's going to do.

"But Landon," I hear Mikaela say. I don't have time to stop. I can't let my mom leave.

"Mom, stop!"

"Landon, wait!"

I turn impatiently to see what is so important to Mikaela. She is pointing to the tombstone.

"Yes, I know, disturbing." Poor girl. I wish she didn't have to witness this.

"But look . . ." Mikaela says, her voice low like she's telling a secret. "At the death date."

I glance back to see my mom fumbling to find her keys in her purse, then I try to concentrate on what Mikaela is pointing at.

"It's today's date," Mikaela whispers.

I kneel, reaching out to touch the numbers. An eerie somberness settles down over us as we all three stare at it.

I try to crack a joke about Mom even getting my fake death date wrong, but it comes out flat and dies right there at my feet. Nobody's saying it, but we're all wondering . . . is it some sort of premonition? Am I going to die today?

Jake touches my arm. "Your mom is leaving—"

I jump to my feet and run. She is already in the car.

As I get close, I notice the car parked next to Mom's. There is a green "U" taped to the passenger window. I turn my focus back to Mom, but she is already inside the car and is starting the engine. I stand in front of the car, trying to wave my hands, trying to stop her. I can see she's losing it right there through the windshield.

I hear footsteps coming toward me. Maybe Jake can try to get her out, talk some sense into her.

Mom and I stare at each other. She's not really going to run me over, is she?

Then I hear the car slam into reverse. Mom is still looking at me as she hits the gas. The car jolts backward and I hear the most sickening thud. I look through the windshield. A small body flies into the air and then there is another thud. My mom screams. I scream. My feet feel as heavy as lead as I rush to the back of the car.

Mikaela is on the ground, blood pouring from her head, her journal open against the concrete, three feet away.

"Jake! *Jake*!" I scream. I look back and he has the door open, putting the car in park. He then rushes to my side. He is pulling out his cell phone.

I take Mikaela in my arms and cradle her little body, my tears wetting her face.

She is lifeless.

15

Jake carried the flowers tucked under his arm like they were a football, and tried to juggle three cans of tuna fish and two bottled waters. The smell of the hospital was, for the first time, inviting. He was here for the long haul. How could he not be?

The card he brought was folded in two and sticking out the back pocket of his jeans. He caught the elevator just as it was about to close.

When it opened, he hurried toward her room. There wasn't a second to lose.

Bette was at the nurse's station. She glanced up at him and he waved.

"Jake, I need to—"

"Give me a minute, Bette. I've got to do something first." He walked right into her room, ready to tell Sam to get lost. He'd rehearsed the conversation a thousand times in his head last night when not a wink of sleep would come. Over the course of the evening, his thoughts turned from anger and rejection to the idea that he didn't, at this point, have very much to lose. Maybe she would never love him. But how would he know if he didn't try? Maybe she would never come out of that coma, but somewhere deep inside he had to believe that she heard him. And if she died, she would know that she was loved.

In the room, the first thing he noticed was that her skin was very pale. She didn't look as peaceful. Her mouth gaped open slightly. Her breathing looked ragged. He quickly set the flowers, tuna, and water down.

"Hope? Hope, can you hear me?"

He pulled the chair, which sat in the corner, right next to her bed.

"It's me, Jake. I'm sorry I left a few days ago. But I'm back. I . . ." The words, as usual, caught in his throat. He pulled the card out of his back pocket. He'd taped it together early this morning, when he returned to the shop to clean up the mess he'd made. It was a rainbow and a river and a sunset and a storm cloud, all taped up together. Inside, the words were jumbled. Together, they didn't make sense, but word-by-word, they held weight.

Hope. Healing. Surrender. Love. Strength.

He looked at her. It was time now. It was time to tell her everything she needed to hear. "Hope, I want you to know—"

"*What* are *you* doing here?"

Jake looked up. Sam stood in the doorway, his arms crossed.

"I thought I told you to leave."

"You did tell me." Jake stood. "I just decided not to listen to you. And I decided Hope needed to hear that she shouldn't listen to you either."

He glanced at the bed, where the card sat. "What is that? Your love note to her?"

And then, before he even knew how to stop himself, he rose, approached Sam—and shoved him.

Hard.

Sam stumbled backward, his eyes lit with surprise. Jake knew it was coming, but he couldn't brace himself in time.

Sam shoved him back.

The next thing Jake knew, he had Sam slammed up against the wall. And then, in a flash, Bette was in their faces, her strong arms throwing them apart from one another. Jake adjusted his shirt, glaring at Sam.

"What are you *doing*?" Bette said to them both, but her eyes stayed on Sam a little longer, Jake noticed.

Jake stepped forward, pointing a finger at Sam. "What are you even doing here? Taking care of a guilty conscience?"

And then, like they'd triggered an alarm, the monitors began beeping frantically. Bette's attention snapped to where Hope lay. Another nurse rushed in, nearly knocking Sam over.

"What's happening?" Jake asked, but nobody answered. A doctor followed the nurse in. Announcements were made over the loudspeaker, codes were being shouted. Jake moved as they brought in a crash cart.

Bette took him by the arm and led him outside. "You have to stay out here."

Sam was already outside and the two stood flanking the door, staring each other down. Sam sneered. "Flowers and a card for a woman in a coma? That's priceless."

"Shut up." Jake glanced in. His card was on the floor, torn in two by all the feet scurrying around.

All he could hear was the chaos of trying to save a life.

GREETINGS FROM MY LIFE

I'm not a fan of the smell of hospitals. It seems like despair and death have a certain stench. The waiting room is not large, but it's as if my mom is a thousand feet away. She sits in a corner chair by herself, rocking ever so slowly, staring blankly into a TV with bad reception. She won't be bothered or spoken to.

Jake sits beside me, rubbing my shoulder as I cup Mikaela's journal as if it is the girl herself. I watch him rise and begin to straighten chairs all around us.

"Are you expecting people?"

"Do you have something else you want me to do?"

I nod, trying not to cry. "Yes. I want you tell me Mikaela's going to get better."

Jake stands there, a chair half straightened in front of him.

"Say it!" I cry. "Say it, Jake! You're the one who knows what to say in times like this. Tell me she will be okay."

His gaze drops to the floor. I try to wait patiently, but he just stands there, not saying a word.

Finally, he whispers, "I can't."

I stand. "Come on, Jake. Here's your chance for the tie-breaker. We're two to two right now! Take the lead."

"I can't," he says, his expression solemn.

"Why not?"

"You were right."

"No. I can't be right. You have to be right this time."

"I don't want to give you empty words."

"You don't believe them anymore? That there are good things ahead, no matter what pain you experience? You don't really believe that?"

"I want to. But life . . . so far, I just haven't seen it."

"I've spent my life not being able to trust words. But the one person in my life who seems to believe what he says is you!" My words wilt right on my tongue. "Don't tell me I've been wrong about you."

"I don't know, Hope." He glances around, seemingly embarrassed, maybe looking for an escape route. "I know what I'm supposed to believe. I know what I want to believe." He eyes my mom for a long moment. "But it's hard." He steps closer to me, just a couple of feet away. "Hope, do you know what happened to your dad?"

I hadn't said it in a long time. It is hard to get out. "Last time I saw him, he went out to get us mint chocolate chip ice cream."

"Do you think he's dead?"

"He has to be. He never would have stayed away on purpose—" My words are cut short by a sudden sob escaping my lips. "Mikaela has to be okay."

His arms wrap tightly around me. I lean into his chest, comforted by nothing more than the warmness of him.

"She wouldn't be in there if it weren't for me," I say.

He draws me even closer. I didn't know it was possible.

"Ms. Landon?"

We turn to find a doctor walking toward us in scrubs soaked with sweat. His dark, curly hair pokes out from his surgical cap. "Are you Ms. Landon?"

"Yes." I meet him halfway.

"I'm Dr. Ryan. We've stabilized Mikaela for the moment, but I'm sorry to say she's in a coma. The next couple of days will be critical."

"Is she going to wake up?"

The doctor gives a slight shrug. "Only she knows that."

"Can we see her?" Jake asks.

"Yes, follow me."

We hurry after the doctor. I glance back once but my mother hasn't moved. We are in the pediatric ICU and it is a sobering sight. So much sadness. So much illness.

The doctor stops and gestures to the room. There is an orange "P" taped to the door. I can do nothing more than snatch it up and wad it into my pocket. These letters are really starting to make me mad.

Inside the room it's almost more than I can take in. She looks so small and so lifeless against the big white bed. It engulfs her. Her head is bandaged. A nurse stands nearby holding what looks like a large needle. We watch her stick Mikaela's foot and suddenly I collapse into Jake's arm. A pain shoots right into my heel. "Ouch!"

"Are you okay?" Jake asks. The nurse watches me too.

"I'm fine." I hobble over to Mikaela's bedside. I can't help the tears, they are just coming out by the bucketful. "Mikaela, it's Hope. Listen to me. You don't have to leave. You have me. You have Jake. Here's the deal, you haven't taken that next risk yet, with that next boy, who's probably really glad you see him behind his weird glasses." I pause, waiting for my emotions to settle down. They don't. "You won't get to kiss him if you don't wake up. You hear me?"

The nurse joins me by the bedside. She is gentle, I can tell. "A lot of coma patients, if they wake up, tell us they can hear what's spoken by their bedsides."

Jake points to the needle she holds. "Does that hurt?"

"Only she can tell us. We're just testing her sensory reflexes for a reaction." She pats me lightly on the shoulder, but it is a stabilizing touch. "I'll be back to check on her."

We stay there for a long time, Jake and me, just sitting and watching her, the monitors beeping in unison, a gray and glum day setting in outside the hospital windows.

"I should go check on my mom."

He nods and assures me he won't leave Mikaela's bedside.

In the waiting room, Mom is there, still staring at the TV, still not responding to my voice. My mother, from past experience, is not one to handle trauma well. Maybe she needs time. I ask her if she wants coffee and she nods vaguely. Or maybe that's just the rocking. So I decide to go find some.

I'm directed to complimentary coffee down a hallway. The carafe barely spits out half a cup. I grab a stirrer just for something to chew on. When I walk back toward the waiting room, I glance toward the nurse's station. And there I see her. Again.

The nurse in the waitress uniform. Or the waitress in the nurse's uniform. Which is it? She looks at me as I pass, just like she did when we were on the street—a look that slows all things around me. It's as if only she and I exist in the world.

And then, my shoulder is knocked from behind. I spill some coffee right onto my shoe. I glance up to see the girl. *The girl.* The one in the purple jacket!

"Hey!" I yell after her, in the exact way nobody would yell in a hospital. "Wait! You! Wait a minute!"

I dump the coffee in a trash and run after her. She darts through an exit door, vanishing once again. But I can't give up. I push open the door. I am now in a gray, concrete stairwell—the same color, it seems, as Mikaela's skin tone now . . . the kind of gray that has not an ounce of warmth to it—cold and hopeless.

I shout downward, though I don't know that's where she's gone. "You don't have to run!" My voice echoes but there is no other noise and I'm left alone. It is not a place I want to be.

I decide to return to Mikaela. I don't like being away from her and I notice this is a change from who I used to be. Hope Landon, when faced with dire circumstances and an uncertain future, tended to run. And here I am, staying.

As I walk toward Mikaela's room, I see Dr. Ryan talking to Jake. I hear them clearly even though I am still far away.

"She has some swelling on her brain. She's not responding to medication as well as we'd hoped."

"What's next for her?" There is a strain in the voice that doesn't match the matter-of-fact question.

"We may have to operate but we don't know if she'll survive the surgery. We're going to watch her a couple more hours and then decide."

"You have to save her!" I say, but I don't stop where they are standing. I go straight into her room. I have to be with her. I have to give her strength, love, whatever it is she needs to feel that she has something to come back to.

And then I am astonished at what I see. My mother. She is draped over Mikaela's tiny body, crying. *Weeping*. Praying in the most guttural way a human is capable of praying. It's the kind of prayer that is all soul and no flesh. It renders the human inadequate and the Almighty the only one capable of doing what must be done.

I stand there a moment, my skin shivering. And then I am at the bed. I don't even recall walking there. My next action, I cannot explain. It is as if I am not even myself. I feel more desperation than I thought a person was capable of feeling.

I grab Mikaela by the arms. I shake her. Not violently, but not in a way that a person with a head injury should be handled.

"Mikaela! Wake up!"

I feel a hand on my shoulder. It is Jake. "Hope, be gentle with her."

I grab her journal, which I had put at the end of her bed, near her feet. I flip it open, tearing one of the pages by accident. "Mikaela, I'll get you everything on your Christmas list." I am flipping frantically through the pages, trying to find her list. And then I notice there is a bookmark sticking out the top. I flip to that page and notice it is an old photo. I scan the list: *Love, Colors, More Time.*

What does it mean? I wonder again.

An answer about my father.

Hope.

I stare at the words, trying to figure out what it all means, what I can do to fulfill this. I glance at the photo again, wondering if there is a clue there. Under the harsh fluorescent light, the picture is easy to see, but I pull it closer to my face anyway.

It is a picture of . . . my father. His arms are wrapped around a little girl. They are in ice skates, standing near a frozen lake. I bring the picture even closer and I lose my breath, my heartbeat, my sense of space and time.

The little girl is me.

And I look just like Mikaela.

I look at her, lying in that bed. It's me.

It's me.

My mom is suddenly behind me. I don't know when she moved or how she got there. "I remember taking that photo of you and your daddy. That was right before he disappeared."

And then I am in a tunnel of images, like I am being swallowed by them, like I'm sliding down a throat. I am reaching up, trying to grab something, but I am only offered flashes of clarity that do not seem to stop me from sliding.

The letters that I've been seeing everywhere, in every color, taped in the oddest places, all come before me.

W-A-K-E-U-P

I do not know where I am. It is both a dark and light place.

But I call out. Or up. I reach. And I plead. "You want to be alive. To love again. You want to live. You . . . me . . . I want to live. I want to live. Wake up . . ."

Wake up.

16

Hope stared into a throbbing white light. Why was she floating, and why were people shouting, and why couldn't she connect all the words in her head?

The shouting settled and when she opened her eyes again, she now heard whispers, except she seemed closer to them then she did before. So why were their voices softer?

She heard her name being called, and then she felt the weight of her own body, like she was, for the first time, aware of gravity. She felt warm and safe. Rested and calm.

A face came into focus.

"Mom . . ."

"Hope! Hope! *Hallelujah*!"

The word instantly grounded her. She was where she should be. She didn't know where she had been, but here she was and it was good. She smiled up at her mom. She felt her mom's cold, fragile hand squeeze hers.

She looked to the left. A lot of cards. Where did they come from? Were they hers?

There was a tray of hospital food nearby, Jell-O and rice and Salisbury steak. There was a strong smell of tuna, something sharply familiar though she hated tuna and would never eat it.

There was a framed photo next to the food tray. It was blurry but she already knew it by heart. It was of her and her father, standing on ice skates in front of a cold, frozen lake. The last picture they ever took together.

"Hope! You're awake!"

There was a man standing over her and she blinked. A doctor? No. Who? He was cute. Had a nice smile. So familiar yet she couldn't place him. She smiled a little, hoping not to embarrass herself. She really needed to get her bearings. Where was she and why were people standing over her? Why was she lying down? Why did her backside feel breezy?

Her attention was drawn back to her mother, who was flapping her hands in the air. "You're awake! Oh my goodness! Goodness, goodness. I told the Lord all I wanted for Christmas was your consciousness."

And there was a lady there too, smiling brightly at her while pushing buttons on a monitor and holding a syringe of some sort. She looked so familiar, a nurse she'd once known. A flurry of activity continued over beeping sounds and excited whispers. She was aware of much but couldn't see beyond just a couple of feet around her.

The man with the cute smile said, "Hope . . ."

"What's going on?" The words feel strange coming out of her mouth.

"You've been in a coma for over a month," he said.

"What day is it?"

"It's Thanksgiving," her mother said. "That gives you one whole month for Christmas shopping." Her mother held up a pencil kit, tied with a red bow. "I got you an early gift. So you can draw your cards."

The nurse, whose voice was familiar and good, took her blood pressure. "Well, well. Sleeping Beauty decided to wake up, huh? You get tired of that tuna smell every day or what?"

"A coma," Hope said again, not sure where that word even came from. She searched the room for an answer.

"Since your wedding day," her mother said. "You got knocked out in the parking lot."

Her memory flashed suddenly to rain and concrete, to voices and to pain—to a purple jacket and a flower truck. To screams, then silence.

There was the guy again, leaning over her. He touched her hand. "I found you in the parking lot on my way out, the day of your wedding."

And then she saw him, at the end of the bed, standing there—the first face she should've seen but didn't.

"Sam!" she gasped. "Sam!"

Something changed in the room. A shifting of some sort. People moved. Gazes fell and others rose. She couldn't quite put it all together, but this . . . this was the man that she needed to see. She looked at her left hand, wondering where her wedding ring was.

"Did we go on the honeymoon to Idaho?"

"Silly," her mom said. "You can't go to Idaho in a coma."

The nurse was back and seemed to be hustling people out of the way. Hope looked for the man with the nice smile, but couldn't find him. "It's going to take a bit for you to understand what you've been through. Be patient with yourself."

"How did I come out of the coma?"

The nurse looked contemplative. "Well, I think a lot of people helped. Your poor mother, she prayed herself silly—though I suspect," she said in a hushed voice, "she was pretty much silly before that. And we did CAT on you."

She had a sense she'd been around cats.

"Coma Arousal Therapy," the nurse explained. "I did that on you, but I had some help. Couldn't have done that without him."

"Who?"

"Lan! Lan!" Sam was again at her bedside, filling the entire side of the bed, it seemed. He looked familiar in an unfamiliar way, like she'd known him before. Of course she had. They were married . . . or going to be. She was going to have to find that out, but the words were still hard to come by. "As soon as I heard you were here, well, I had a lot to process, of course. I mean, I had my own grieving to do, as you can well imagine. But that's what I always loved about you . . . you took me at *my* pace."

"Sam?" He seemed to be acting so weird.

"I've been such a jerk." And then, from his back pocket, he pulled out a card, bent in half to fit in the pocket, crumpled at every corner. "The card says it better than I could. And no card could make up for what I did. I just got scared. But being without you proved to me that I love you. I just needed that proof, you know? I'm not a take-it-by-faith kind of guy."

Behind him, Hope saw the guy with the smile. He stood in the doorway but the smile was gone.

Sam continued. "I want to throw you a wedding! On my parents' yacht! You won't have to do a thing. You've been in a coma—who would make a coma chick throw herself *another* wedding, right? I don't think they make a card for that kind of a jerky move."

Then, just like that, the man behind Sam left. Hope felt an emptiness she couldn't explain, and then a memory arrived like a letter to a mailbox. It was a letter, in fact, that she saw . . . a letter from Sam, slipping from her fingers, floating to the ground, breaking her heart in two and three and then a million pieces.

"I'm sorry about everything that happened to you," Sam said.

"I'm not." It was the first two words that felt right and solid on her tongue. "I think it was the best thing you could have done for me. You woke me up."

"But I'm back now." He threw open his arms like he was the gift she'd been waiting for.

"No, you're not. We're not. Ever."

"All right now, all right! Time to let the lady have her space." The nurse shooed everyone out, telling them she needed thirty minutes or so to run some tests. The room grew quiet and Hope didn't know what to say. But then the words started flowing.

"Who was that man here, with the really nice smile?"

"His name is Jake. He found you and has barely left your side for over a month."

"He looks so familiar. I know about him, but how could I?"

"What do you know?"

"His wife left him. He was very sad about it."

The nurse looked at me. "Between you and me, I don't think he's told another soul except you the whole story."

Hope nodded because somehow she knew that.

"I'm Bette." Hope watched her take notes and push buttons. "The neuro doc is on his way to take a good look at you, but by all accounts, you're going to be just fine. Things might be fuzzy for a while, but you'll be okay."

Hope looked out the window. She was drawn to the sunlight. The doctor arrived.

"I'm Dr. Ryan," he said, grinning at her. "You gave us quite a scare, you know that? We didn't think you'd wake up. And then we almost lost you. You're a fighter, I'll give that to you."

Had she and this doctor met before? It was like this was a dream, and somewhere else was a reality.

He shined a light in her eyes, asked the nurse to run some tests she'd never heard of.

"For any of your coma patients," Hope asked, "have they ever . . . have they ever told you they saw stuff in a coma, like people and faces, before they woke up?"

"Sure. I mean, just like in a dream, you see people you know, things that are familiar to you. Some of what you hear around you, in the room, can bleed into your dreams."

"And what about people they hadn't met yet, in real life . . . but then they see them when they wake up?"

"That's not medically possible."

"In what realm is it possible?"

The doctor smiled mildly at her and patted her shoulder, before turning to the nurse. "Let's make sure her electrolytes are in balance, okay? Hope, I'll be back to check on you later."

Bette continued to do her thing. Hope's attention was drawn to all the cards, all over the room.

"I don't know this many people."

"Pardon?" the nurse asked.

"Where did all these cards come from?"

Bette smiled. She grabbed a handful and laid them carefully on the bed in front of Hope. "I think you'll find one signature more than any others."

Hope opened the first one. It was signed *Jake*.

17

"Your legs are strong. Your mind is right. You're on your way to your new life. A lot of people have been praying for miracles for you, sweet girl."

"Thank you for everything, Bette," Hope said, hugging her. Then she noticed the little bride and groom, still sitting on the bedside table. She walked to it. Once it seemed so big—it seemed it meant everything. Now it was just a small piece of plastic. She took it in her hand and tossed it in the trash.

Bette watched the symbolic moment, her hands clasped solemnly in front of her.

Hope felt lighter than ever. Just then a woman rounded the corner into the room, wearing pink scrubs and pushing a wheelchair.

"Candy here will take you down to where your mother is waiting with the car," Bette said.

Hope looked at Candy and laughed.

"What?" Bette asked. Hope shook her head, and Bette grinned. "Another person from your coma world?"

"When will it end?"

"Maybe it won't," Bette said with a knowing smile. "And maybe that's a good thing."

Candy grinned and rolled the wheelchair forward. "I hear somebody's been released! Glad to see you looking so alive!"

Hope sat in the wheelchair, put her bag on her lap and looked up at Bette. "I hope he understands I needed some time to think—to come to terms with my life—to realize I know a good thing when I see it."

"Sounds like a greeting card," Bette laughed.

"You think he will even talk to me?"

"I think it's worth the risk to try. Bring him a peace offering."

"Tuna?"

"Something less potent, more romantic."

"Got it." Hope reached out for a hug. "Thanks for everything, Bette."

"You'll forgive me for poking your poor little feet?"

Hope laughed. "I don't know what was worse—needles or tuna."

Candy rolled her out. As they approached the elevator, Hope let out a laugh.

"What is it, doll?" Candy asked.

Hope pointed to the guy walking by, thin as a rail, a tangling of IVs hanging off him. "It's just that I saw him once . . . at my house . . . he stole my—never mind."

"You sure they cleared you for release?"

"I was this kooky before, I assure you."

Downstairs, she was loaded into the car. She couldn't wait to get back to Poughkeepsie. It felt like the longest drive ever. She didn't even need to ask. Her mother knew to take her straight to the nursing home.

"Not too long, now. Doctor's orders to take it easy."

"Can I have a moment alone, Mom? With Grandma?"

Her mom smiled and handed her the Columbine flower Hope requested she bring. "I'll just wait out here for you."

Her legs still felt a little shaky as she walked in. The home was quiet and she went unnoticed down the hallway to her grandmother's room. Tinny Christmas music blared through the intercom system in the ceiling. Cheap garland wrapped in tinsel was strung this way and that. A small, plastic pine tree stood humbly in an out-of-the-way corner.

A lot had changed, but this had not: her grandmother sat in front of her window, quiet and still and but a whisper of who she was. Some cards were missing, Hope noticed, from the grouping by the window.

Hope knelt in front of her, eye level. "Hi, Grandma. It's me. Hope." She handed her the Columbine flower.

And then, there was a blink. And a look. Her grandmother was *looking* at her. *Into* her. "That's what your daddy named you."

Hope felt breathless as she nodded. "Yes, Grandma. It's me."

"I will never understand why your Momma wouldn't let us have a funeral for him. After the accident that night. I told her it was wrong, to let you hope we'd find him." She spoke as clearly as if she'd never been lost inside that mind and body of hers.

Hope didn't want to lose her back into wherever she'd been. "What are you talking about, Grandma?"

"After his car went into the Hudson, when he was out getting you ice cream. Mint, I believe it was. Even though they never found his body, we all knew he was never coming home. I wanted to tell you, but she wanted to hang on to that . . . she didn't want it to be real . . . there was another world she wanted to live in, where things might be made right someday."

Hope shuddered. Was her grandmother speaking the truth or nonsense? She watched her brush the Columbine flower against her shoulder. Why was she suddenly speaking now?

A lot of people have been praying for miracles for you, sweet girl. Bette had told her that at the hospital during her recovery and now it seemed those prayers were transpiring right in front of her.

"Grandma, are you sure?" Hope whispered, but she knew in her heart it was true.

"Such a sweet boy. Such a sweet, sweet boy. Good manners. Shy smile."

"Who?" And then, like that, her grandmother was gone. The light in her eyes vanished and she gazed out the window, then looked at Hope again, as if she'd never seen her before in her life.

"Well, hello, young lady. Can you get me a flower?"

Hope stood and took a couple of steps back. She noticed the missing cards again. Where had so many of them gone?

THE COLD WINTER wind snaked around the heavy headstones, grazing their legs as it went. Her mother huddled against her.

"Why are we at the cemetery?" Her hair was standing straight up in the air, doing its own hallelujah wave, in the wind. "There's not even a grave here."

"I know, Mom. That's the point. I need you to hear me. Okay?"

"Okay, I've never spent enough time listening to you, and I want to. Because I noticed, when you were in that coma, you weren't talking and—"

"Mom."

"Yes?"

"Dad is dead."

"No, honey. He's just . . ."

"Mom. You know he's gone. You don't want to know it, but you do. He loved you more than anyone else on this earth . . . except me." Hope laughed through her own tears. "You know, if he had somehow survived that accident, he would have come home. It's time to let go."

It started as the tiniest sniffle, and then it grew to a sob so freeing, Hope imagined that it felt as if every lie she'd ever held on to was being carried off by the wind. Her mom turned and buried her face into Hope's neck.

"Mom, let's . . . you know."

And for the first time since her dad disappeared, Hope was the one who did the praying.

"THANK YOU SO much for driving me," Hope said. "I can't drive for two more weeks."

"Are you kidding me? I wouldn't miss this for the world." Becca pitched a thumb toward the backseat. "She's cute, I'll give her that, but she literally sucks the life out of me. Milk. Energy. Sleep. I got nothing left except to observe how other people live their normal lives."

"Don't look at me! I'm nothing normal."

"Well, you're not dull, I'll tell you that. Dumped at the altar. Attacked and thrown into a coma. Wooed while unconscious. And I thought having a baby was exciting."

"What ever happened to that girl?"

"What girl?"

"Who attacked me."

"Your mom didn't tell you? They caught her just a mile down the road. She was from the Children's Home. The news said they sentenced her to community service at the YMCA." Becca's eyes widened. "What? You look like you've seen a ghost."

Hope shook her head. "Maybe I just saw what my life might have been if I hadn't had a mom who prayed so much for me."

Baby Abigail let out a tiny cry from the backseat. Becca nodded toward the building. "So, this Tuna Guy—you think he's the real deal? Sounds fishy to me."

"Becca, you were right."

"About?"

"It wasn't my geography that needed to change. It was me."

"Huh?"

"Never mind." Hope smiled. Maybe reality bled into her coma life, but she'd found just the opposite to be true too. "Okay, it's now or never. You're waiting out here, right? In case I have to make a run for it?"

"You got it."

Hope got out of the car, took a deep breath and stood in front of Heaven Sent Flower and Gift Shop. The last time she'd seen that sign it was on the side of the truck and only read *HEAVE*, which was exactly what she did.

The building number was 352. No surprise there. Large snowflakes began to fall lightly across her face. For fun, she stuck her tongue out to catch a few.

But there was no time to waste. She opened the front door of the shop and little bells rang. Two elderly ladies greeted her in unison. Their sweaters matched and they looked like sisters.

She spotted him, his head down, at work on something important. When he looked up, his face lit exactly the way she thought it would.

"You're out!"

She wore a playful, mischievous grin. "I know who you are."

"The guy who sat by your bedside, bored you silly 'til you woke up?" He set his pencil down. The two ladies giggled and moved to the back of the shop.

Yeah, she had her flirt on.

Out of her bag she took a hand-drawn card, filled with every color imaginable, the whole rainbow and more.

Two caricatures were sketched on the front of the card. She watched his face and she knew he recognized himself and her. She really loved to see him smile.

It read: *Do You Like Me?* She flipped to the inside: *Yes, No or Maybe So.*

He looked up at her, his eyes awash with . . . delight?

Yeah, delight.

"Don't say no," Hope said.

"Hope, I . . ."

"Don't say no." Comatose, she realized, makes people bold.

He walked to the other side of the counter and stood very close. "I'm not. I simply wanted to point out that on the inside, you're asking me to make a choice but you don't say what you think. How you feel. We need a rewrite."

"I think . . . I'm um, my thoughts . . . they're telling me we need to believe again, believe it's worth the risk. Believe our pain has brought us to this place. Sappy, huh?"

"Just right. I'm glad you're here. I wanted to ask you a question. How does a girl in a coma send a guy greeting cards?"

"What do you mean?"

He reached behind the counter and pulled out a stack of envelopes to hand to her. There was no mistaking the writing was her grandmother's. Hope pulled out the first card. She'd made this one on a Wednesday sitting under a tree at the park, simply signing it Hope. One of dozens over the years.

It struck her right then, that this was the boy her grandmother always talked about, the shy one with the gentle heart—the one she had no interest in since the day he gave her that first card in grade school. It was her grandmother who could never resist a guy with intimate knowledge of flowers.

It left her breathless and hopeful all at once—so full-circle in an otherworldly sort of way. She stared into Jake's eyes.

"What's a girl gotta do to get a job around here, writing her own stunningly witty greeting cards? Maybe a line of 'pony up' cards."

"Well, this is a family-owned business. You have to be family to—"

And then she went all cliché on herself to interrupt him and plant a kiss on his lips. They melted into each other. It was the corniest, mushiest greeting-card moment ever. "You're hired," he said, his finger brushing her cheek.

Somehow I already knew that.

Discussion Questions

1. What was your favorite part of the novel? Why?

2. Who is your favorite character and why?

3. Who did you want Hope to end up with and why?

4. In the novel, Hope goes through a crushing blow, being abandoned at the altar. What is the most disappointing experience you've had? How did you respond to it?

5. Where do you look for hope in the midst of difficult circumstances? What encourages you?

6. Like Hope, have you been able to use humor to get through difficult times in your life? If so, how have you used it?

Do you know of creative ways to use humor to help others going through a difficult time?

7. Cici, Hope's mother, seems to bury her pain by pretending bad things don't happen. Do you know anyone who uses this coping mechanism? Have you used it yourself to try to avoid dealing with pain? What was the result?

8. If you were writing your own greeting cards, would you write make-up cards or break-up cards?

9. Write a sample greeting card of the type of card you wished you had received when you were in pain over a trial. If you think someone may be helped by it, make it into a card especially for that person.

10. Did you enjoy the story in the real world or in Hope's coma world better? What was it you liked best about it?

11. What do you think is the biggest mistake Hope makes along her journey? How could she have done things better?

12. Did you understand the symbolism of the lady janitor in the hallway at the YMCA, that she represented where Hope feared she'd end up if life didn't change? Do you face fears about where you will end up one day? What are you doing to combat those fears?

13. Hope has to overcome a lot of fears to chase after her big dream of being a greeting card writer in NYC. She leaves the safety of her job and her home. What is your biggest dream? Have you chased after this? Is there anything holding you back from trying? Are there any big moves you need to make in order to go for your dreams?

14. What do you believe about the verse, Romans 8:28, that talks about how God works all things together for his good?